LYAH BETH LeFLORE

Last Night a DJ Saved My Life

{A Novel}

HARLEM MOON
BROADWAY BOOKS
NEW YORK

Published by Harlem Moon, an imprint of Broadway Books, a division of Random House, Inc.

PRINTED IN THE UNITED STATES OF AMERICA

HARLEM MOON, BROADWAY BOOKS, and the HARLEM MOON logo, depicting a moon and a woman, are trademarks of Random House, Inc. The figure in the Harlem Moon logo is inspired by a graphic design by Aaron Douglas (1899–1979).

Visit our Web site at www.harlemmoon.com

Book design by Jennifer Ann Daddio

Library of Congress Cataloging-in-Publication Data
LeFlore, Lyah Beth.
    Last night a dj saved my life : a novel / Lyah Beth LeFlore.—1st ed.
        p. cm.
    1. Music trade—New York (State)—New York—Fiction.
    I. Title.
PS3612.E3498L37 2006
813'.6—dc22
                                    2005057433

ISBN-13: 978-0-7679-2118-3
ISBN-10: 0-7679-2118-6

10 9 8 7 6 5 4 3 2 1

FIRST EDITION

I thank God for His blessings,
mercy, and the opportunity to live my dream.

For Mom, Daddy, Hope, and Jacie . . . my foundation:
Mom—you are my shero. Thanks for teaching me how
to pray and showing me how to smile in the face
of adversity; Daddy —for standing by my side
like a rock, always, your Sunflower; Hope and Jacie—
we've weathered many storms in our lives, but we
persevered and came out stronger and smarter.
We are Shirley's Girls!

Jullian, Noelle, and Jordy—the world is yours.

Minnie, Annetta, Monroe, Floyd Sr., and Aunt Barbara—
as always your spirits live through my work and words.

Finally, for every girl who believes in fairy tales and
rainbows, and knights in shining armor—
keep dreaming and believing in the power of love . . .

Acknowledgments

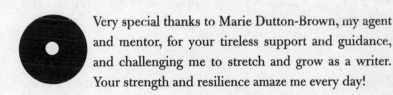 Very special thanks to Marie Dutton-Brown, my agent and mentor, for your tireless support and guidance, and challenging me to stretch and grow as a writer. Your strength and resilience amaze me every day!

Janet Hill Talbert, my editor and friend. Another one down, many more to go! Thank you for your vision, belief, and commitment, and for allowing me to share my voice with the world.

Clarence Haynes, for your valuable creative input.

Many thanks to Stephen Rubin, Bill Thomas, Rachel Rokicki, Catherine Pollock, Julia Coblentz, David Drake, Rebecca Holland, and the rest of the Doubleday/Broadway family.

DL Warfield, another St. Louis Homie-Done-Good! You are an incredible artist and I thank you for a brilliant cover that embodies all that Destiny is.

Alan Haymon, as always, for your unflagging support and friendship.

Special thanks to the following individuals for their professional support and friendship: Patrik Henry Bass, Jeff Burns, Margena Christian, Laini "Muki" Brown (my "Spiritually Tough" sista), Vanesse Lloyd-Sgambati, Mondella Jones, Khalid Williams and Ashleen Jean Pierre of MBA, Tynisha Thompson, Tavis Smiley, Dawn Staley, Angie Wells, Pam Eels, Lola Ogunnaike, Tia Williams, Gilda Squire, Adam Bonnett, Stephens College and President Wendy B. Libby and Richard Libby, Jabari Asim, Jamie Foster Brown, Shay Smith, Leslie Christian-Wilson, Bill Beene, Ira Jones and First Civilization, my homegirl Deneen Busby, and Jacqueline Lee of Diageo/Crown Royal for your enthusiasm and support the moment you laid eyes on the masterpiece DL created.

Thanks to my supportive family: The Davis and Bradley descendants, the LeFlores, the Bohrs, the Robnetts, the Jarmon descendants, the Price-Moore's, Nicholas (Aunt Barbara is smiling down from above), John Drew Lindsay (my big brother and legal counsel).

My cousin girlfriends: Karen (we are more like sisters, and I thank you for your love, generosity, and giving me a place of solace), Missy, Passion, Jamina, ShaRee, Sydney, Gigi, Susan, Tracey, Kim.

My other big sisters: Lesvia, Barbara "Babs," Kathleen, Daphne, Teresa, Kathi, Sable, Delphine, Crystal G., Dr. Pam, Allison, Pam H.

My fabulous, talented, and spiritual girlfriends (old and new): Dion (it just keeps getting better and more fabulous with time), Mamie (we are survivors!), Leah, Leslie (thank you for Noah!), Tizzi (let go and let love), Africa, Connie, Dana, Josie, Crystal F., Wendy W., Sonia W., Angie R. (keep your head up, Mami!), Mary ("Coco"), Lajuan, Keita, Monifah, Myiti, and Wanda.

And to my male friends who've supported my dreams throughout my career: Charles Berry, Gerald Levert, Bennie Richburg, Mike City, Jaleel White, Scott Crawford, Alan Bovinett, Tim Brown (thank you for finding me again), Reggie "Rock" Bythewood, Richie Owings, Aaron Mitchell (for the inspiration), and Edwin Pabon.

Huge thanks to all the independent and African American booksellers, book clubs, and media across the country.

There's not a problem that I can't fix

'Cause I can do it in the mix

—LAST NIGHT A DJ SAVED MY LIFE

Last Night a DJ Saved My Life

C.R.E.A.M.
(Cash Rules Everything
Around Me)

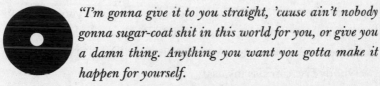 *"I'm gonna give it to you straight, 'cause ain't nobody gonna sugar-coat shit in this world for you, or give you a damn thing. Anything you want you gotta make it happen for yourself.*

"A woman's approach to life should simply be: Get in, get yours, and get out! Life is too short and there's too much money out here to be makin' to be wastin' time with a Negro who ain't got nothin'!"

I was just six years old when my mother told me that. She didn't teach me much, but Juanita Day's specialty was making money and men—old ones, young ones, ugly ones, fine ones (like my daddy), but never lazy-no-money-havin'-cheap-watch-run-over-shoe-wearin' ones.

Juanita was one woman who didn't let anything or anybody get in her way, either. I never saw her pick up a Bible or set foot in a church, but she believed God created two types of people: those who want what you have, and are always scheming on you; and those who want to align themselves with you because it looks good on their social résumé (in other words, the how-can-I-be-down-wannabes). Juanita said the best way to avoid both was not to trust anybody.

I've pretty much followed that philosophy my whole life. It works well in my line of work, where everybody's beautiful, fabulous, and paid. Some are genuinely decent people, but a lot of the others are trapped in that superficial lifestyle of "bling and bullshit."

They're quick to say things like, "Oh, Destiny? That's my girl!" or "Yeah, me and D are tight!" The whole time, those same people are hatin' and trying to snake me out. That's why I never get too personal. I'm a businesswoman. I play the game to make my money.

To me, honesty and loyalty are two of the most admirable qualities a person can have, and only a handful of people I know possess both—Ainee and Uncle Charlie; my two best friends, Izzy and Rico; and Josephine, who in my adult life has become something of a surrogate mother to me. And then there's Jenna. I guess you could call her my protégée, but that seems a bit too formal. She's really more like an *extension* of my extended family. For them, I'd give my life. Everybody else can kiss my ass.

I don't give a damn if you're on fire and I'm the last person on earth with a bucket of ice water. If you're not one of those six people I just named, then, like Flavor Flav said, "*I can't do nuttin' for you man!*" You probably think I'm some cold-blooded bitch. Cold-blooded, no. Bitch . . . sometimes. We all have our days.

Maybe some psychoanalyst would say, "Destiny Day's perception of life and relationships is such, because of her dark and painful childhood." I agree my childhood wasn't as innocent as most small-town girls. I mean how many girls are born in what my Granny referred to as "the den of sin"? That den of sin otherwise known as

2

East St. Louis, Illinois. A small, predominantly black town that's a spit's distance across the Mississippi River from St. Louis, Missouri.

The best part of East Boogie (that's what the folks from St. Louis called it), was that it had some of the most talked-about after-hours partyin' in the Midwest. People would say, "Watch your back *and* your pocketbook in East Boogie." But they'd bring themselves right on across the river and get their party on 'til the moon lost its fight with the sun.

I remember for the most part regularly hearing gunshots, walking on those dirt sidewalks in the blazing-hot summertime, and folks sounding off about crooked politicians. But it wasn't so bad. The good thing about small-town living, particularly in the black community, is that everybody knows each other and they look out for you.

As a kid, it seemed like everywhere I went—the neighborhood grocery store owned by Mr. Earl and Miss Bird, whose breasts were so big she always looked like she was on the verge of tipping over; one-eyed Winky down at the gas station, who used to sneak a peek up Juanita's skirt when he fixed our car (he always gave her a discount when my daddy wasn't around); and Miss Stella over at the beauty shop who had booty for days (her breath smelled like cigarettes and stale beer, and she talked real loud and liked to be all up in your face)—they all knew my name was Destiny and who my mama and daddy were.

I didn't spend much time in East Boogie, though. By the time I was ten years old my fairy tale had come to an end. Reason: drugs, the typical ghetto tragedy. That's the breaks, right? But don't shed tears for me. We've all seen this movie before. When you're livin' foul it catches up to you . . . eventually.

Juanita Hayes didn't have any family. One might say she was a wanderer who wandered right into Carlton Day's life. Lore has it that she came from the Southside of Chicago by way of Detroit. How she ended up in a lil hell-raising town like East St. Louis, I'll never

3

know. A woman without a past, who gave a church boy hope for the future.

Carlton had a kind, innocent spirit that provided the right amount of security for what the whispering folk (you know, those same good people at the grocery store, the gas station, and the beauty shop) called a "loose woman." Juanita was too much for him, no matter how hard he tried to keep up with her. He just couldn't.

I never looked at Juanita and Carlton like a child does a "mommy" or "daddy." They were more like a big sister and brother. There's a whole lot more I could say about them, but I'll just sum it up like Rod Stewart did in his classic, "Young Hearts": *Young hearts be free tonight. / Time is on your side.*

But time wasn't, and I don't want to talk about it anymore. Would you?

Nah . . .

New York, and who I am now, are a long way from Miss Roxy's fried-chicken-and-tripe sandwiches and Juanita and Carlton getting high out of their minds. At thirty five years old I've got a lovely life. I'm at the top of my game as *the* premiere party promoter in New York City, smiling all the way to the bank, and free of male drama. I set the rules with the men in my life, and they either play by them or they've gotta go.

Juanita told me that when she first looked into my eyes she saw I was destined for greatness and that's why she gave me my name. Carlton, on the other hand, was just happy I had ten fingers and ten toes. Destiny Day . . . pretty cool name, right? It fits. I may be like Juanita when it comes to money and my insatiable thirst to fill my cup of life to the rim, and swallow it in one huge gulp, but let me be clear, I'm not *like* her. I'm never going to make the same mistakes she made.

4

Disk One

To the Beat Y'all

{1} LADIES FIRST

{2} LET'S GET IT STARTED

{3} PUMP UP THE VOLUME

{4} DON'T BELIEVE THE HYPE

{5} THE BREAKS

{6} WHAT A MAN

{7} YOU CAN'T PLAY WITH MY YO-YO

Ladies First

Josephine is a stickler for time and hates it when I'm late for tea. Maybe I should call? On second thought, I'd rather not hear her mouth twice. I stepped off the curb at 140th and St. Nicholas and scanned the Avenue. A few gypsy cabs race back and forth, but they're all occupied. Not even the occasional yellow taxi is in sight. I'm thirty minutes late and these Jimmy Choos were not made for walkin'.

I check my watch, zip up my mink-lined leather jacket, and slip on a pair of oversized Jackie O sunglasses. Although the sky's bright and clear, looks can be deceiving. Today's crisp fifty-degree temperature is a reminder that March is a lot closer to January than it is to July. Mother Nature can be extremely unpredictable this time of year in New York, and tomorrow she could blast us with a dose of snow and freezing rain.

I think she does it just to remind us that she's still running thangs. Ahh, the power of being a woman. We can change our minds any damn time we please and nobody better say a word. Therefore, since Mother Nature tends to be hormonal, a girl must be prepared in the City at all times. Your Birkin bag has to be stuffed with extra amenities like a pashmina, flip-flops for an impromptu nail-shop drop, and a compact umbrella, amongst other necessities—baby wipes, tampons, perfume, hand sanitizer, and condoms.

My cell phone rings. I hurriedly fish through my bag to answer it (the downside to toting around all those lovely amenities). By the time I find it, the screen reads: *Call missed.* It was Malik. I hit redial, but I get his voicemail. To further irritate me, somebody just nabbed a cab with my name on it, barely two feet away, because I was too busy fussing with the phone. *Shit!*

My voicemail alerts me. I hit the MESSAGE RETRIEVE button.

You have one new message . . .

MALIK: *Hey, Mama. Shit's been crazy and I'm in DC in the studio, 'bout to head to Atlanta. I get back tomorrow. Hit me on my Black-berry. I lost my other cell.*

I roll my eyes. The usual.

The Lowdown

IDENTITY: Malik (meaning "King") Sekou Jaru, aka hip-hop record producer and all-around music-industry power player. Godson of late jazz great Miles Davis. Son of famous jazz musician/producer "King" Jaru, founder of Jaru Note Records, whose producing résumé is a who's who of greats in the jazz world.

STATUS: Single, probably for life. A sista's cool with that. Nice and simple is how we both like it.

JUST THE FACTS: Minimal Baby mama drama, gives the fierce sex-down, likes to splurge on baubles for Destiny, and his ice is always twinklin'. He has that hustler mentality that drives me mad crazy.

Hearing Malik's rugged voice did what it always manages to do . . . put a tiny smile on my face. We've been hanging out for almost a year, the longest time I've ever dated a guy. We aren't exclusive, I'm always going to keep me a couple on the side, but I guess I'd have to consider Malik my "main squeeze."

At last, a gypsy cab pulls over and I'm on my way. The sound of native tongues chanting faintly pumps through the car speakers. I instruct my soft-spoken African driver where to go and lean my head back, thinking about Malik's message again. I've told him over and over, we've got a good thing with no preset guidelines. Just have some respect for my time. When I see him tomorrow, I'm going to give him the biggest hug and longest kiss, right before I punch him for leaving town and not telling me.

I see The Uptown Tea Café just ahead at the corner of 118th and Madison. The rattle-rattle-thunder-clatter of the well-broken-in Lincoln Town Car slows to a stop, and I pass the driver six bucks and exit.

The Uptown Tea Café always gives me peace of mind. I try to get my fix of chamomile, controversy, conversation, and calm regularly from Josephine. Honey, Josephine Rosalita Williams-Eliott-Schultz-Sanchez, also known as Dame Josephine, is something else and summed up simply, quite a woman of the world. I want to be just like her when I grow up. Josephine is a pint-sized punch with a figure that's almost as good as mine. I said *almost*.

Much props to thirty-five. My body isn't as fabulous as my best friend Izzy's, that girl's got the metabolism of a twelve-year-old. However, it's pretty tight for a woman who's five years from crossing yet another major threshold where gravity, by all known reports, is likely to take a major stab at my self-esteem. I just have to keep my good eye on the carbs. A solid size eight is what I like to be. Since thick is the new thin, I'm definitely keepin' some meat on my bones.

Dame Josephine's creamy toffee-colored skin has that eight-glasses-a-day glow. She wears her hair in one long braid down her back. I've never seen a stitch of gray up in there either. The few faint crow's feet around her eyes and her bony, slightly wrinkled hands are the only giveaway that she's seen as many sides of life as she claims she has.

I met Josephine during my brief stay at NYU. One day Izzy and I stumbled into a cute little coffee shop and Spanish bakery in the West Village (hence the Sanchez, her fourth marriage). Josephine was cussing out her then-husband Mario right in front of all the customers and wasn't the least bit embarrassed.

After she finished laying him out, she turned right around and it was business as usual. I thought it was cool how this spicy woman, dressed in a flowing Spanish-inspired skirt and a T-shirt, and draped in a colorful shawl, wasn't taking any mess off her man. She became my instant surrogate mother.

I pushed open the café's large, ornate antique doors and removed my sunglasses. The Uptown Tea Café had a cozy opulence with its mahogany wood interior and furnishings and plush velvet seating. I headed straight to the back of the room to a small round table that was surrounded by three low, stuffed chairs. It was on an elevated platform and enclosed by long velvet drapes that were pulled back.

"You're late!" Josephine said, entering the room from the kitchen. When somebody made Josephine mad, she let the world know with her no-time-for-the-pleasantries attitude.

The Lowdown

KNOWN MARRIAGES: Four (my hero!)

AGE: Unknown. She's got a secret hookup with the Fountain of Youth. I gave up trying to figure out exactly how old she was years ago, but concluded she must be in her early sixties, because she talks about participating in sit-ins during the Civil Rights movement, and the day Dr. King died, and working on the Poor People's Campaign.

OCCUPATION: Spiritualist, activist, diva, and owner of The Uptown Tea Café. Life is her muse.

Dame Josephine flowed through the room with a youthful glide, dressed in her usual, what I call oasis glam. Today she was wearing a Japanese kimono-style top, loose pants, and sequined slippers. I was about to give an explanation, but I couldn't get my mouth open before she cut me off.

"I *had* decided that I wasn't going to speak to you, but then that Negro Abraham Paul decided to lose his damn mind and traipse around here like he was some kind of royalty. I almost kicked him square in the behind when he asked me if his ex-wife could come and stay with us for a while until she gets on her feet. Then he made some stupid joke about how 'Maaaarvelous' it would be to be surrounded by all the women he's loved. The nerve of him! I'm not his concubine!"

She was fussin' and cussin' about the sometime love of her life, Abraham Paul. He's a poet and musician who's been writing his life story as an opera for the past five years. They hooked up a decade ago, and he's been her live-in ever since. He also helps out here at the café.

"So, lovey, you get a break today for being late. *Very* late." I didn't explain.

I sat at my regular table in the back silently, while she prepared our usual: two piping-hot cups of jasmine tea, yummy grilled-cheese sandwiches, and tomato and basil soup. My afternoon tea-time with Josephine was filled with talk about our favorite subjects to debate: men and love.

"Darling, I'm going downtown for my writer's group. How about I bring you back something?" Abraham Paul said, attempting to kiss her on the lips, but she gave him nothing but cheek. He's a lean, wiry man with a robust voice. Always dapper and elegant in his fine tweeds, linens, wools, cashmeres, and cottons, reminiscent of the way men dressed during the Harlem Renaissance. I think he came from Northern black aristocratic money. No one ever told me that, but he carries himself in such a manner. "Ahhhhhh, Destiny, how are you, sweetheart?" he said, giving me a warm pat on the shoulder.

"Oh, enough of the nice-nice. You know you're in the doghouse. How about you surprise me?" Josephine said unenthusiastically, but Abraham Paul skipped right out the door as if everything was perfect in paradise. He knows Josephine well enough to just ignore her fussing.

"Love can be a beautiful thing, except on a day like today when I want to just choke Abraham Paul!"

"You always say you're going to put him out, but you never do," I said.

"I have pity, that's why I let him stay. Besides, I'm too old and too tired to be bothered with putting him out for real, and who would take out the garbage? And who would I have to fuss at?" She chuckled.

"Josephine's gangsta hand is strong!" I declared.

"Chile, maybe in one of my past lives. You'll see, wait until you get my age. You'll realize that all that running around with all these knuckleheads wasn't worth the drama."

"How old did you say you were again?" I tried to get her age out of her on the sly.

"I didn't," she snapped, and then she smiled, moving right past my question. "You'll learn someday, my dear, that you're cheating yourself with all these superficial relationships. You know what that means?"

"No, but I'm sure you're gonna tell me."

"I'm talking about empty calories and zero nutritional value. Speaking of superficial, where's Waldo?"

So now Malik was Waldo in the "Where's Waldo?" children's books. Waldo's always lost somewhere in a maze of artwork, and the trick is finding him in places like crowded cityscapes.

"I see somebody missed their calling to be a comedian," I smarted, taking a bite of my sandwich.

"No, I just haven't heard you mention him the last couple of times you've been over here. I just assumed he was missing again," she sipped gingerly from her teacup.

"You thought he was *missing again*," I said, mimicking her, continuing to eat.

"No mention usually means out of sight."

"Okay, let's just put it all out there, Dame Josephine," I smirked. "Truthfully, Malik has a lot of issues to work through."

"Issues, that's a nice word."

"Excuse me: issues that, thanks to his mother, stem from his feelings of abandonment as a child."

"Chile, you've got more excuses than a politician. You're a great talker, but do you *really* believe what you're saying? Malik reminds me of my second husband, William "Willie" Williams. I should've known something was wrong with him, having two first names. Willie and Malik are like that lab rat running on the wheel."

"Huh?"

"Yep, just running and running, but they never seem to get anywhere. They say they're trying to get to that cheese right there in front of them. But they're too stupid to realize the cheese is dangling from a string. They're never gonna catch that cheese, it's just there to keep them running on the wheel."

Josephine laughed. She was always giving me analogies from her own life experience. I waved her off. Her little anecdote seemed to be for her own amusement.

"Getting back to your original Waldo question, Malik *has* called."

"And . . ." Josephine said, sipping her tea.

"*And*, he's in D.C. on his way to Atlanta, trying to finish an album from a new kid he found down there." Josephine's eyebrows went up in surprise as she looked at me.

"I know," I said, "same story different day. I should stop taking his calls. And *not* because of this whole superficial-relationship theory you have, but because at thirty-five, I have no patience for his b.s." I smiled. "I'm just torn because he's so great in bed!"

"Destiny, you are a mess!"

"I'm serious, Josephine, if Malik wasn't so adorable, I would've dropped him a long time ago. All I'm looking to hire is a Maintenance Man, somebody who can stop by to fix the plumbing every now and then. If I've got a leak, he can patch it up, and keep my pipes in working order. You know what I mean?

"My problem is that I can't get rid of a man fast enough. I think things get complicated anyway when men and women hang out too much. Consistency equals commitment. Men don't like that word and neither do I! That's why I'm a firm believer in the hit-it-and-quit-it school of thought."

"You'd better be careful, with all these men running around on the downlow and AIDS!"

"Oh, I always make them strap one. I need to live so I can make money!"

14

"Chile, I'm about to put you in the doghouse with Abraham Paul for talking so crazy!"

"I'm serious, I keep myself a stable of stallions: Malik, Curtis, my little sweetie Peter, and I'm always taking applications. Malik is just number-one for *now!*"

"Destiny, I've seen a lot in my life and I still say you need to start cuttin' some of these jokers loose. You love these bad boys who are just plain . . . bad!"

We let out another round of belly laughs and settled in for more tea.

I know Josephine means well with her been-there-done-that speeches, but I've got my own set of beliefs. I don't try to force them on anybody, either, but I will say this: The whole happily-ever-after, love-marriage-and-the-baby-carriage theory is all hype. I love the freedom to come and go as I please. Juanita was right. Life *is* too short. So, I made my choice a long time ago.

I decided the love thang just ain't for me.

Let's Get It Started

I raced down FDR Drive in my Range Rover. I keep the Rover in a garage near my apartment building. Like most New Yorkers with cars, I save driving for downtown trips, going to Jersey, or late nights at the club.

Grandmaster Flash and The Furious Five's "The Message" was tonight's anthem. The East River shimmered, reflecting the tiny lights that outlined the Brooklyn and Manhattan bridges. The water below swooshed and crashed to the beat of the classic hip-hop sounds blasting out of my speakers.

Rico, my personal makeup artist and best GBF (gay boyfriend), was riding shotgun and busy rummaging through his portable makeup kit in desperate search of the bronzer he *insisted* I needed. I checked the dash . . . 11:35 p.m. as I exited the Drive at 14th Street.

"You's about to walk up in the party lookin' like Shockadelica bringin' it, the way I beat your face!" Rico loved experimenting with color against my cinnamon skin. He *can* do some makeup, or as he likes to call it, "*beat a face.*" So, I get to take full advantage of the perks.

The Lowdown

HISTORY: Birth name, Fredrick Carter, Jr.

ETHNICITY: Black but he's got a thing for Puerto Rican boys. He has a tendency to pass for Dominican, hence the use of his "stage name" Rico.

HEIGHT: Six foot

BODY: Thin and chiseled, he gives you that brooding intensity of a younger, sexier Djimon Hounsou.

AGE: In his own words, "Never ask a diva her age. That's just rude. Didn't your mama teach you nothin'?"

We met back in the spring of 1989. He was my neighbor when I moved to the East Village after I withdrew from NYU. I loved that cheap, sardine can of an apartment. Rico used to tell me stories and jokes about growing up in Harlem, struggling with his homosexuality in a household run by a mean and strict Pentecostal preacher-daddy, and with a mama who said very little and did everything she was told to do.

When Rico came out on his sixteenth birthday, "The Good Reverend" *threw* him out. Even on his deathbed, his father refused to see him. Rico was just happy that with the passing of The Good Reverend he was able to reconcile with his mother. I guess that's all any child ever really wants . . . a mother's love.

17

Scenes from the Velvet Rope

EXTERIOR: MARQUEE NIGHTCLUB
11:45 P.M.

There was a mob of people trying to get inside Marquee. Four bouncers dressed in black were at the entrance. I tapped my assistant, Jenna, on her shoulder. She whirled around wearing a headset and a tightened facial expression. She hates it when I catch her off-guard.

We gave each other a round of hugs and girlfriend kisses. Rico slipped in a couple of air smooches, too. Jenna was holding a clipboard with tonight's guest list. At my events, the clipboard is crucial, with pages upon pages of every name from Cameron Diaz to Beyoncé, including top fashion-magazine editors, athletes, and power brokers. A *must*! Without it you're not in the "hot" party business.

"It's a zoo," she said with a strained smile.

"It's Thursday," I replied.

"I'll wait for *you* at the bar," Rico said, nodding at me and then walking inside.

"By the way, it pisses me off when you do that." She was referring to my surprise arrival.

"Girlie, pressure keeps you on your toes," I said flashing a smile. Miss Thing ought to be used to my unannounced entrances after five years.

The Lowdown

THE NAME & THE FACE: Jenna Cohen, cool Jewish-Asian-Cuban mix of a girl (I always tease her that she's a mutt).

BACKGROUND: Dad is *the* Elijah Cohen. You know, big-time attorney to the stars. Yep, that's Daddy Dearest. She's determined to make a name for herself on her own, the old-fashioned way! Jenna's crazy. There ain't no way my daddy's gonna have all that juice and I not take advantage of it.

PHYSICAL STATS: Girlie is tiny and waif-waisted with the face, proportions, and honey-blond mane of a Hollywood big-screen darling.

Jenna's Nextel walkie-talkie beeped.

"Wassup, Nikki?" She shouted into her headset mic. Nikki is one-third of "The Girls." That's what I named my crew of working girls Jenna supervises. Jenna's my only full-time employee. The Girls mainly work on party nights, for large events, or to help Jenna on heavy office days. Nikki's a sista attending NYU. She's smart, focused, and passionate, and she has the stamina to be a helluva publicist one day.

"We've got a problem at the back door!" I could hear Nikki's voice crackle over Jenna's headset.

"I'm on my way!" Jenna huffed into her walkie-talkie, giving me an exasperated look.

"Deal with it. I'll handle this madness. Holla if you need me." I winked as she handed me tonight's clipboard.

Jenna's my right hand. I've groomed her well, and no matter how challenging the situation, I know she's got it under control. Investing in headsets and walkie-talkies for the staff was the smartest move I could've made, and *her* suggestion. They are our lifeline, and keep us connected when I've got a demanding A-list-only crowd like tonight.

We have to be within a press-of-a-button away, because when there's a party, I might have Jenna, The Girls, even security running all over the venue, making sure the guest list is organized; the front of the venue isn't too congested; no undesirables (aka uninvited guests) are trying to crash the party; the bathroom attendants are stocked with gum, tissue, deodorant, mints, lotion, and perfume; we have the right champagne in VIP; and the list goes on. When you demand and expect the best, you get the best.

I quickly organized the guest list, and just in time. The crowd started pushing and shoving, desperate to get inside the club. I stood behind the velvet rope. In my world, unhooking the velvet rope is like opening the Pearly Gates. It's *that* serious!

Holding the velvet rope tight, I motioned for one of my regulars to come through. "Back up! Back up! If you're not on the guest list you're not getting in!" I announced. I saw a girl mouthe, "*Bitch!*" I threw her back an equally *bitchy* smirk. Before heading inside, I gave security the nod to turn *her* and everyone else who wasn't on the list away.

Pump Up the Volume

I'm the queen of my domain. People kill to get into a Destiny Day party. I have what people call "the other nine-to-five." Most Americans punch into their J-O-B at nine a.m. and spend their entire day pushing papers and clock-watching. When five o'clock rolls around they make a mad dash for mass transit or prepare for rush-hour gridlock; fight their way home, scarf down dinner; finally put the kids to sleep, exhausted. And as they lie in the bed staring blankly at the ceiling, trying to psych themselves up to face the monotony of life again the next day, I'm slipping on a pair of Manolos and a slinky frock, ready to rock the night away.

You name it, I got it on lock, all the clubs—Marquee, Show, Deep, PM, Lotus, Tangiers, Mission, Bed, and anything in Manhattan that's new, coming, or hasn't been thought about yet. New clubs

pop up and disappear on the hour in New York City, and club own-
ers give me first dibs because they know I'm a guaranteed money-
maker. If you're not hip-hop royalty, a product of wealth, or of
über-model status, forget about coming to my parties.

"Girlie, we need a spa day after tonight!" Jenna said, joining me
at the bar where Rico was waiting.

"My treat!" I replied, giving her a girlfriend high-five.

"Hello! That makes all this stress worth it!" We shared a laugh.

Twelve midnight, and right about now is when the scene kicks
into overdrive. Marquee's ultra-sexy vibe transports you on a head
trip, reviving the heyday and frenzy of New York's famous Studio 54.

My eyes catch a glimmer from the glass-beaded chandeliers
overhead. The downstairs dance floor is packed with Pharell
Williams and Paris Hilton clones and supermodel wannabes. I blow
a kiss to DJ Peter, who returns a flirty wink from the dj's booth. With
the fader and two wheels of steel in hand, he's in deep concentration,
contemplating what to toss at the crowd next.

DJ Peter, aka Peter Silverman, or as I like to call him, Peter Peter
Pussy Eater. I know I'm so nasty, but it's true. He's one of the best
I've ever had—bedmate and dj. Hmmm . . . Where to begin? Nice
Jewish boy, raised in Hell's Kitchen back when the pushers and
prostitutes collided with the struggling artists and musicians, a place
where poverty had no color lines and all cultures gathered.

One night back in the early nineties, I checked him out spinning
on a Sunday night at Plan B on the Lower East Side and was
amazed. He had skills, cuttin', mixin', and scratchin' on the wheels
of steel. He precisely *and* intuitively took the room from Run-
DMC's "It's Like That," into David Bowie's "Fame," and right on
into Lisa Lisa & Cult Jam's "I Wonder If I Take You Home."

We've been together ever since. I manage him, too (fifteen percent, oh yeah, extra cha-ching). But I never double-dip. Bad business. I only take my percentage on outside gigs. So what that we mix

business and pleasure? Who could pass up a great body like that: tight butt, six-pack, big hands *and* feet (and you know what they say about big hands and feet). I'm convinced he was a brotha in a previous life.

"Legendary," Rico said handing me a freshly mixed Crown Royal Lust. Old school CR, chilled and shaken just right with a splash of cranberry and peach, was my choice elixir to kick off club nights. "These kids are carryin' tonight!" I nodded in agreement, and tossed back my drink quickly. "And DJ Peter is pumpin' it!" Rico had his own way of communicating. He was speaking in what I referred to as gaybonics. "Legendary" was my pet name; "carryin' " meant the crowd was partying to the fullest; and "pumpin' " meant the dj was playing great music.

It was time to check out VIP, so Rico and I jetted up the club's massive staircase. My Alexander McQueen flounce skirt shimmied and bounced with each step. I worked my three-inch Christian Louboutin stilettos like a pair of flip-flops.

"You know you got candies and cookies and all types of snacks up under that skirt!" Rico teased, patting me on the butt. I glanced back at him and smiled. Rico always looked amazing. He was giving me very Old-Hollywood-meets-b-boy-Purple-Rain in a purple velvet Versace suit, lavender dress shirt, and sparkling white Air Force Ones.

As soon as we walked into the upper-level lounge of the club, DJ Biz Markie scratched in the Gap Band's "Outstanding." Hip-hop is cool, but there ain't nothin' like old-school R&B. I headed straight to my best friend, Isabelle Grace Santos, aka Izzy—the Jersey-born effervescent partygirl with a big heart, a bad temper, and the talent to drink any guy under the table. Izzy's the closest I've ever come to a sister.

Izzy was standing next to my reserved table pouring a glass of champagne and glowing. We hugged each other, and she handed me a glass and began dancing in place. All eyeballs, male *and* some female, were suddenly glued to her swaying hips.

The Lowdown

STATS: Thirty-six, but don't tell her agent. Saucy, sassy, 5'10", an amazing body with perfect C-cup breasts, an ungodly tiny waistline, and the colored girl's calling card—a big round booty. She could've easily been a model.

I can't believe we've been friends for fifteen years. It seems like we met yesterday. I was a freshman at NYU and had just started throwing parties. When we met, she told me she had been on her own since she was sixteen, just like Rico. Izzy worked retail and waitress gigs to make ends meet. By the late eighties, girlfriend had become a club rat and figured out a way to use her street-trained dancing talent and her good looks to make money on the emerging music-video scene.

She hit the big time when Al B. Sure!, Bobby Brown, Levert, and Keith Sweat were all at the top of the charts with hits like "Day and Night," "Just Coolin'," "Roni," and "I Want Her." She was the lead dancer in all their videos and out on tour. So, if you've ever wondered "Where Are They Now?" she's right here.

Izzy's dramatic eyes, deep-bronzed, glowing skin, and thick, dark hair can be attributed to her Puerto Rican roots (the *only* good thing her drug-addicted mama ever gave her). She's got a Spanish accent, too, but girlfriend can't speak one word of it. I blame it on her unstable childhood. Well, okay, she managed to pick up some words from her grandmother, who she calls *Abuela*, and she occa-

24

sionally tosses around common Spanglish phrases like *"Mira, Mami, aqui."*

"Izzy, where were you? I waited for you to see if you wanted to ride with us, but we had to roll," I asked, grabbing myself a glass.

"You went to see D-Block, didn't you?" Rico smarted holding up his glass.

"I went to see *D-Roc!*" she snapped.

"Oh, that's cold, Rico. The prison reference is in poor taste!" I said.

"Thank you, Destiny," Izzy said, rolling her eyes at Rico. "He's coming here tonight, so you two play nice!" Izzy gave us a pleading look.

I hate that my girl only has eyes for the dogs of the world. Damon "D-Roc" Douglas, teen R&B heartthrob in the mid-eighties, busted for drugs, then served nine years in prison. That was ten years ago. He's been trying to make a comeback ever since. They hooked up six months ago.

Izzy's convinced D-Roc is her soul mate. I'm convinced her blind eye and deaf ear aren't going to do anything but cause her more pain than she deserves. I hate to be the dark cloud, but I think the whole thing is a ticking time bomb. The scary part is that I don't know when it's going to go *kaboom*! But it's coming.

We finished off that bottle of champagne and wasted no time popping another cork, as Biz Markie brought us out of the old school and into the new school with a slammin' new joint by Mary J. Then The Biz took it all the way to the next level, scratching in some of that Neptunes funk. The entire VIP lounge lost control!

Beautiful brown, black, yellow, tan, and white bodies were swaying all over the room, in a sweat-drippin' choreographed groove. You've got to love the power of music. It moves beyond gender, race, and language.

R&B and pop diva Garcel arrived, surrounded by her personal security and a small entourage of girlfriends. There were no free VIP tables, and she needed a set up right away. Before I could flag down a bouncer to alert one of The Girls, Nikki entered the VIP area and briskly high-stepped through the maze of people in a pair of four-inch stiletto boots and a minidress that showed off her ballet-trained legs. Her warm copper skin matched her soft, tousled, shoulder-length curls. Nikki's large expressive eyes were blinking quickly as she approached me. "Destiny, we're all over it!" she said, whispering loudly in a tightened voice over the music.

"You're killing me with the lip service!" I said impatiently. "Just get the other girls up here to help you ASAP."

"Gotcha!" she said, reaching for her walkie.

Chryssa, my Asian-American Princess, was right behind her. She's a hardcore New Yorker who knows what she wants and goes after it. Her blunted, straight, black mane was bouncing and shaking with every move as she rushed around VIP clearing tables and pushing couches together. In a flash, Nikki had set up glasses and complimentary bottles of champagne, vodka, orange and cranberry juice, and water on the tables.

"Wassup, Garcel, I'm Destiny and welcome to my party. Your table's right over there," I said, extending my hand. I made sure to give the personal touch when celebrities showed up at my parties.

"Hey, Destiny, I've heard a lot about you," Garcel replied. We'd never formally met, and I'd been trying to get her to come to one of my parties for a while.

I motioned for the final third of The Girls, Heather (Jenna's hire), to escort her to her booth. Heather looked nervous, and she was having difficulty maneuvering the superstar through the congested crowd. I told Jenna from the start that her little Southern belle was wimpy and weepy—our "Weakest Link."

Jenna really wanted to help Heather out, and I gave the poor child a shot. But the City ain't for everybody. Grandmaster Flash said it best: "*New York, New York, big city of dreams, and everything in New York ain't always what it seems . . .*" Heather ought to be sipping on mint juleps in her garden somewhere.

I continued making my rounds to the other party guests, then met up with Rico and Izzy on the dance floor, where we twirled and twisted to the pumping, pulsating music. The night was heating up.

Three and a half hours later, Izzy was wasted and still waiting for D-Jerk to show up. It was almost four a.m. and the party was winding down. I settled up my business with Jenna, The Girls, and club management and was ready to call it a night.

Rico helped Izzy into the front seat of the Range Rover, buckled her in, and then climbed into the backseat. I hopped in the driver's seat, started the engine, and waved goodbye to Jenna, who looked like the night had left no mercy.

Stevie Wonder's "Lately" kicked in softly. I whipped the car onto 10th Avenue and jetted up to 23rd Street, hit a right and was at the FDR in no time. I love driving in the wee hours of the morning. The East River is calm, the roads are empty, and the sky is blushing from the hint of daybreak.

"Des, I love you. Don't be mad at me. I love D-Roc, too. You think he loves me, Mami?" Izzy murmured.

"Shhh, Iz. You're drunk. Go back to sleep." I smiled, patting her hand. Before I could say anything else, Izzy was snoring. The sad part is my girl doesn't even have a clue that D-Roc's probably got two or three more just like her. I think the Spinners said it best: "*It takes a fool to learn / that love don't love nobody . . .*"

Don't Believe the Hype

I woke up and hit POWER on the stereo remote, my latest purchase, a Bang and Olufsen surround-sound masterpiece. Nothing like some good funky Cameo to get the blood pumping and that butt in gear. I climbed out of my big, overstuffed, leather-upholstered king bed, untangling myself from the luxurious Frette sheets, and stretched.

My bedroom was a cozy retreat. A great mattress to drift away to the land of the forgotten after a long night is my only prerequisite. You can't hustle in the nightlife scene and not have comfort at your beck and call. The walls, a deep textured crimson, are covered in paintings by Faith Ringgold. Dame Josephine is always preaching that "The hip-hop generation needs to stop wasting all its money on clothes, jewelry and poppin' bottles and invest in Black Art."

A few years ago I started putting my money to good use. Ring-

28

gold is a good friend of Josephine's and I was able to buy several pieces from her "Dinner At Aunt Connie's House" collection—a series of portraits of strong, courageous black women from Rosa Parks and Harriet Tubman to Zora Neale Hurston and Bessie Smith. Waking up seeing the faces of these women on my walls gives me a renewed sense of pride every morning, and reminds me that I can go out into the world and do anything I set my mind to.

I dialed my voicemail.

You have two new messages, twenty-two saved messages.

Obviously, I haven't done a very good job of setting my mind to cleaning out my mailbox.

MESSAGE ONE:

Curtis: Destiny, I miss you and that beautiful smile and wanna see you. How's my friend? I'm getting hard just thinking about her. Call me.

(Damn, a brotha's pressed!)

The Lowdown:

IDENTITY: Curtis Chatsworth III

STATUS: Married. Fell out of love a long time ago. (Yes, I know dating a married man is a major no-no for women who have scruples. Not that I don't, just not in his case.) Curtis is one of the biggest entertainment lawyers in New York. Get this Armani-clad brotha behind closed doors, and it's all about the freaks comin' out at night.

He's a major power player, and far from a square. Raised in the 'hood in Newark, he got a BA and his MA from Columbia, and then a JD from Stanford. Oh, and I almost forgot to mention, a PhD in Cunnilingus.

29

MESSAGE TWO:

Curtis: Hey, where are you? I really want to see you.

Note to self: Hello? Can somebody get the message to him that it's not attractive to beg? I hung up the receiver, slipped the twelve-inch version of "Let It Whip" into the CD changer, turned the volume up louder, and did the Electric Slide right out of my undies and tank and into the shower.

Fifteen minutes later I was refreshed, recharged and ready to take on the beast . . . Life.

I walked out of my bedroom and into the living room, turning the speakers on in the rest of the apartment. Izzy was sound asleep in the loft bedroom. Not even blasting the Dazz Band will wake that girl from her comatose state. The office *used* to be set up in the loft, but for the past three weeks my large stainless-steel dining table has been temporarily doubling as the office–slash–conference room.

I insisted Izzy come here, after losing her Brooklyn sublet, until she saved up enough money to get a new place. She's spent more time "in between" apartments than anyone else I know. Girlfriend's been a regular gypsy, jumping between her abuela's house in Jersey City, different boyfriends' apartments, and finally the Brooklyn spot. I'll be happy when she gets settled.

I plopped down on my large chenille sectional, picked up the television remote, and pressed POWER on the giant plasma screen that was attached to the far wall. After a few minutes of channel surfing, I landed on CNN and hit mute. This was my daily routine. The feel-good music playing on the stereo helped me get through the headlines of the day's worldwide tragedies slowly crawling across the screen. I picked up the cordless to call Ainee, who I hadn't spoken with in two weeks. Note to self: MUST GET BETTER ABOUT THINGS LIKE THIS.

"Ainee, it's me!"

"I was just thinkin' 'bout you. You musta read my mind," she said in her usual warm and motherly tone. "Why haven't I heard from you, child? Watchu doin' up there? Are you eating right?" Ainee had a million questions. I'm used to it. I just let her talk and proceeded to light up a cig.

"Don't worry about me. I'm a big girl, Ainee. I just gotta make sure you and Uncle Charlie are taken care of," I said letting out a puff of smoke.

"You know me and your uncle worry about you, living that fast life. Lord, you so much like your mama. You won't let no grass grow up under your feet," she laughed. "But you sweet and givin' like your daddy. Carlton had a big heart. I suspect that's why he loved your mama so much. You deserve to have that kind of love, Destiny. When you gonna find a nice young man to marry?"

Why was she starting up? It seems like lately that's all she ever does is worry me about getting a husband. I held the phone away from my mouth and took another big puff, inhaled, and slowly released a cloud of ringlets. I imagined sending out rescue smoke signals.

"Ainee, you know I love you, but my life is great just as it is. Please understand I'm just not the marrying type. I like having my own space and callin' my own shots too much."

There was a long pause. My words were a hint for Ainee to get off my back about that whole marriage thing.

"*Please*, stop worrying, Ainee."

"I'll shut my mouth and keep you in my prayers. It's just that I saw how your mama and daddy came and went, and I know all about that fast-paced livin'."

I didn't like it when she started bringing up the past, talking about Juanita and Carlton.

"Destiny, it's dangerous out here in these streets."

"I'm not in the streets, and I don't mess around with, or know anybody who messes around with, gangsters *or* drugs, Ainee."

"Well, I just know that nightclub life *brings* trouble."

Ainee was subtly trying to compare my lifestyle to my parents', mainly my mother's. I heard mixed stories growing up about the so-called "trouble" that got them killed. However, the general consensus was that Juanita set Carlton up (that "general consensus" being my paternal side of the family). They said Juanita was the smart, streetwise one. I've never met any of my mother's people, so all I could go by was my Granny saying things like, "that low-life woman this," or "that low-life woman that."

By the time I was ten, my mama and daddy were dead, and I had to grow up real quick, because my Granny died six months later. I think it was because she had lost her only child the way she did. She was heartbroken. A parent never thinks they're going to bury their child first.

I ended up with Granny's baby sister, Ernestine. I call her Ainee (pronounced A-NEE, because I couldn't say Ernestine when I was a little girl). Ainee and Uncle Charlie took me to live with them in Markum, Illinois, a small, working-class, tight-knit suburban community just outside Chicago, where people went to church on Sundays, had good family values, and stressed education. But I never lost my connection to East Boogie in my heart.

I quickly shook the thoughts of my stolen childhood out of my head. Thinking about Juanita and Carlton stirs up mixed emotions, both sadness and anger, because I never got the chance to have a real "mommy" and "daddy" like the kind you see on television. They never saw me grow up, and I'll never see them grow old together.

"Destiny, men and women need companionship when they get up in age." Ainee was trying to send me to the retirement home at thirty-five. "That's why I want you to get yourself settled. You should've finished college, that's what you should've done."

That's another pill I've had to swallow for God knows how long. I made the decision sophomore year at NYU to forfeit that full four-year scholarship to be "*A what? A club promoter. Do Jesus!*" Ainee almost had a heart attack right there at the dining room table during Christmas dinner when I broke the news.

"Ainee, I know it still upsets you that I gave up my scholarship."

"Well, baby, it's just that you're so smart. You could've been a doctor or a lawyer."

"But I'm doing what I love to do, and I make more money than I could've ever made with that bachelor's degree."

"Humph! I'll let it be. I just don't know how long I'm gonna be around, and I wanna see you happy, child."

"Ainee, don't talk like that. You aren't going anywhere anytime soon. Let's talk about something happier, like how's the unpacking going?"

"Lord have mercy, I still can't get over all this house. I guess you must be doin' alright 'cause this house you got me and Uncle Charlie sure is nice. This is more room than we know what to do with." She laughed.

Yes, I did it. Achieved the NBA players wassup-y'all-I-bought-my-mama-a-house dream. They'd never owned a home, and property being so cheap back in Markum compared to New York, I wanted to give them something to show my thanks for putting up with me.

"Just don't forget where your blessings come from," she insisted.

"I know, Ainee. Me and God have an understanding."

I noticed my BlackBerry buzzing and five new messages on my cell. "Ainee, I gotta go. I love you, and give my love to Uncle Charlie, too."

"I love you, baby! Be safe up there!" She laughed again. "And maybe you'll meet a nice man and change your mind about getting married."

"I doubt it," I said sweetly, with a touch of sarcasm. "On that note, I really gotta go!"

Conversation over. It's hard explaining my life to somebody like Ainee. All she knows is her forty-plus years of marriage, going to church, what Uncle Charlie has told her about life, and living in Markum. My life, on the other hand, is way outside their realm of thinking, and for the most part that of most people. She equates happiness with having a family.

"Wake up, sleeping beauty!" I buzzed in Izzy's ear. She swatted the air, attempting to squish an imaginary fly. I shook her harder. "Heifer, wake up, we gots ta roll!" I shouted. She groggily rolled over and sat up.

"Shut up! I've got a hangover!" she said sleepily.

"That's what you get for being an amateur," I said, ripping the covers back.

Izzy could always get dressed fast when she was hungry. We stepped out of my Harlem abode on 140th Street and headed down the block to St. Nicholas Avenue. The brownstone I live in had been converted into three condos by a black developer. My building is just a quick walk from the epicenter of blackness, 125th Street.

The mercury reads a slightly brisk but pleasant sixty-five. Looks like Mother Nature's hormones are stable today. As we approached 125th, the smell of fresh fish, fried chicken grease, and sandalwood made for an interesting mixture.

"New-ports! WassupIgotthemNew-ports!" A b-boyed-up young Blackman inconspicuously whispered in passing. Brothaman was getting his hustle on.

Standing outside a hair-braiding shop were four African women; one, young and dressed in a Kente cloth print dress and head wrap, called out, "Braids! You get your hair braided!" There was a cluster of two or three more down the block doing the same thing. Uptown, you could get hooked up with silky twists, dreads, braids, or even a fly weave in no time.

For other sistas, the choice may be the Puerto Rican and Dominican sistas who can whip one of their famous "doobies" (also known as the fierce wrap) on you at lightning speed, and all for twenty dollars. Whatever your flavor, vibe, or style, slammin', fab hair Uptown is all around, and a woman has no excuse to have too many bad hair days.

Farther down the block, we ran into my man Unique, the self-ordained "bootleg king" who was giving free previews of the latest Will Smith flick via a mini flat-screen strapped to the front of his sweatshirt.

"Wassup ladies! Yo, I got that hotness!"

"Not today, Unique, not today," I smiled.

Izzy and I made our way down the lively Avenue filled with people, *my* people, who had the corners jam-packed. Just for fun, we flirted with the brothas posted up on the block, scoping us out. I love black men, and from the roughnecks to the refined, Harlem has 'em, representin' all shades cocoa, caramel, café au lait, and chocolate.

In all of New York, there's no other block, borough, or 'hood that matches the hustle, flow, attitude, and flavor of Harlem. I may be a transplant, but I've made Uptown the place where I rest my head. I consider myself a New Yorker, and this *is* everyday living.

The Breaks

I opened the door to Carol's Daughter on 125th Street and Izzy and I were greeted with the floating aroma of red clover, roses, eucalyptus, and lavender. Rico manages the boutique-style natural body and hair products store, but he constantly reminds us all that it's "just temporary," until his "TV or movie ship comes in."

He's hoping some high-profile celebrity will snag him to travel the world and make them beautiful. I'm the first person to endorse the "dream big" campaign, but you've got to put the work in, too. It's not going to happen by osmosis. Rico's problem is that he's more focused on "boys" than doing makeup.

I scanned the store for Rico while Izzy browsed, testing and smelling the latest arrivals of shea-butter moisturizer and passion-fruit-scented hair oil. I started using Carol's Daughter in the early nineties when the owner made the body products in her Brooklyn home, and I've been addicted to the brownsugahhoneykissed handmade oils and body goods ever since.

"Hey Destiny, hey Izzy," Imani, the assistant manager, called out from the rear of the store. She's a soul-sista who makes Erykah Badu look conservative. "Rico said come on back."

"The Legendary!" Rico passed out his usual greeting for me. *Kiss, kiss* on each cheek as we entered the stockroom. "And look at you, La Doña!" He gave Izzy a repeat performance of the *kiss, kiss* routine. "Did y'all see that man I met last night?"

"That's the problem. It's all about the boys when it needs to be all about your book!" I stayed on Rico 24/7 to get his portfolio done so he could get out there and hobnob with some of the artists I know. But no matter how much I love him I am not putting my reputation on the line for Rico to half-step.

"Chile, I'm gonna get it done when the time is right. It's called cash-flow shortage! Anyway, don't you want to hear about the cutie I met last night?"

"When?" Izzy asked.

"Chile, you was drunk. You wouldn't remember!" He rolled his eyes.

"Rico, you meet a cutie every night," I said.

"No, his name is Jorge and he's beautiful, Destiny."

"*Ay, dios mio*! He's La'in?" Izzy didn't pronounce the "t". She put her hands on her hips, "Rico, just tell me—is he legal?"

"Yes, he'll be twenty-five in a week or so, but never mind that! He's a sweetie."

Rico has a fetish for younger Spanish men, and most of the time they're unemployed. "So what does he do for a living?" I asked.

"I knew you were gonna go there, Destiny. That's why I don't like sharing my business witchu! Yes, he *does* have a job!"

"Don't get indignant, the last three didn't." I gave Izzy a girl-friend high-five.

"He's a masseur," Rico said defensively. "Well, he's working on saving his money to go to massage school. So right now he's dancin' down at Crash."

"Oh, yeah, the gay club over there on Thirty-Ninth, between Fifth and Sixth," Izzy said.

"What? He's a go-go dancer?" I said with surprise.

"Crash is a very popular club. He makes *very* good tips!" Rico said, folding his arms across his chest.

"Oh, now you've got an attitude," I laughed. "I've got nothin' to say."

"Good, 'cause don't nobody say nothin' about them tired brothas you been draggin' around. Malik, Curtis, Peter, and ooh, Black. Stop the madness! If you ain't goin' to the Academy Awards with his ass, you need to cut the umbilical cord!"

"First off, Black was cut off a long time ago, and at least my men are all paid and bringin' somethin' to the party."

"I'm still buggin' that Rico's got a dancing massage therapist! That's hot!" Izzy taunted.

"I know you'd best not say nothin' or I'll get started on D-Block, the ex-con crooner!" Rico glared at Izzy.

"No, you di'n't!" Izzy's mouth fell open.

"Yes, he did!" I teased.

My cell rang. The caller ID flashed: MALIK'S CELL. "Finally! My boo." I smiled. They both gave me appalled looks. "I know that sounds reeeeaaaally ghetto, doesn't it?"

"He got you open, Mami."

"They say all a woman really wants is a roughneck," Rico said.

"But there's something even more exciting, and that's a rough-neck who's paid, smart, in fresh sneakers, a crisp white tee, and wear-ing a nicely starched but broken-in pair of jeans, with the right sag, in all the *right* places. I really ought to be ashamed of myself. I'm too damn old to be checking for a brotha with a sag. Malik is damn near thirty-seven!"

"Legendary, I don't think I've ever seen the man in a pair of dress slacks and shoes."

"I don't think he owns any," I said. Oh well, I may not be an advocate for falling in love, but they also say every woman has "one" who makes her heart flutter, and right now I can feel mine beating between my ears. Maybe I'll play it right and not answer, make him wait like he always makes me. "Can you believe I haven't heard from Malik in over a week? Then all of a sudden I get a message from him yesterday. I *need* to let him know he's dispensable!"

"Yeah, right! Give her a minute, she gonna crack," Rico said, looking at Izzy as if he was about to cash in on a bet.

"Don't count on it," I snapped in protest. "I know what to do with a man like Malik. You can't let yourself be available all the time. Just wait. I will conquer this beast!"

"Who you foolin', Ma?" Izzy taunted as we headed toward the front door of the store.

"Imani, I'm out for lunch, get that new shipment on display, please!" Rico called out, pointing where *this* and *that* ought to be placed.

"Let's lunch, ladies!"

We were barely out of the store when my phone rang again. I looked at the screen, at Izzy, then at Rico, back at the screen, then at both of them, then finally gave in and answered.

"Hey, Mama." There was that rough-and-ready, ride-or-die signature greeting. Malik had one of those voices that automatically made you want to undress when you heard it.

"Hey back." Yep, I was smiling, doing a piss-poor job of keeping up my tough-girl act.

"I'm heading over the GW Bridge, I'ma scoop you in about twenty minutes."

"I might be busy." I tried to stand firm. Izzy and Rico played the whistling-Dixie routine in the background.

"D, quit buggin', you know I'm goin' through some shit right now tryin' to finish this album, and today is a fucked-up day for me. I need to see you and I got something for you, please." The magic words. I agreed to see him and hung up. A smile crept across my face again.

"Don't try to front for us, Mami. You know you love that man."

"You're making more out of it than it is. Malik just needs to talk. And let's clear this up, I *like*, I don't *love* Malik. There's a big difference."

"Is cool, do watchu gotta do, Mami, even if it means kicking your girl to the curb," Izzy said.

"She betta if she gone eat tomorrow!" Rico had once again pushed the limits of creativity—using that old-timey phrase coined by Southern folks.

"That man is fine!" Rico said.

"You got that right, Rico. Izzy, you'll get over it!" I said.

Izzy and Rico bade me farewell and continued to bicker down the rest of the block. This was their regular Desi-and-Lucy routine. We may give each other a hard time, but it's all in love. I know it may sound clichéd, but in this world, true friends *are* few and far between. I can count mine on one hand. He may be a drama queen, but like I told you before . . . if the boy can't do anything else, he *can* beat a face. Makeup is his life, and if I had two wishes, the first, of course, would be for Izzy to get her own place. The second would be for Rico to do makeup full-time.

What a Man

The Twenty-Fours on Malik's brand-spanking-new, black-on-black Mercedes-Benz SL 500 rolled to a slow stop. I opened the door. He was blasting classic Biggie. Hey! *"Kick in the door wavin the four-four . . ."* I slid into the passenger seat, bobbing my head. I had re-fluffed my spiky-curly hairdo. Ah, the beauty of having a short haircut! I was glad I had put on a cute outfit today, too.

Malik liked it when I wore tight low-rider jeans that showed off my butt. Plus I had on my favorite black leather Gucci jacket and boots. I tossed my large metallic handbag onto the backseat. Malik was wearing his regular flavor: jeans, a Sean John lightweight goose down, white shell-toe adidas, and a black skully, looking appetizingly good. He gave me a deep lingering kiss.

"You hungry?" he asked in a soft and somber tone.

"I could eat," I said, smiling.

Malik turned off Lenox onto 116th. Amy Ruth's Home Style was the spot to get all the good soul-food eating you could want in Harlem. Once we were seated, Malik took the liberty of ordering our regular: Sweet tea, collards, black-eyed peas, fried chicken, cornbread, and mac and cheese, and two Heinekens to wash it down. We topped everything off by splitting a slice of red velvet cake. I thought my stomach was going to burst.

Malik removed his skully. He was fresh from the barbershop and looked like a sweetfaced little boy. My sensitive thug.

Straight outta the South Philly streets. Malik's daddy may have been a famous jazz musician and producer, but he left home when Malik was three to go on the road and tour. His music was more important than being a father and family man. That's when Malik's grandmother stepped in to raise him.

We had seen a lot of the same pain and struggles. I was proud of the fact that despite the street odds, my baby was smart. He had gone off to a small college down in North Carolina on a football scholarship and vowed to be successful and take care of his grandmother. He never really wanted to be in the music business, but I guess, just like me, he couldn't fight the genes.

Malik has become one of the biggest power players behind the scenes in the music biz. He has all the jewels and paper to floss, but he grew up fighting to get his. My man is a mover and shaker with a small stable of in-demand producers, and an artist named Freedom that the industry had been hyped about for the last two years. Except where was this *highly anticipated* album everyone's been waiting on, that Sony Records paid an advance of a million dollars for?

How we met . . .

Occasionally, I venture downtown to the Village Vanguard to hear jazz. It gives me peace of mind. One particular night the marquee read: "KING" JARU AND FRIENDS: TERRENCE BLANCHARD ON TRUMPET, RON CARTER ON BASS, HERBIE HANCOCK ON PIANO, AND "KING" ON DRUMS. Talk about living legends. I quickly purchased my ticket and headed inside.

I noticed a tall brotha enter the joint, and I immediately peeped out his savvy street swagger. He sported his trademark, fresh-out-the-barbershop fade, and his watch, bracelet, and diamond-and-platinum link necklace were more *bling bang* than gaudy. Okay, so I blushed when he asked if he could join me. I was alone and brothaman couldn't understand why.

"I do this all the time. Music is like my religion. People go to church by themselves, don't they?"

"True!" I could hear his strong Philly accent. He was surprised by my candor.

"Why not come to the club to hear music by myself?"

His face lit up. His lips, his teeth, his smile, made me want to kiss him. A kiss for me can be just as important as making love. I wanted his lips on mine at that very instant, but I held back. I knew it would be worth the wait.

The rest of the night we went back and forth about jazz. Who was the coldest: Coltrane or Rollins; Miles or Diz; Wynton or Blanchard, and on and on. The *one* thing we did agree on was Monk having been one of the baddest pianist/composers that ever lived.

After the show, my goodbye was interrupted by his spontaneous invitation for me to hang out for a few at the club. He said he had a surprise. My stomach got all jittery when he took his strong arms and gently moved my body behind his. I clutched the back of his shirt. He towered over me like a giant human shield. He smelled clean. I know it sounds corny, but his scent reminded me of that Irish-Spring, just-out-of-the-shower freshness. He grabbed my hand (his was soft, yet masculine) and led me backstage.

"Pops!" he called out.

A man with long silver dreads, equally towering, and smoking a fat one, turned around. His father was "King" Jaru, world-renowned jazz producer and drummer. I felt like such an idiot, having gone on and on about jazz, a world that was second nature to this man. I gave Malik one of those *how-you-gonna-play-me-out-like-that* looks.

After introducing me to the rest of the musicians, he walked me out to my car. I gave him my number, and before I could get a good-bye out, he took me in his arms and kissed me. You know, one of those good, long, juicy but not sloppy, lust-filled kisses, and it was all I imagined it would be. That man almost had a sista fallin' out right there on the spot.

● ● ●

"Watchu daydreamin' about, D?" Malik asked, interrupting my walk down memory lane.

"About how long we've been hangin' out."

"Oh, c'mon, you not about to get all female on me, are you?"

"Negro, please! You know that's not my style. I'll leave that to those wimpy girls," I laughed.

"Nah, I'm just teasin' you. I'm glad we tight like this. I can talk to you like we boys."

"And then there's the incredible sex!" I said, blowing him a kiss across the table.

I could always keep it real with Malik. So many times men have to deal with women sweatin' them or vice versa. Malik knew I was the kind of woman who would never blow up his spot as long as he came straight with me.

"Thanks for hanging out with me today, D," he said, clearing his throat. "I'm under a lot of pressure with Freedom and the record label."

"I know, that's why I'm here. Despite the fact that I think it was pretty inconsiderate of you to leave town for almost a week and not even tell me you were going away, or call me when you got there. Nothin'! What's up with that?" I said, stroking his hand.

"I'm sorry, D. Sometimes there's so much happening I don't know whether I'm coming or going. Shit's crazy."

"Hey, we're both busy and have lives. It's just about showing the other person some courtesy. You feel me?"

"I feel you. C'mon, let's go for a ride," Malik said smiling.

Malik turned off 125th Street onto the small service road that runs parallel to the West Side Highway. We were as far west as you could get in Manhattan. The Hudson River was just over a short fence. He parked. Biggie's "Ready to Die" was playing softly.

"Remember back in the day when you had the Tunnel on lock?" Malik said, reminiscing wistfully.

"The Tunnel put me on the map!" I said. Biggie's "Party and Bullshit" came on in the background. "Ooh, that was my song!" I closed my eyes, trapped in the music. "*I came into the world ready to party and bullshit . . . !* Whew! How blazin' was that track?" Biggie's song was taking me back to the early nineties all over again.

In ninety-three, I used to do Sunday nights at a club called The Tunnel (remember over there off the West Side Highway? Yeah, you remember). It was during the same time 'Pac was shooting the movie *Above The Rim*, and he and Biggie came through the party like Batman and Superman around midnight. The crowd went bananas.

"Them thug-ass Brooklyn heads are wildin' out, fightin'!" one of my bouncers alerted.

"Get 'em outta my spot, now!" I was screaming frantically at security to "toss 'em to the streets!"

Big and 'Pac walked onto the stage. "Where my party people at?" Tupac's gruff voice had seen more pain than men twice his age.

"Drop that shit!" Biggie ordered, sounding like a ten-year-old exhaust pipe, his words running together (folks back home in Markum would refer to it as being "tie-tongued"). DJ Clark Kent dropped the needle on the wax. A chilling hush fell over the crowd. You just knew all of hip-hop was about to be baptized and anointed by two disciples of the ghetto. It was mystifying. They rocked the mic, freestylin' to Biggie's "Dreams." Martin and Malcolm reincarnated in the form of urban street soldiers. They took the entire club to the mountaintop.

I still can't believe we lost two of the illest lyricists in the game, over some bullshit . . . *Party and bullshit* . . .

● ● ●

Malik and I were both lost in thought. The river's choppy waves splashed against the rocks that lined the shore. Malik held me close.

"I gotta make this music shit hot again with Freedom, D."

"You will when they put the record out."

"Nah, I'm thinkin' I might have to do it renegade-style if the label keeps trippin'. I wish I had the money right now to just buy him out the contract and do that joint independently, press the record up, get it to dj's to promote it."

"You know DJ Peter and all the dj's who spin at my parties will definitely play it. Screw the record company."

"It would cost me about two hundred G's to pull it off, but a lot of cats out here owe me favors. I know I could get hot producers to lace me for cheap, and for the video, I could go to any one of the big hip-hop video directors. Damn, it doesn't matter. I've still gotta hit cats off with cash.

"It's just not possible right now. Most of my crew is on my payroll. I've got to make sure my two kids are taken care of. My cash is all tied up."

"If you didn't have to take care of all your boys . . ."

"D, chill on that. Brothas got kids to feed. Bottom line, I need an investor." He looked at me. "Or one hot party on the level you operate on and I could make some fast paper."

He laughed. My eyes went wide. I know he didn't think I was about to just throw *my* checkbook at him.

"Hold up, D, I see the look on your face, and that shit hurts!"

"It's just that I don't operate like that. I have to see a solid business plan before I . . ."

"I'm not coming to you to get money!"

"I thought . . ."

"To hell with what you thought!"

"Malik, baby, please!" I reached for him. He pulled back. "Baby, you have to really think stuff like this through. I mean do you have a plan on paper?"

"D, I'm from the streets. I know how to battle with the hustlas *and* the white boys. I make hot music. That's what I do! On the real, I don't need your help, but if I did, at least I know where we stand. You definitely just showed me the truth."

I took his hand in mine and squeezed it tight. "Don't play games with me to see if I really have your back or something. You know the truth. I believe in you and I am supportive. I'm sorry." He reluctantly took me in his arms. I rested my head on his chest and began rubbing it. I soon had him as placid as the now-quiet Hudson. The chorus to the Biggie classic echoed in my head, "*Biggie give me one more chance . . .*"

An hour later, we nestled in my bed. Malik's body shuddered in my arms. He made a quiet, deep grunt. I followed it up with an embarrassingly loud moan. This brotha was too cool to make any noise. He thrust himself in and out, up and down, deeper and deeper inside me each time. Me coming, him coming, both climaxing. Tiny earthquakes erupted between our naked bodies.

When we were finished, Malik rolled over and sat up on the edge of the bed, removing the condom. I reached inside the nightstand and ripped open a feminine wipe. I kept a stack of packets there for times like this when I didn't feel like rushing off to shower.

Malik was six-two and strong. I rubbed his belly, then kissed it. He had developed one of those I'm-makin'-more-money-than-I-know-what-to-do-with-so-I-can-afford-to-eat-out-every-night-at-expensive-restaurants, music-industry guts. In other words, the lifestyle of making hit records, and fancy eating, blowing at least three, four, five hundred dollars in one sitting, to treat all his boys and any other groupie who decided to tag along, didn't allow much time for an exercise regimen.

"I almost forgot." He picked up his jeans and reached in the pocket. "This is for you." He placed a platinum-and-diamond tennis bracelet, with a pavé-diamond "D" dangling from it, on my wrist. I pounced on the bed with excitement.

"I love it! But wait, I can't take this," I said, seductively sliding behind his body. "This could be Freedom's video or a number-one single from a hit-making producer."

"Don't insult me, D. I have to make sure my girl is happy. How does that look if we're hanging out and I'm rockin' jewels and you're not?"

I ran my hand up and down his tattooed biceps, admiring my new gift. As I traced the outline of the Psalm Twenty-Three inscription on his left forearm, I thought back to how Juanita would talk to me when she was drinking, like I was grown, about love and life. She liked the blues and sad songs. Her favorite was the way Aretha sang "Today I Sing The Blues." Ree Ree would wear that song out 'til it screamed uncle. It was like the blues walked right in and camped out at our house.

"The worse kind of loving is the kind that's good," she'd say. I didn't know what she was talking about, but I was intrigued by the way she closed her eyes, wrapped her arms around herself, and danced in the middle of the floor. She was graceful and pretty like the ballerinas I saw in my books.

"A man's promise don't mean shit, you know that, Destiny. Watch what he does and what he spends, and not what he says. Talkin' sweet don't mean shit," she laughed, taking a sip of the dark liquid that looked like Coca-Cola in her glass. After a few glasses she'd be sliding out of her seat and slurring her words, but when I drank soda pop it didn't make me do that. She let me have a little swig of hers one time and it burned my throat and chest. She laughed at me.

"Yeah, a man can do a whole lot, like buy you nice clothes, take you fancy places, and kiss you real sweet." She closed her eyes and twirled around. "Sing it, Ree Ree! Humph, what a difference a day makes. My life used to be good before you came along."

I lowered my eyes. "Damn, I didn't mean it like that, Destiny." She touched my face. "I just mean I never thought I'd be sitting here being somebody's mama. Fate is a motherfucker." Juanita cracked a smile and reached out her hand and grabbed mine. "Come on, dance with me." We began to dance. Juanita always had the blues, but that night we chased them off good. I know it because the next day I saw her smiling and hugging Carlton like nothing had ever happened.

I couldn't stop thinking about the pressure Malik must be under. It takes a lot of strength to go up against a machine like a major record company, but I know if anybody can figure it out, my baby can.

Malik blazed up a blunt and took a long toke. He hated that I smoked cigarettes and drank like a fish, but he was a weed-head. We always debated one vice against the other. He blew out a puff of smoke and turned toward me, running his fingers across my cheek and lips, flashing a bedazzling smile. I blushed and disappeared under the covers, but not before inviting him back in for Round Two. Now that's some good thug luvin'.

You Can't Play with
My Yo-Yo

Saturday is catch-up time with Jenna. We usually spend half the day working, and the other half hanging out as girlfriends—you know, doing the brunch thing, shopping, mani-pedis. Since neither one of us was in much of a mood to work today, I decided we should get our to-do list done as quickly and painlessly as possible and put most of our energies into Saturday slumming. Translation: lots of girl talk and snacking on fattening brain food: pizza, beer, and chocolate!

Today couldn't be a better day for all of the above, either. Izzy's gone MIA for the past twenty-four hours. She's probably holed up somewhere with D-Roc. It would be nice if he could at least keep some money in her pocket. I'm not complaining, because when I was struggling trying to get started doing small clubs here and there around town, Izzy was rollin' in the dough. Dancing in music videos kept *her* paid, and *me* with a meal more often than not.

I try not to make her feel uncomfortable about staying here, but it gets challenging. Sometimes there's entirely too much activity going on. I have enough action happening at the clubs. When I'm home I like two things: my space and listening to my music. I love Izzy, but I'm going to rejoice on that happy day she moves.

"Okay, what's our week looking like?" I asked Jenna, semi-distracted, checking my voicemail.

"I can do better than that," she said. I got our club lineup for the next week, including the following Tuesday."

"Hold that thought!"

YOU HAVE ONE NEW MESSAGE . . .

Ainee: Destiny, it's Ainee. I'm just callin', baby. I didn't talk to you last weekend. Me and Uncle Charlie doin' fine. We love you. I'm praying for you, too. I saw a really nice-lookin' young man at church Sunday. He's got a good job and comes from a nice family. Oh, well, we love you.

"Urgh!"

"That must be Malik."

"I wish. It's Ainee. I forgot to call back home." I hung up.

"Des, you've got to do better. Your aunt and uncle are getting older, and you never know."

"You're right, but everything's so hectic. Ainee will understand. I'll try to remember to call sometime this week. Anyway, let's move on . . . quickly!"

"Okay, we've got Couture Funk at Lotus on Wednesday."

"Perfect, make sure DJ Peter plays all the sexy sounds that the beautiful people like." I give each of my weekly parties a name. Couture Funk attracts the trendy high-end fashionistas and the hip, young, big-screen actresses and actors.

"We've got dj's Elle, Selly, Naomi, and Miss Saigon for our Femme Fatale party at Joe's Pub on Thursday."

"Hold up, you can't have an all-female dj line up without featuring DJ Jazzy Joyce or Samantha Ronson, and see if Spinderella is in town and can come through. Ladies ten dollars, guys twenty!"

"Bubbles and Beats is Friday at Club Bed. Veuve is the champagne of the night. Finally Tuesday we've got Electric Essence at Club Flow."

"I like all of that. Bottle service only in VIP at Bed, and DJ Peter needs to keep the hip-hop, R&B, and reggae going all night at Flow. Open bar 'til eleven, get Crown Royal to hook it up. At midnight, we'd better be getting fifteen to twenty dollars a head. Put it all together and send out an e-blast to all the record labels, modeling agencies, magazines, and industry big-mouths. Okay, enough work, let's break out the double chocolate fudge brownies!"

"Yummy, I'm PMSing, too. This is just what the doctor ordered," Jenna said, quickly putting away her work folder.

"*I* don't know about *you*, but I feel like some old-school hip-hop."

I searched frantically through my CDs that lined the living room's back wall. My collection was somewhere in the thousands, I'm sure. Hiking, reading, or tennis may work for some, but Destiny Day's "thing" is all about the music and a sista *is* picky. You can't just slap on any old record.

I pulled the CD of choice from the shelf, carefully lifted the disc out of the jewel case, and placed it in the CD player.

"Des, you're acting like it's the Hope Diamond or something."

"Music *should* be handled with care. I damn near need twenty-four-hour security to watch Nina, Luther, Prince, the Stones, Parliament, 'Pac, Aretha, and The O'Jays!"

I slowly pressed PLAY on the stereo. Eight bars of percolating, pulse-pumping congas kicked in . . .

"Aw yeah! Can you feel it? It's Nile Rodgers's famous throbbing bass. The thump that makes your body melt into the rhythm, and you know that what you're hearing is definitely not a test. No, this is that *real* hip-hop music."

"Des, I have never met anyone who loved music as much as you do."

"It's in my DNA," I said, breaking into the first line of the Sugar Hill Gang's hip-hop opus, "Rapper's Delight." I spun around and did a smooth body-wave move. Jenna doubled over with laughter. "Girl, that was my jam! Ooh, I almost forgot to show you the latest!" I said, flashing my wrist and the dangling blingrific "D".

"My eyes! My eyes! I've been blinded!" Jenna said, dramatically shielding her face.

"That's right, my baby keeps me icy!"

"Yeah, if only you could get a little consistency from that man."

"Who cares about consistency? This way we never get sick of each other."

"That bracelet's amazing, but I don't think you really feel that way."

"Of course I do, Jenna. As long as the paper is rollin' and the diamonds are sparklin', I'm cool. Malik will never be far away. If I really need him, I know how to track him down."

"He may never be far, but he's never within reach, and that's what's important. Really, who wants to always have to exert so much energy tracking a guy down?"

"I'm cool with it, Jenna. And you know I can *always* call up Peter Peter Pussy Eater."

"That's so crass and impersonal." Jenna's reaction was like an animal releasing her scent to mark her territory.

"Jenna, don't tell me Peter's your crush." I was strangely taken aback.

"Don't be silly, Destiny."

"Hey, I just saw how uncomfortable you got when I referred to him as the *Pussy Eater*."

"It's not a nice reference," she said, clearing her throat. "I know that's your piece. And I do not have some schoolgirl crush on him, don't worry."

"Oh, I'm not worried, you're my girl, but you know the rules."

"Yeah, yeah, never shit where you eat. 'My money is my money, and my men are my men,' " she said, mimicking me.

"See, now you're trying to be funny!"

"For the hundredth time, I don't have a crush on Peter. The point of all this is that you're always playing Mother Hen to all of us, and now it's my turn to make sure you're okay. I see that you care for Malik, but remember the old saying, Destiny, 'Money can't buy love,' girlfriend."

"I'm not looking for love on *that* level, so stop worrying. Anyway, who cares if it can or can't buy love, it certainly *can* buy some spectacular baubles like this one!" I brandished the bracelet again.

Malik may not be what Jenna, Rico, Izzy, or Josephine considers to be the "perfect relationship," aka consistency and dependability, but who cares—he has *great* taste.

"I give up! You have all the answers, so I'll just stay tuned for another episode of the Fabulous Life of Destiny Day!" Jenna proclaimed.

Just then, Rico rang the buzzer on my door. When I opened it, he was wringing his hands and had a worried look on his face.

"Destiny, I really need to talk to you," he whispered loudly, pushing his way into my apartment.

"Rico, I'm meeting with Jenna. Can it wait?"

"Girl, don't worry," Jenna cut in. "I know what I have to do for work. I'm heading out. I need to get a mani-pedi." She'd sensed the urgent nature of Rico's unexpected visit. She collected her things, gave a round of goodbye hugs, and jetted.

"Rico, what was that all about? How rude. Wait, I know that look. It's Jorge, isn't it?" Rico didn't have to say a word. When he has that woe-is-me look, it's always boy trouble. "Rico, I told you that boy was too young for you to be messing around with. He's barely legal, he's unemployed, and you're stressed out, chasing him all over town! Baby, you're almost forty years old! What are you doing?"

"Don't ever bring up a diva's age, *that's* rude! Anyway, age is a state of mind, and Jorge is not running all over town. I just need to borrow some money until next week."

"Rico, you've never been good at managing your money, but ever since Jorge's been around you've been even worse, and extra broke. This is the second time I've loaned you money in two weeks."

I pulled five one-hundred-dollar bills out of my wallet.

"Destiny, this is the last time, I swear."

"I know it, because the bank's closed!"

"Jorge had an emergency and I just had to take care of something."

"Jorge needs to get a *real* job."

"Destiny, we all have our man issues, *please*."

I knew my friends well enough to know when not to push or back them into a corner, just like they knew when to let up on me. I dropped the issue.

"Hey, I picked these up for you while I was at the newsstand," I said, changing the subject. "Maybe they'll inspire you to work on *that book*," I hinted, handing him a large shopping bag.

"Ooh, you know I love *Italian Vogue*! And *W* and all the international trades! Chile, look at Miss Beyoncé! She ain't workin' it like she needs to. I could beat that face backwards. And look at Christina Aguilera! They got my girl looking like a drag queen! Now look at Tyra. You know that's my dream to do her. I could really do magic on that face. Ooh, let me see who they got to do this makeup. Humph! He ain't all that."

"I'm giving you these magazines for inspiration, not for you to bash other people's work. You need to get rid of all that negativity and channel that into your own creativity."

"Preach, Oprah! I'm working on it. But I gotta get the right people for my book, and it takes money to get a photographer and set up a shoot."

"If you weren't trying to play sugar daddy to Jorge, you'd have your book. I'm not trying to bring you down. I just want you to be able to win at this."

"Destiny, I know you got my best interest in mind and I'm not going to let you or these brownies down!" Rico stuffed a brownie into his mouth.

"Pig!"

"Don't hate me because the calories don't stick!" Rico teased. Then he pulled up his shirt to show off his six-pack and shoved another brownie into his mouth. I plopped down on the couch and joined him. No point in letting Jenna's PMS cure go to waste.

{1} START ME UP

{2} SYMPATHY FOR THE DEVIL

{3} RAPTURE

{4} PIECE OF MY HEART

{5} 19TH NERVOUS BREAKDOWN

{6} GET OFF OF MY CLOUD

Start Me Up

Manhattan Avenue is a stark contrast from the hyper-speed activity of 125th Street and the other busy main throughways in Harlem. I love how the neighborhood is lined with trees and brownstones. Trees that are rooted in the rich history and culture of black people; concrete and brick that hold secrets and stories from the *beginning* of Harlem through the Renaissance; and now, that same concrete and brick will carry a part of the new urban regentrification. Then you have a few dilapidated and abandoned buildings, worn from the struggle, still hanging around, waiting for their turn.

I love my loft condo, but I wish I'd had the foresight six or seven years ago to buy one of these babies before downtowners and white folks got wise that the New Harlem Renaissance was on the way and caused the prices to skyrocket into the millions.

I could see Curtis's Range Rover parked ahead at the corner of 124th and Manhattan. I made a U-turn, pulled into an available spot, and rushed across the street. I glanced at my watch. There was plenty of time to frolic before I had to be at the club tonight.

I walked into Perks, our favorite meeting place for the past six months. Perks is that kind of old-school watering hole with a laid-back-in-the-cut, colored-folk feel, a real R&B joint. Perks is unassuming and virtually off the radar of people in our business circles. Close your eyes and imagine the dj doing a slow fade from Percy Sledge into Mary J. Yep, that's Perks. It is exactly the type of safe-ground for two high-profile industry-ites (one of course being married).

. . . and there Curtis sat . . .

He was at the bar with his back turned. My eyes scanned his stately, six-two frame. His style was conservative and sophisticated. He has a penchant for well-tailored high-end suits and fine Italian leather dress shoes. The cuffs of his custom-made dress shirt were accented by sterling Tiffany cufflinks, and an expensive Swiss watch peeked out of one sleeve.

"Hey, you," I whispered, leaning in to his ear.

"Wassup, sexy?" Curtis stood up and gave me an enormously long and tight embrace.

"Wow, I know it's been a couple of weeks, but maybe we should see each other less often. I like these kinds of greetings." I ran my manicured hands across the lapels of his suit jacket.

"I just missed you," he said, snuggling his nose into the nape of my neck as he removed my jacket. "You smell amazing." My backside brushed against his rock-hard penis. "See, you got me going already."

It didn't take much for Curtis to get aroused. Poor man, had a wife at home, but to say the brotha was sexually deprived was an understatement. He was long overdue for a fix. I kissed him again on the lips. Perks allowed us the freedom to act like high school love-birds.

Curtis Chatsworth III. Where do I begin? In 1992, when I started taking on the New York party scene in a major way, Curtis was one of the first big power players on the rise that I met. He was in-house counsel for MCA records. He was fresh out of Stanford Law and the talk of New York.

Curtis introduced himself to me at one of my parties, and said he was so impressed he just had to take me out to dinner. A few dates and several hours of mind-blowing sex later, he hooked me up with an exclusive contract to get all the MCA black music acts' album-release parties for the next year. It was the beginning of a beautiful relationship.

Curtis and I were cool and lovey-dovey for about six months straight. I always knew he had a girlfriend. Hello, forget about OPP, I'm down with POPP (penises of other people's people). But then the Negro up and got married on me. I laid low for a while, figured he needed to settle into married life. But we ran in the same circles, so there was bound to be a reuniting of sorts.

Thirteen years later, I get a call from Curtis. He's uptown, in my neck of the woods, and he wants to see me. I remembered walking past Perks with Josephine one evening, and I gave him the address. I met Curtis and we picked up right where we'd left off. Perks quickly became the "perfect creep spot" for an evening cocktail and a flirty interlude, if we didn't have time to swing by my apartment and slip in one of our body-rocking bump-and-grind sessions.

"You called earlier, what was so urgent?" I asked sitting on the stool next to him, crossing my legs.

"I have good news."

"What?"

Curtis motioned to the bartender. She brought over a bottle of chilled Korbel.

"I know this isn't Cristal or Veuve, but it was the only thing they had cold," he said referring to the bottle of bubbly. Nothing against the less expensive brands, even though my taste buds prefer the finer champagnes (Curtis is a major cheapskate, has been ever since I met him). "I thought we could celebrate me hooking you up with a fat deal with Garcel."

"Multi-platinum, pop-sensation Garcel? I just met her the other night."

"She told me, *and* while we were in Europe I told her she had to give you an exclusive for the party for her debut album."

"I love it that my man has my back," I said raising my glass for a toast.

"Why don't you show me," he winked, lifting his glass and tapping it gently against mine.

I planted the biggest, wettest, most passionate kiss on Curtis's lips. We grabbed our glasses and moved to the back of the room, where a table in the corner provided more privacy.

"Damn, I really missed you." Curtis kissed me again, discreetly slipping his hand under my skirt and inside my panties.

"I missed you too," I whispered.

"What did you miss?" he whispered back, growling suggestively.

"I missed kissing you . . ."

"Yeah, . . ."

"I missed the way you suck on my nipples . . ."

"What else . . . ?"

"I missed making love to you and feeling you inside me . . ." My eyes rolled back euphorically.

"You've got me so hard," he quietly grunted, gently massaging me.

"I wish I was sitting on top of you right now . . ." I said close to his ear.

"I want you to come all over me . . ."

"You're gonna make me come right now . . ."

"Do it baby, come for Daddy, come for me!"

Mmmmmmmmmmmmmmmmmmmmmmmmm.

Moments later, I was in the restroom and patting myself dry. Afterward, I splashed cold water on my face and smiled at my reflection. Curtis had come through for a sista yet again. See, I knew there was a reason I kept him around. He wasn't into trickin' (you know the fine art of ballin', aka a high-paid, highbrow brotha's limitless spending on trips, shopping sprees and yes, buying the bar out for you and your friends), but he was sure to always bring me some good business.

My cheap sneak excursions and skill for giving amazing head, in exchange for the ability to tap into his resources, were far better than a weekend romp in a suite at the Delano on South Beach or a trinket from Fifth Avenue. Now, if I could just learn the "booty clap" (the technique of droppin' it like it's hot and moving your rump shaker-video 'ho-style). Izzy swears it's done wonders for her. Imagine the payoff.

If I could develop that skill, I could have this cheap Negro securing me a multi-million-dollar deal with Nike. I can see it now: my own clothing line, shoes, jewelry, lingerie, cosmetics, movies! Move over, Puffy! Put some clothes on, Kimora! There's a new diva in town who's ready for her closeup and a nude billboard in Times Square!

Oh, come on, don't go all Gloria Steinem on me! I've got plenty of self-esteem and self-respect. However, I'm a firm believer in the philosophy that if you're spending time with a man, giving up the goodies, a brotha needs to come up off some jewelry, a business hookup, a trip to an exclusive day spa . . . something!

Sympathy for the Devil

"Are you going to be okay, Iz?" I asked, putting on my blinker and exiting the Holland Tunnel on the New Jersey side. Izzy stared out of the passenger window, lost in thought.

"I'm fine, Ma," she said, biting her bottom lip. "I'm just glad you're with me." I could see her knuckles turning white from clenching her seat.

"Iz, you gotta keep your temper under control."

"That *bitch* better not be there."

"She's *not* a bitch, Iz, she's your mother." Izzy gave me a cold glare.

Izzy had gotten an urgent call from her *abuela* about an hour ago. Her grandmother was vague, but it all had something to do with being scared that Izzy's mother, Carmen, was going to "do something bad." We weren't sure whether she meant to herself or to Abuela. We hopped in the car immediately.

"You know, when you're angry you can do things you regret, Iz. I think when we get there you need to chill out and let your grandmother tell you the whole story before you just go off and start kickin' ass like last time."

Izzy's mother is a crackhead, and she does what crackheads do best—sell your television, stereo, cell phone, and steal from your grandmother's pocketbook, right in her own house. She's probably occasionally sold her body to get a hit, too. Izzy's always resented her for getting hooked on drugs, and for running her father away when Izzy was a little girl.

They've had a tumultuous relationship since Izzy was about twelve or thirteen. But the breaking point came not long after Izzy's eighteenth birthday. It was the last time she lived under the same roof with Carmen at her grandmother's house. Carmen was so high that she hit Izzy, but as far as Izzy was concerned, she was legal and just as grown as Carmen. Iz swung back and it was on. After that, she left and got her own place.

Even if Izzy has to borrow money from me to do so, she goes to visit her *abuela* at least once a month to make sure she has groceries and money, since Carmen is always stealing from her. But it's been almost eight years since she's actually *seen* Carmen. Izzy manages to keep her visits short and sweet to avoid any confrontations.

"I hate going through this crap. Thas why when I left the las' time, I made it clear that I never wanted to see her again. As far as I'm concerned I got Abuela, and I had my father. I don't have no fuckin' mother!" Izzy's eyes welled up, but she was so furious the tears couldn't break through.

Seeing her like this brings back memories of when her father was dying. He left when she was three, and she didn't reconnect with him until she was twenty years old, just a month before he died. Izzy always hid her pain behind her laughter and smiles, but his death was a major breakthrough for her emotionally. Helping her get over his death really sealed our friendship.

Izzy's grandmother's house was only a five-minute drive from the Holland Tunnel once we crossed into Jersey City. Her block is in a typical family-friendly, predominantly Puerto Rican neighborhood and lined with row houses. Izzy helped her grandmother do some renovations about two years ago when she got a nice payday for a series of Pizza Hut commercials she booked.

Her grandmother was standing at the door smiling when we pulled up. Mrs. Santos's short, plump body type had you fighting the urge to pinch her cheeks everytime you see her, like you would a small child. "Isabelle! Destiny! Come in! *Mira aqui!*" She gave us both big hugs and rushed us right into the kitchen, where she had a big pot of rice and beans on the stove.

I hadn't seen the inside of the house since the renovations were completed. Usually, if I drive Izzy over from the City, she runs in, out, and we bounce. I don't want a run-in with Carmen any more than Izzy does. I was impressed with the updated fixtures and modern furniture. Izzy had succeeded in moving her *abuela* out of frilly curtains and doilies (both of which I always teased as being *very* Puerto Rican), and into mini-blinds and the age of Pottery Barn. Her grandmother still has a hundred different pictures of Jesus all over the walls and pictures of Izzy at every stage of development on the shelves, end tables, mantel, and any open shelf or counter space she can find.

Black people and Puerto Ricans are a lot alike in that respect. I don't care how bourgeois you are, you know your Auntie or Big Mama has pictures of all the grandkids—even some kids who *aren't* really in the family—all over the place, and either the Bible opened up to her favorite verse, a picture of Jesus on one of the walls, or both, and nine times outta ten, a pot cookin' on the stove.

The latter being just what Izzy's *abuela* had on . . .

The whole house smelled like Spanish seasonings and simmering garlic and onions from the chicken roasting in the oven. The aroma had my mouth watering.

"Where she at, Abuela?" Izzy demanded.

"*Mira*, chu so skinny, Isabelle. An look at chu, Destiny. Sit, eat, now," she piled both our plates with food. I loved to hear her *abuela*'s silent "e's" and "t's", and the way she rolls her "r's" and makes her "y's" sound like long "e's." If I ever get some free time, I'm gonna sit my butt down and learn Spanish. How fierce would a sista be? Think about it, a woman who can speak proper English when conducting business, Ebonics when dealing with the homies—and with some Spanish, I could corner the Latin market.

"Thank you, Mrs. Santos," I said, digging in. I was focused on our mission, but right now my stomach was calling.

"I'm not hungry, Abuela," Iz barely picked at her food.

Her grandmother was stalling, but it was one helluva delicious tactic.

"I happy you came. Carmen es sick," her grandmother said, putting her hand over her mouth. She spoke English for the most part, especially when I was around.

"What did she do to you?"

"She . . . she started yellin' an screamin' an throwin' theens all over. I try to stop her, an she raise her han'," her grandmother was shaking. "I foun' dis,"—she held out a syringe wrapped in plastic—"an, when I say somethin' she start to scream and say theens to me, very bad theens. She say she kill me."

"I'm gonna . . ." Izzy caught herself before finishing her sentence. "If she shootin' up, she gotta go, now!" She threw her hands in the air.

"Isabelle, *por favor*, calm down. My Carmen need help," she said, making the sign of the cross, breaking down in tears.

69

"Ma, don't tell her nothin' about me." We looked up and Carmen was standing in the doorway smoking a cigarette. It was like looking at Izzy's reflection, but Carmen's once-thick black hair was now brittle and thin; her beautiful, soft eyes were sunken and empty; and jaundice had replaced her youthful complexion. Her frail body was worn from drug abuse. The thought of how beautiful she once was made me look away.

"What chu doin' here?" Carmen's voice was raspy. She blew out a puff of smoke.

"Carmen!" Izzy's grandmother shouted. Then she started praying.

"Don' tell her my business, Ma!"

"I don't care what you do on the street, Carmen, jus' don't bring it up in here. An' if you ever touch Abuela, I'll kill you!" Izzy grabbed Carmen and began shaking her. Carmen's weak body collapsed in her arms.

"No! Iz!" I shouted, pulling Izzy away from Carmen.

"No, no, no, Isabelle!" Her grandmother put her hands over her face and started praying and crying.

"I'm sick. They jus' told me. I got AIDS, and my liver is no good. So hit me! Hit me! It don' matter." Carmen slid down the wall, "Nothin' matters. I'm gonna fuckin' die anyway!"

"I gotta go, Abuela!" Izzy stormed out with tears streaming down her face. I didn't bother stopping her. I helped Carmen into a chair, got her grandmother calmed down, and left as fast as I could.

On the ride back Izzy was silent.

"I know you're not okay, girl, so there's no need for me to ask you. But what can I do?"

"Nothin', Mami. I'm never goin' back there."

"Iz, your *abuela* needs you, Carmen needs you." She didn't respond. "You gotta be feeling something. Talk to me."

"I don't feel nothin' and right now, I just need a drink."

"Okay, we can handle that." I pressed the gas pedal and zoomed back through the Tunnel. In no time we were parked and sitting at the bar at the Soho Grand Hotel, washing our worries away with a round of stiff martinis.

We didn't need to talk about it. We had our own sacred "Surviving Sistas" code. Translation: My ear was available if she felt like talking, and vice versa. Izzy would have to deal with this on her own time. When she got ready. And when that time comes, I'll be there to help her work it out. Women like us were born strong. We didn't have a choice.

Rapture

I make it a policy not to answer phones or pages during meetings. I like the client to feel like a priority. However, some fool has been blowing it up since my lunch meeting at Jean Georges started with R&B and pop princess Garcel Kelly, and the MTV executives in charge of production and development. Oh, and I forgot, Garcel's overbearing stage-mama-manager, Sharon, who's flamboyant and a major bigmouth. I shifted uncomfortably in my chair trying inconspicuously to make out the message on my annoying BlackBerry screen, but to no avail. Every time I tried to sneak a peek, someone fired off a new litany of questions.

"Um, Des-ta-nee, wassup wit security? You know it's some haters out here, and um, Garcel gots ta have lots of security." Mama Kelly probed. She was just plain country. A spectacle from head to toe, and her hair an ever-changing color wheel. I had only seen various photos in magazines, but it was something to behold in real life. Today was strip-club, pole-dancer red. She looks like she just walked out of a Bronner Brothers hair show. Mounds of weave, curled and fried, glued and stitched to the top of her head.

Her outfit, just as spectacular, was a clash of the designer titans, if you will. She's overdone in that Ab Fab kind of way. Someone played a cruel joke on this woman and told her that Gucci, Baby Phat, Prada, and Christian Dior were all related and should be worn simultaneously.

Before I could answer the question about security, she cut me off, "Unuhn, Garcel gots to have this," her mama smacked in between big chomps of beef tenderloin, using her index finger's brightly colored acrylic nail tip to pick at a chunk of meat that was lodged between two front teeth. "Uhnuhn, Garcel, don't do that!" She was about to push me to the point of slapping a gag order on her. "Oooh, Des-ta-nee, is Fiddy-Cent gone be at the party? I love me some Fiddy!"

Great, Mama was a groupie, too! It's true you can take the fool out of the 'hood, but you can't take the 'hood out of the fool. Garcel just sat in a demure pose like everything was normal. I wondered what in the world she was thinking. This girl seems the total opposite of her mama.

Garcel's decision to go solo from super-platinum singing quartet, G.L.O.W. (short for Garcel, LeVonne, Olivia, and Wanda), made headlines. It was her popularity as the lead singer that had propelled the group to sell a whopping sixty million records worldwide. She finally kicked their sorry asses to the curb. Everyone knows she's the star, has always been the star, and those other girls don't stand a chance on their own (you didn't hear it from me, but one very pushy manager mama also played a major role in the others getting the ax).

This will be my first venture into live television. I'm throwing more than a party. It's an all-out promotional extravaganza for Garcel's new album, "Single 2 Mingle." The release date of September First is almost six months away, but the single drops late summer and the record's going to be huge.

The record company, Garcel and her management, and MTV want a star-studded party that will feature a live performance and twenty-five wardrobe changes. They're all thinking L.A. or Miami for this shindig, but I'm thinking an end-of-the-summer blast, Labor Day Weekend. And there's only one place for this level of fabulosity . . . the Hamptons!

"Mrs. Kelly," I politely interrupted.

"Call me Sharon, all them formalities make me sound old." This woman thought she *was* the star. She was trying to dress and act as young as her daughter.

"Okay, Sharon. I know you're big on Miami and Los Angeles, but I mean seriously, MTV viewers have seen South Beach and Los Angeles a million times. Plus, between you and me, Christina Aguilera, Christina Milian, and Britney are all going to be doing big parties in both South Beach and Los Angeles before Garcel's first single even drops. All due respect, but in my opinion, Garcel sets the trends. She doesn't follow them. I'm thinking a Hamptons, Labor Day soirée!"

"Aw, naw! Garcel ain't gonna be no sloppy seconds! I like the way you said that: 'GARCEL SETS THE TRENDS, SHE DON'T FOLLOW THEM!' Let's do the Hamptons fo sho! Plus, I been wantin' to get up there. Hell, yeah! Diddy and all them got houses up there!"

This woman has given me a headache. My BlackBerry is still going off like somebody's losing their mind. I finally see the message: I HAVE TO SEE YOU . . . NOW! I shake my head, laughing to myself. Crazy-ass Curtis. I excuse myself and quickly click away to the bathroom.

"Curtis, baby, you're killin' me. I'm sitting with Garcel and a table full of folks right now," I say, trying to be cool and not curse him out for blowing me up all through lunch. I mean after all, he did hook up this whole Garcel party contract.

"I need my Destiny to be fulfilled!" he said.

"You are insane!"

"Damn, baby, I miss you. I've got a small window of time, c'mon. I'm hard just thinking about you."

"Curtis, you're always hard."

"Whateva, B, I'm harder now!"

I loved it when he flipped his pseudo-conservative image for down-and-dirty, but the real deal is that Curtis stays hard and horny.

I checked my watch. There was always room in one's day to slip in a guaranteed orgasm. "I'll be wrapping up in about forty. I didn't drive, so pick me up at the Trump."

"I don't want to see Garcel, c'mon Destiny."

"Curtis, pick me up. I'm not hearing all that."

Click.

Destiny always gets her way.

We concluded our meeting.

Smooches!

Ciao!

I promised to get back to everyone right away with numbers for the proposed Hamptons event.

Garcel was whisked away in a blacked-out Escalade, the MTV'ers in a taxi. With perfect timing, Curtis's Range Rover pulled right in front of the hotel, stopping just short of my Sergio Rossi. My beaming face reflected off the car's dark-tinted windows, and I jumped into the passenger seat and lightly pecked Curtis on the lips.

He looked like one of those models in GQ. His style always fascinated me. In one word: impeccable.

Suit: Giorgio Armani . . . $3,000.00
Shoes: Ferragamo . . . $500.00
Watch: Baume & Mercier . . . $20,000.00
The Sex: Priceless!

"Fuck that shit, until they give you the paper you deserve we ain't signing shit! You the *star*!" He slapped and gripped my thigh as he emphasized *star*. I loved to see Curtis in action when he was talking to one of his clients. He was like Dr. Jekyll and Mr. Hyde. One personality was straitlaced and Mr. Ivy League, the other was grimy and hardcore. He disconnected one call and quickly speed-dialed another. He looked at me and put a finger to his lips. I rolled my eyes and gave him the one-handed "jerk-off" gesture.

"Yeah, sweetheart. I'll be home in time." When he said the word "sweetheart" it sounded stale and emotionless. "Tell your father I already reserved our tee time for tomorrow."

Yadayadayadawhatever.

He pressed END.

"The wife is always on your ass."

"Shut up, Destiny." Curtis swerved wildly, pulling the car over to the side of the road, leaning into me. "That pretty little mouth of yours is always smarting off." He kissed me forcefully. "I'm gonna put something in it, if you keep on!"

"Is that a threat?" I challenged, my mouth pressed against his.

"Damn, you turn me on so much!" His hand shot up my dress and just as his fingers reached inside my panties I grabbed them.

"Drive!" I ordered.

We groped and fondled each other for the next sixty or so blocks. Today was our lucky day—an open parking spot in front of my building *and* an empty apartment. Normally, Jenna was at my condo running calls, but I had sent her out this afternoon to a few showrooms to see what the new season was bringing, and Izzy was at an audition.

By the time I put the deadbolt on the door Curtis was standing in all his God-given talent. He lifted me up and I wrapped my legs around his smooth olive-hued back. Curtis's physical prowess was exceptional. He ran five miles a day, was an avid golfer and hiker. His body was statuesque and made me think of sweet caramel candy. I ran my fingers through his thick black waves.

Curtis ripped open my Diane von Furstenberg wrap dress, tossed it to the floor, and threw me on the bed. He unzipped my boots and tossed them across the room. I hit POWER on the stereo remote and "selection three," my favorite hit-it-'n'-quit-it quickie CD of the Isleys' classic slow jams, underscored our afternoon romp.

Curtis slipped his tongue around my Cosabella thong and went to town, working it up and down the walls of my vagina, in and out, round and round until I tightened and swelled. He was driving me insane. So what, he had a wife who was too busy planning lavish social affairs, attending board meetings, and redecorating their ten-thousand-square-foot abode to pay attention to him. Yeah, yeah, sure his wife's father was the first black CEO of Pacific Motors. Big deal—she was rich by default. This man was too perfect to waste away up in some mansion in Long Island.

I sensuously bit my bottom lip, and Curtis went in for the kill, flicking his tongue back and forth gently over my clitoris. I don't normally like to use the Lord's name in vain, but . . . *free at last, free at last, thank God Almighty, my orgasm was set free at last!*

My body shook and quivered, and just when I thought heaven couldn't get any closer, he snapped on a condom and slid inside me. (Look, I might be with a married man, and I know you're still shaking your head talking about "that's just plain wrong, girl." But I'm being safe. I'm not trying to catch some kind of venereal disease or worse.) But I just have three words: a-ma-zing!

We lay still, his head resting on my breast.

"I wish I could stay. I hate going home to *her*."

"Curtis, you do this every time. Why are you with *her*, then?"

"Destiny, you just don't understand things with *her*. It's all very complicated. *She's* got me over a barrel." (We never used "her" name when talking about "her," even though I know it's Gina.)

"Baby, if you're not happy with *her*, just leave *her*. You're successful and rich by your damn self."

"Yeah, but *she's* got me by the balls."

I didn't want to hear him complain another moment. This was the same excuse he used every time. My whole thing is, as paid as he is, couldn't he have paid her back a long time ago? Of course he could have! Please, he was the music business's budding Golden Boy, legal eagle making tons of money when they met. Brothaman had a lock on all the hottest producers making hip-hop smash hits, before the rest of the world realized the power of sampling. I just don't get it. Why stay in something that makes you so miserable?

We got up, and he began to dress. I quickly rushed off to the bathroom.

"What's the hurry?"

"You know I can't stand being all wet and sticky."

"I love your body," he called out.

I turned the shower on and stepped in to take a quick rinse-off. "Explain it all to me. You and *her* don't have kids together . . ." I said, drying off and slipping into a Juicy Couture velour sweatsuit and a pair of UGG boots.

"Don't go there, Destiny."

"I'm sorry." His wife being infertile is a touchy subject. "Look, you don't love her! And to make matters worse, you have to make an appointment to sleep with *her*. What are you sticking around for?" Now I definitely wasn't trying to jockey for position with a brotha. Hell, I needed a committed relationship like I needed a hole in my head. I just hated to see someone I liked so much so unhappy.

"Destiny, I don't want to ruin this by talking about *her*. It stresses me out."

"You know what, Curtis? You need to look at your life and start thinking about a little something called happiness. We only get one life, at least here on this earth, and you're withering away with this woman."

"Just kiss me," he said softly, taking me in his arms. I almost felt bad for Curtis. I was his only source of solace, but at least all this good pussy will leave him in better spirits until the next time.

Piece of My Heart

Men in the music business will make you lose your mind, if you let them. Malik is going to be the last A&R-slash-producer-slash-manager, or any combination of the above I ever deal with again! Didn't he know *I* invented the idea of putting business first? I'm the most flexible human on this planet, but this is downright unacceptable!

Malik gave me his word he wouldn't disappear tonight. After spending a thousand dollars on tickets for us to attend Wynton Marsalis's private benefit concert and cocktail party for Jazz At Lincoln Center, I'm ready to go postal on his ass. Wynton called *personally* to invite me! Damn, we've been doing so well since Malik got back from Atlanta last month, hanging out between his studio sessions, grabbing dinner or a movie when we can. But now I see we're back to this b.s. again!

The last message I sent to him via BlackBerry read: *Cocktails start at seven. Pick me up by six o'clock. Don't be late!*

Hello, it's *now* six o'clock and I have yet to hear back from him. *Where the hell are you?*

My fingers typed another message at lightning speed into my BlackBerry. I fired up a cigarette and took a long drag, turning up the stereo another few decibels. The speeding-car guitar licks of "Rock the Casbah" echoed my rage.

I could've taken someone else and saved myself the aggravation. Decision made. I'll go dateless. Destiny Day never lets a man get the best of her, and she's not about to start now! Malik's gotten way too cute playing that peek-a-boo, "Where's Waldo" card, calling when he feels like it, disappearing for days.

I poured myself a glass of wine, downed it, slipped into a fab Armani slip dress, threw on a pair of come-get-it-right-now, four-inch Giuseppe Zanottis, and was determined to set the night on fire—solo.

Post-extravaganza cocktails were held at the Mo Bar inside the Mandarin Oriental Hotel. Thirty-five stories high and surrounded by glass, the room was lit up like New Year's Eve. I was just about to settle into my two-hundredth glass of Veuve and engage in major dialogue with Denzel. He commented that I smelled like "an exotic fruit basket." I giggled. My BlackBerry buzzed.

No this asshole *wasn't* calling me in the middle of my Hollywood moment. Perhaps Denzel was going to demand that I co-star in his next big-budget flick. How would I prepare for the sex scene?

My BlackBerry buzzed again.

I looked at Denzel. I looked at the BlackBerry screen. I looked back at Denzel, then back at the BlackBerry screen. I suddenly had a flash of that famous Esther Rolle moment in the Evans's kitchen. *"Damn! Damn! Damn!"*

The message read:

Wassup, Mama? I got tied up in the studio in Atlanta and took a later flight. I'm sorry I missed the party. I'm down at Quad mixing. I'll make it up to you. I miss you—Malik

Forget Denzel! In a matter of seconds, I had drained my glass, kissed Denzel goodbye (on the cheek of course; I heard Pauletta don't play that!), grabbed my mink wrap, clicked out of the Mandarin at sixty miles per hour, hopped into a waiting taxi, and instructed the driver to get to 49th and Seventh Avenue in a hurry. He did. The taxi came to a screeching halt, and I opened the door and tossed a ten to the driver.

Buzz. Buzz. Buzz. I impatiently pressed the studio intercom.

"Studio," a voice crackled through the tiny intercom.

"Malik's session!" I was irritated, beyond tipsy, rocking back and forth on the narrow heels of my ornate stilettos. I lit a cigarette and took several quick, short puffs on the elevator ride up. The car crept to a stop on the fourth floor. The doors opened slowly and Malik's boy Talib was waiting there with a big fat grin on his face.

"Hey mama, wassup?"

"Don't give me that shit, Talib. Where the hell is Malik?" I stamped out my cig and pushed past his six-three, two-twenty body. Then Malik's cousin Amaru entered from a side room. Homie was just as big as Talib. Was it the champagne, or did they just grow 'em like that back on the old Philly block?

"Wassup, D? Watchu doin' here?" Amaru said.

"Oh, cut it. You know I'm lookin' for Malik!"

"Yo, is Malik here, Ta?" Amaru asked with a confused look.

"I haven't seen him. I been at the other studio and I just got here," Talib said. They both had dumb expressions on their faces. Lovely. I was engaged in mind-numbing buffoonery with Tweedledum and *Tweedledumber*.

The Quickie Lowdown

Talib, Malik's homeboy, who grew up with him back in Philly and now carried the official title of "My Man." (Definition according to Webster X's Unabridged Dictionary: An affectionate name for a black man's trusty sidekick whose duties include everything from chauffeur to beverage-, bag-, and booty-fetcher at the club. And no, there isn't an official W-2 form for this job.)

Amaru is Malik's other homie from around the way. He says he's trying to be a "manager," but I've yet to see one rap artist or singer that he manages.

Just then Malik came out of the bathroom. His normally crisp white T-shirt and starched jeans were slightly rumpled, but the bling on his neck, wrists, and finger still had him looking like a vision of hip-hop-bad-boy royalty. He had on a Phillies hat, ghetto-cocked to the side.

"I can't believe your punk ass flaked on me, and then your *weak-ASS crew*"—I emphasized that part, pointing to his boys—". . . is trying to play me for a fool, Malik!"

"You're drunk, D," he smirked.

"Tell me something I don't know!"

Malik pulled me by the arm into the bathroom and slammed the door. Here I was, furious, veins popping out on my neck and forehead, looking up at him, and this man smiles. A million-dollar boyish grin that made my heart melt. My panties were instantly soaked.

"You're killin' me, D. I'm tryin' to finish this record and you're buggin' out! C'mon, shit's—"

"Yeah, yeah, shit's *crazy*." I rolled my eyes.

"I promise I'm gonna make it up to you." He stepped closer to me and I found myself trapped. He stared deep into my eyes and blinked slowly. His eyes were filled with the pain of his childhood. I could always connect with him, because we both knew the rough side of life. Two people both determined to be "somebody," make money and have "things," lots of things. We had defied the ghetto odds.

Except Malik's ties to the streets were much deeper than I could ever imagine. His life was in so many ways *still* there. No matter how successful he is or may become, he'll always keep that element around him. Like bringing every homeboy he ever had growing up to New York to live with him. He's afraid to let go. Maybe he thinks if he does, he'll lose himself. I don't know.

"You're gonna miss my ass when I leave you for good," I said, shifting coyly.

"You ain't goin' nowhere."

"There's stiff competition out there."

"You're ridiculous," he said, and then kissed me deeply. "You know you're crazy, right? You gotta stop trippin' D."

"Whatever! You messed up today. Big time!" I closed my eyes and fell into his grip, and he lifted me up and placed me gently on the bathroom sink.

"I *said* I'm gonna make it up to you, Mama," he said in between licking and kissing my earlobes and neck.

"Whatever you do, better come in carats," I smarted, dropping my mink wrap to the floor. The satin straps of my dress slid off my shoulders. He nibbled on the back of my neck.

"I didn't know a two-hundred-dollar bra could look so good," he smiled, admiring my La Perla.

"You *ought* to, you paid for it," I said, closing my eyes. Malik pushed my dress up and began massaging the insides of my thighs with his large, powerful hands. He worked his fingers up and inside the soaking wet walls of my vagina and lightly stroked my clitoris.

"Mmmmmm, Brazil is one of my favorite countries," he smirked, referring to my well-maintained Brazilian wax job.

Malik was strong and commanding, yet gentle and tender. He kissed and sucked, and kissed and sucked, and fondled and caressed, running his tongue over and around my hard nipples. I sighed softly. I could feel the heat surging between my legs, my thighs tingling, and all sense of speech escaping my mind. I sighed again.

"Shhhh!" he commanded.

I grabbed him by the waist of his pants, ran my hands over his rounded belly that seemed to make me even more excited. The buckle of his belt clicked open and I anxiously unbuttoned his pants. Malik's manhood was large, hard, and thick. I could feel the blood pulsing through its shaft as I gripped him tightly in my hands.

"I missed you," he said.

"How much?"

"Too much."

I slipped a condom out of my evening bag. I kept one on me at all times, just in case I got lucky. A sista liked to get her groove on, too, and like I told you before, I'm not about to be irresponsible. I don't care how good the sex is.

He rolled the condom over his long curving penis, and gently yet forcefully made his way inside. I gasped, stifling the sound of sweet release in my throat. I wasn't about to confirm everyone's suspicions outside, and go out like a complete hoochie mama. He let out a long breath. I had him in my clutches again, wrapping my legs tighter and tighter around his back, grinding my hips up and down. Destiny had regained her power.

"You missed this, didn't you?" I whispered.

"Yeeesss," he struggled to get the word out.

"Tonight was an important night for me," I said through gritted teeth.

"I know—*uhhhh!*—I know—*uhhh!*—but you can't be comin' up in the studio wildin' out!"

"You can't keep disappearin' thinkin' you can come in and out of my life when you feel like it!"

It was a showdown and power struggle of the wills. The harder I clenched my thighs and forced my way down on him, the harder he thrust. My hands gripped his broad shoulders. His hands gripped my buttocks. It all made for a very dramatic build and the perfect, climactic moment. We both let out deep, exhausted groans. He wrapped his soft lips around my right nipple, sucking it gently, then releasing it.

I wet a thick wad of paper towels and furiously wiped off the residue from our bathroom quickie. We exited in silence, only to be greeted by the thumping bass line seeping through the studio booth's walls. He held me from behind while the tiny elevator transported us to the lobby level. We hit the street and were met by a chilly gust of wind.

"I can have Talib or Amaru drive you home," he said, kissing me on the back of my neck. "I gotta finish working."

"I thought you were driving me home," I said, wincing. "No thanks, I'll pass." After all that, he still didn't get it. I was not going for one of his boys driving me home.

"D, please don't start showin' out again," he pleaded, handing me a wad of cash, hailing a taxi. "Here, buy something really nice for yourself and we'll hang out this weekend. Maybe go down to D.C. Freedom has a show at Dream."

I covered up my anger and smiled. Thinking how *O-V-A-H* this whole thing we have is. Fuck Freedom. The artist who's been working on an album for only God knows how long. You'd swear this was about to be better than Prince's comeback.

"Nah, I've gotta work this weekend. I'm giving a big party. I'm gonna be crazed, but hit me when you get back," I said. I kissed him goodbye and disappeared into the cab. I looked at the money balled up in my hand . . . three hundred dollars. The audacity of him trying to put "us" on the level of a meaningless exchange between a prostitute and her john. I can't even get a pair of Manolos with this!

19th Nervous Breakdown

I grabbed my usual table at the Café. Josephine entered from the kitchen and sauntered over in a colorful, long, free-flowing dress and shiny metallic thong slippers. I had already prepared myself for a scolding, since I hadn't been by the Café in three and a half weeks.

"I know what you're gonna say," I said, flashing Josephine the palm of my hand, anticipating an earful of questions about my whereabouts lately.

"Oh, you do, do you? So tell me, since you have the power to read minds." Josephine sat down across from me and folded her arms across her chest.

"You're gonna fuss at me, because I haven't been by here to see you."

"Oh, Lovie, you *are* a mind-reader!" Josephine teased. "No, I just figured life had swallowed you up momentarily. I knew you'd be back when it spit you out!"

"I guess you could say that," I replied. We laughed. Josephine certainly had a way with words.

"Soooooo . . . where's Mr. Waldo?"

"No comment—we're not talking about him! I just came by for a nice lunch!"

"I know you don't think I'm letting you off the hook that easily. The way you've been standing me up around here? If I was a bettin' woman, I'd say there's trouble in playa's paradise."

"Outside of the fact that Malik can't seem to get our timing right, we're cool."

"Timing? That's a new one."

"What I mean is, we're good for about a week or so, then I may not hear from him for five or six days. But I'm not trippin'. I'm just flowin' like always."

"Isn't that hard to do?"

"What?"

"You know, the flow thing."

"More women should try my way. It sure beats getting your heart trampled on or beaten to an unrecognizable pulp. I refuse to let that happen. The problem is that women out here need to stop being such wimps when it comes to men, and the first step is to dismiss the fairy-tale fantasy crap about that four-letter word, L-O-V-E. Why does every woman seem to be waiting in vain for some knight in shining armor to come and whisk her away to the land of make-believe? The sooner a woman faces reality, the sooner she can stop looking at L-O-V-E through glitter-sprinkled glasses."

"Ahh, to be young and out of touch with reality. Perhaps, if I'd been more in touch with reality, I would've bypassed all the others and just waited for Husband Number Four. Mr. Sanchez was a *keeper*, and I was just too foolish. Rest his soul, but I guess God had a better plan for me. Maybe it was giving me the understanding that I had a good thing but I hadn't treated it with care. So, He took it away.

"When I was young I had your kind of thinking. I thought I was invincible and that there was always something better out there. I'm older and wiser now, and this time I won't be so hard-headed. Abraham Paul gets on my last nerve sometimes, but there's something quite comforting in knowing that I won't have to spend the rest of my life alone." She laughed. I laughed. We clinked our teacups.

"No, Josephine, I just think God created some women to become wives and mothers, and *then* He gave some of us the good sense to know we weren't cut from the same cloth. Seriously, what is marriage? A piece of paper that usually ends up not being worth the ink it's written on! Or a ring that's as meaningless as the receipt. Trust me, it's only going to end in divorce."

"Hmmm, I never accused you of wanting marriage. But it's interesting *you* mentioned it. I will say that love is an exceptional thing, marriage is a beautiful thing, and the best part of that beauty is alimony!"

We let out a round of raucous laughter.

"Destiny, you are a woman with a heart of steel. I can't wait to see the day that love knocks you right off your feet."

"Keep waiting!"

"Bravo!" Josephine stood up and began clapping. "Finally, someone who's figured out a way to fight the universe! You must have *some* superpowers, girl."

"Maybe I do."

"Well, Wonder Woman, you can drop the act. I see it all in your face. Some man's got a hold of you. And like I said, if I was a bettin' woman, I'd say it's Waldo."

"The word *hold* is a bit much. I'll admit I *have* become more interested in being with Malik than spending time with anyone else. And yes, when I don't see him, I miss him. When I don't see him and don't hear from him, he makes me mad. It's driving me crazy."

"Honey, with Malik you've gotta be ready to handle the truth, and right now you aren't open to the truth."

"What truth?"

"The truth that he may never give you what you need."

"Oh, he gives me everything I want."

"See, you can't *hear* me. Not what you *want*, what you *need*. But until then, I hope you've had a revelation and decided to leave other people's husbands alone."

"I'm not going that far!"

"You're gonna learn, girl, that married stuff is no good. Imagine what you'd feel like if you were his wife."

"I can't, because I have no desire to be his or any other brotha's wife!"

"Deary, you sit and you listen to this Curtis person tell you how unhappy he is . . ."

"And how happy *I* make him," I gave her a devilish grin.

"If he's so unhappy, why's he still with the woman?"

"I have no idea, but women are not stupid, Josephine. She must know he's messing around on the side. I say it's her fault. I am *so* not interested in hearing all the war stories about the pain and suffering these women go through in relationships. They need to get over the 'love done me wrong' speeches. Most of them bring this so-called pain and suffering on themselves. If Curtis's wife was handling her business, he wouldn't be out chasing me down."

"You ever heard of a little thing called karma? Let me tell you something. I've been on both sides of the fence. I look at you and Curtis and I can tell you right now how it's going to end. It's called Husband Number Three, Mr. Marty Schultz. Marty came from old, dusty money." We laughed. "No, I'm serious, the man's family shit and money came out! Marty loved him some Josephine. He followed me all the way to Kenya, he loved me so much!"

"What were you doing in Africa?"

"Oh, child—Africa, Egypt, India, Europe, I've traveled all over the world. He just happened to catch me at that time of my life when I was reconnecting with the Motherland. But that's not the point! That's the problem with young people. You don't listen! No more interruptions, now!"

I gave Josephine my silent "girl scout" cross-your-heart oath and sat back in my chair to hear the rest of her story.

"When I met Marty, I had just walked out on Husband Number Two. We don't like to talk about him." Wrinkles formed across her forehead at the mere thought. "One day I was walking out of the Schomburg Center as he was coming in to make a large donation. Schultz Beverages . . ."

"You mean *the* Schultz Beverages, as in the king of ginger ale and beer?"

"Bingo, baby! Despite his family's wishes we married in Kenya and he stayed there with me for another three months. When we came back to the States, old man Schultz was enraged. He got over it after Marty promised to cut himself off from the family. Oh, but I nipped that in the bud real fast.

"White folks always gotta go to the extreme. Josephine was not about to live like a poor church mouse. I could do bad by myself!" We gave each other a rowdy-sista high-five. "Let's just say I was influential in pushing him to go back to daddy.

"We lived large—galas, formal dinner parties every night, you name it. Then Marty decided he had to cheat on me. Now, he'd had many affairs in the past. I knew about them. A woman always knows. At first I didn't care because I had my gowns and jewels, driver, mansion.

"But one day I woke up and realized the money meant nothing. We were just going through the motions. The way I saw it, we didn't have children so there was nothing to hold on to. Marty got scared at that point. He fought to make me stay. He vowed to stop messing around. He knew that when I left there would be a void. No one else would ever *be* Josephine."

"No offense, but how is that situation similar to me and Curtis?"

"Hush up! My point is that I knew, just like every woman in that situation knows. There's going to come a time where that woman is going to get fed up. You don't know what's really happening at that house."

"He has to stay with her for financial reasons."

"Destiny, the man's rich! Stop being so stupid! He must love something about her."

"Well, it doesn't matter; I'm not trying to have him leave her to be with me."

"Then what do you want? What if he left that woman today and showed up on your doorstep?"

"I don't know. I'd tell him to go back home or something. I damn sure don't want a husband!"

"Then what do you want? I bet you don't even have a clue."

"I've got plenty of life left in me, Josephine."

"That's not what I'm sayin'. What do *you* want in life? You're young, but honey, in five years you're gonna see how fast life starts movin', and you need to make up your mind right now if you wanna still be doin' the same thing five or ten years from now. Jumpin' from man to man, not carin' who you hurt in the process, and burnin' life's candle at both ends. That's a short life. A short *unhappy* life."

"It doesn't matter—all of it's getting boring anyway."

"Destiny, it's time to try something new." Josephine reached across the table and patted my hand. "I've got customers."

"By the way, did you at least walk away with a piece of his fortune?" I asked.

"I may be a fool for love, but I'm *not* a fool!" She winked.

I'd almost forgotten about being hungry. I picked up the menu and decided to try something new, something I'd never tasted before. Maybe the curry chicken salad or the wild-mushroom-and-barley soup, and a cup of raspberry-mint tea. That may not seem like such a big stretch to you, but for me it was. Whenever I ate here at the Café, I always got the same one or two dishes on the menu.

Surprisingly, Josephine asking me what *I* wanted in life had really made me think. What *did* I really want? Does the money and the hustle get old after a while? Does juggling men get old after a while? Maybe if I was putting more into being with Malik, I would get more out of it. I agree that trying something new might not be a bad thing. Hmmmm . . . I guess today I'll start with the menu.

Get Off of My Cloud

My apartment was buzzing with activity. Jenna was making calls to venues and lining up production details for Garcel's big album-release party in the Hamptons, while I worked out some budgetary details with MTV on one of the other lines. We're close to five months out, but for a party of this magnitude we have to lock in the major details now.

At the same time, DJ Peter was stressing me about setting up some meeting with label executives to get his music heard.

Nikki organized files, Heather busied herself bringing in my laundry and dry cleaning, and Chryssa sorted through a shipment of next season's wardrobe picks, courtesy of Tracy Reese. She'd personally sent over three stuffed-full garment bags from her showroom for me to select a dress from her upcoming summer collection for

Garcel's party. In the middle of all this madness, Izzy was on the couch, listening to her iPod, preparing for an audition.

My private line rang. Damn, it was Ainee.

"Hi, Ainee, I'm so sorry I haven't been able to call. Did you get the money I sent?" I said, preoccupied with paperwork.

"We got it, baby. It just isn't like you not to call. Are you okay up there?" Ainee's tone was worried.

"I'm fine, Ainee. I've just been forgetting to call. I got your messages, though. It's just a crazy time and I'm kinda in the middle of work." I started to scroll through my BlackBerry.

"Well, we're doin' fine here. The big church picnic is this weekend . . ."

"Oh, really?" I was half-listening, half-returning pages.

"Yes, Lord! I sure wish you could make it back here sometimes for it. I told you about that young man at church . . ."

"Oh, yeah, but I don't think I'd be right for him, Ainee," I said, putting her on speaker.

"Yes!" Jenna screeched. "With a lot of ingenuity and begging, we've got the Star Room for the party!" We gave her a round of applause. The Star Room was *the* place in the Hamptons, and no small feat to nab during a big holiday weekend.

"Destiny, what's all that noise?" Ainee shouted through the speaker box. I'd forgotten she was still on the phone.

"Ainee, I'm sorry, but my meeting just started. I'll try to call you this weekend. I love you, and tell Uncle Charlie I love him, too!" I hung up without even saying goodbye. All I could think about was that we'd secured the Star Room and beat out all the other Hamptons heavy hitters on the most popular weekend of the summer. "Jenna, that was great, now all we need to do is focus on a killer list of celebrities so this sucker can be splashed all over the magazines. And, Peter, I really want the music to be sexy. Lots of Garcel! Maybe do some special remixes."

"Yo, D, speaking of remixes. I need to get set up to start makin' some beats for some of these artists that be comin' through the spot."

"Peter, it's comin', but I don't think you're ready yet. A remix is one thing. Right now Kanye's got all the heat and Timbaland and the Neptunes are still gettin' the good artists."

"But with your connects I could get tracks on those same artists' albums. D, Jenna has heard my shit." All eyes shifted to Jenna.

"Since when did you become a studio groupie?" I asked sharply. "I thought I was supposed to hear your tracks *first*, Peter! Wassup wit that?" There was silence. "Some-freakin'-body tell me what's going on!" I shouted, glaring at Jenna.

"I'm, well . . . I did, um, hear his beats kinda by accident, and truthfully they are hot, Destiny," Jenna said, recoiling.

"I pay you to be my assistant, to *have* my back, not go *around* my back!"

"Destiny, I do have your back."

"D, why are you always thinkin' somebody's out for you?" Peter interrupted.

"Because I *know* people, so don't go there, Peter! This is between me and Jenna. You are my artist and I know what's best for you, and I know when the timing is right in the industry to put you out there."

"People said the same thing about Kanye!"

"I know you ain't *even* trying to compare yourself to Kanye West."

"I'm just sayin', I signed with you to manage me, because it's all about who you know, but you don't even believe in me!"

Peter got up, stomped to the door, and yanked it open. I ran right after him and caught him before he could storm out.

"Peter, wait!" I grabbed his hand on top of the doorknob and gave him a pleading look. He relented, slamming the door shut. Jenna jumped, and Chryssa, Nikki, and Heather all looked at me in shock, followed by Izzy, who had by this time removed her iPod ear-phones.

"What the hell . . ." Izzy-come-lately chirped.

"We don't need an audience!" I shouted. They slowly went back to what they were doing. I leaned in close to Peter. "Don't do this, baby," I said, lowering my voice, cupping his face in my hands.

Artists can be temperamental, and I was not trying to have my number-one dj and star attraction quit on me. You don't find a white dj with the skills Peter has every day. He was going to be a huge pro-ducer. My retirement fund was banking on him. I had to keep him happy, but I also had googobs of other priorities right now, and his Dr. Dre dreams would have to wait.

I gently pulled Peter's face toward mine and kissed him. "It's cool. Just let me hear the beats and I'll make some calls when the time is right." Peter turned away. I turned his face back toward me again. "I promise, soon."

"No bullshit, Destiny. I haven't stepped to anybody 'cause I'm tryin' to respect our relationship." I kissed him again. He acqui-esced. I had him back under control.

"I got you, baby. Now chill—I'll see you tonight at the club," I whispered, nibbling on his ear.

"Okay."

"And maybe after, too."

He smiled and left.

As soon as Peter was out the door and out of earshot, I went bal-listic. "What the hell was that all about, Jenna? You gassed him up to come over here when I've got more important work on my plate."

"Destiny, I'm sorry." Jenna's jaw tightened.

"Whatever! I *don't* think I need your opinion about music."

"Des, chill. Jenna ain't tryin to do what you do!"

"Shut up, Iz! If I didn't have control over my artist, I wouldn't be a very good manager, now would I? Bottom line, I'm not ready to put

Peter out there as a producer yet!" I lit up a cig. "Now, we've got work to do." I took a long drag. I couldn't waste any more time.

Jenna and The Girls gathered around the table to finish going over the plans for Garcel's party. The atmosphere was tense. When I dismissed everyone, Jenna packed up her bag and left without saying goodbye.

"Des, that girl works her butt off for you, and that was wrong," Izzy said, placing her hands on her hips in disgust.

"Iz, if I need your opinion I'll ask."

"You need to watch how you talk to people. I'm out. I've got an audition."

"Good!"

Izzy quickly gathered her belongings and left, too. I didn't care. This is Destiny's show, and if anybody doesn't like it they can step off and keep steppin'.

Disk Three
Turn the Beat Around

{1} LOVE TO LOVE YOU BABY

{2} BLAME IT ON THE BOOGIE

{3} DISCO INFERNO

{4} LOVE ROLLERCOASTER

{5} LOVE HANGOVER

{6} I WILL SURVIVE

Scenes from the Velvet Rope

EXTERIOR: LOTUS NIGHTCLUB
9:42 P.M.

I needed some fresh air and a cigarette. Yeah, I know it's a contradiction. I should quit. I'm working on it. Actually I did this morning, but I officially un-quit about twenty minutes ago when I arrived at Lotus, a swank nightclub in the meatpacking district. With developers rediscovering this area in the past several years, top designers like Stella McCartney and Marc Jacobs have set up shop, there's a sprinkle of great restaurants, and many popular clubs liven up the nightlife scene. It's become the new SoHo.

I dialed Malik's cell for the third time, but got his voicemail again. I decided against leaving a message. He promised he'd stop by the party. I hoped he made good on that promise. I picked at my fingernail, chipping away at what *was* a fresh manicure. I blew out a cloud of smoke, as if when it cleared he'd suddenly appear.

Jenna poked her head outside the front door of Lotus, aborting my thoughts. I was glad. The last thing I needed to be doing was spending valuable time worrying about some man.

"They have patches for that stuff, you know." She was trying to lighten the mood. We hadn't said more than ten words to each other since she stormed out of my apartment that afternoon.

"I don't need a patch or anything else. I can do it on my own. It's not a real habit, anyway," I said, cracking a smile.

"Oh, that's right—you're Superwoman!" she retorted. "Here, take a look at this." Jenna was Johnny-on-the-spot, wearing her usual headset and holding her clipboard with tonight's guest list on it. I could tell she was still mad at me from our spat earlier. I was already over it.

"What's up?" I asked. "You still mad? You know, once I say how I feel, I move on."

"I'm really not trippin'." Jenna is definitely immune to my outbursts. She's been with me five years, and she's the yin to my yang. She's got that laid-back, it-will-all-work-out-fine attitude. Not me: I'm diligent, merciless, and relentless when it comes to the nightlife world. I have to be. If I miss a step, another hungry wolf is waiting in the wings.

"I know you don't love me any less. It's over, and you don't have to worry about Peter."

"I know," I smarted. "Look, Jenna, you do a great job, and when you're friends with the boss it makes it hard sometimes to separate the business and the personal. I'll just be blunt: don't get caught up in who I'm personally screwing."

"Des, I'm beyond clear on the personal stuff."

"Good. And I hate to say it, but on the business side I've noticed that you've been slipping lately. We've got a lot of big projects coming up, and you've got to focus more. No excuses."

"You're right, no excuses!" She was just about to turn around and head back inside. "By the way . . ." she smiled and held up my brand-new Chanel bag. I put the cigarette in my mouth. Jenna tossed me my purse, and I caught it with both hands.

"Those things cost too much money to leave them lying around." We burst into laughter.

In my own defense, I'm hard on Jenna, but I give her her props, too, and I pay her damn well. Plus, who wouldn't sell their grandmother to rub elbows with a Who's-Who list of superstars in entertainment, sports, and business; live the glitzy, crazy life on the A-List club scene; enjoy the perks that include driving the boss's new

Range Rover; and sport high-end fashions courtesy of all the major designer showrooms?

Speaking of fashion perks . . .

I glanced down at my feet and smiled at my four-inch bejeweled masterpiece of a pair of shoes. Normally, I get freebies, but I paid cold, hard cash for these babies. The perk part is that I got them a season early. Jimmy Choo has truly outdone himself this time! Ooh, they're bad! The kind of shoes that when you wear them, you need no introduction or drum roll, folks simply back up and let you toss that bad boy through the door and it screams "THE QUEEN BEE BITCH HAS ARRIVED! HELLO!"

I looked up as the infamous Victor "Black" Wilson stepped out of the back of his black-on-black, tinted-out SUV. I ran my fingers through my cropped hair, took one last drag of poison, dropped the burning butt to the ground, and carefully stamped it out with Jimmy.

Tonight's "big" party is for his new clothing line for women, Blaque. That's right, another former rap-impresario-turned-music-mogul-turned-fashion-icon-and-designer. However, Black is doing it better than most of the competition. He's created a two-hundred-million-dollar fashion empire with VBW, a casual menswear line; Victor Exclusive (what he calls the "ghetto flashy" equivalent of Ralph Lauren's Purple Label); and now Blaque, top-of-the-line sportswear for women.

I got the party's liquor sponsor to spend one hundred G's for this party, and when I told him that for the fabulous guest list he wanted it would take another hundred, he took it out of his pocket. Destiny Day Productions earned a cool fifteen percent. Not bad for a night's work. Black wants the world to know his new flavor of the month, Michaela, is the face of Blaque. He wants a party so memorable that the industry will be talking about it until next year.

"Still got it, huh?" Black said, hugging me and inhaling my skin's scent deeply (Black's the kind of boy your mama told you to stay away from). He tried to slide his right hand down over my ass. I grabbed it mid-motion. Who the hell did he think he was? I didn't care how much money I was getting paid for this party. Ass-grabbing is not part of the deal.

"Watch yourself, sweetie, you don't get those kinds of benefits anymore. Let me tell you a little secret." I leaned in extra close to his ear and whispered in my most seductive voice. "The day Destiny Day loses it, and ain't fine no more, brothas better start lookin' for pigs in the sky."

This is our routine. Black and I have what they call a good old love-hate thang. I used to let him hit it every now and then, but it's gotten old, and he's got too many baby mamas. We've still got insane chemistry, but sleeping with him isn't worth the drama.

"Saved by supermodel," I said, rolling my eyes. Miss Michaela came slithering up behind Black. She was wearing a feathery Cavalli number, and the baddest bejeweled Chanel shoes attached to the longest legs I'd ever seen. (Note to self: Toss out these Jimmy Choos *im-mee-chit-ly*.) Michaela also had the perkiest breasts I'd ever seen, nipples at attention as if on cue. One word . . . fake! *Fake, fakitty, fake, fake!* Oh, did I mention they're fake?

"I thought you stopped." Black was referring to the cigarette butt still glowing on the ground next to my right foot.

"I did. But Negroes like you stress a sista out," I said, extending my hand, inviting Black and Michaela into the club, but not before taking one more look up and down the street for Malik.

"Shall we go inside?" Michaela oozed.

"Absolutely!" I replied eagerly, looking around again. Hey, don't fault me for keeping the faith that the brotha will show. I shook it off: *I'm over it now*. Stressing over a man is definitely not a good look for Destiny Day.

Love to Love You Baby

Black's face froze in amazoment as the three of us glided into Lotus. He was arm-in-arm with two of the most talked-about women in New York, me and Michaela. It had been my brainchild to transform the swank, laid-back, bi-level lounge feel of Lotus into a decadent underwater sex den with partially nude models, males and females, some as provocative human trays, serving sushi on their bodies.

Jenna was standing front and center, on her job keeping the flow of the party in line. "You good, Des," she whispered, running her fingers through her straight mane. That was code for "is the client happy?" I winked, mouthing *thank you*. I admit I do get crazy with the controlling thing at times, but she understands me.

Jenna used to be pretty intense herself (she was borderline neurotic), until she started practicing yoga religiously. I tried yoga for about a week. Forget about it! It was too quiet and my thoughts were too loud. But after firing two assistants, I'd finally found someone who could deal with my shit and not buckle under the pressure.

Black nodded his approval. I let out a silent sigh of relief and winked again at Jenna, who had been discreetly taking deep breaths herself. I've been throwing parties for over a decade, and the big, money-maker, high-powered ones like this for the last handful of years. But I still get nervous when it comes to pleasing the client.

The usual suspects . . .

Access Hollywood, Extra, ET, and photographers from *In Style*, *People*, *Us*, and a slew of other popular mags rushed us. I let them snap a few poses and quickly ducked out of the paparazzi's view. On cue, a muscular, well-oiled, honey-colored Puerto Rican hottie dressed in nothing but a pair of sheer genie pants and skivvies (you know those itsy-bitsy Speedo-like boy panties) handed me my regular Crown Royal Lust.

I scanned the room, gingerly sipping my drink. Tonight's party was definitely a hit. I'd taken sexy to a whole new level with this party, and Malik was missing it all. He could've been here with his artist, Freedom, spreading the buzz about the album. I could've even had DJ Peter leak one of the tracks he's been working on. This party was going to be all over the media tomorrow, local and national!

A few rounds of flashbulbs later, I slipped into my third Lust of the night. DJ Peter, on the ones and twos, took it back . . . waaay back. *Oooh, no he didn't?* I smiled. *Oh, but he did!* Patrice Rushen's "Forget Me Nots." That was DJ Peter's subtle message to me. The blue-eyed soul man strikes again!

He winks.

I wink back.

I'm ready to dance. The music and the cocktails are officially taking hold. I can't lie. I do wish Malik were here so I could give him a private dance. I close my eyes, musing at the thought, then throw up my right hand, pumping it in the air. I'm in the zone, bobbing my head, swaying my body from left to right.

Nobody better bust my groove. I came to party! I open my eyes and catch a glint of DJ Peter's diamond-encrusted watch, and his cute buzz cut and boyish face. He tosses back a shot of Patrón and smiles again. He might be nice to take home tonight, especially since Malik's a confirmed no-show.

"Get yo asses up!" DJ Peter shouts over the mic as he starts the record yet a third time, but not before I've instructed a bevy of scantily clad mermaids and genies to bring out bottles of Cristal and trays of champagne glasses.

Millions would die a thousand deaths to live this life. That's the illusion. A person can really get caught up, too, and start believing her own hype. Not those of us who are smart, though. Never get too comfortable or you fall off. It's about keeping that dough coming, and I've got two words for tonight: "cha" and "ching." Black Wilson knows and everybody else knows that if it's hot . . . Destiny's got it on lock.

Blame It on the Boogie

"I drink and drive for a *living*!"

I shouted this at Peter, snatching my car keys out of his hand. To no avail; he insisted he drive me *and* my car home and snatched them back. He was worried about my safety. Oh well, I am buzzed and would be mad as hell if I woke up tomorrow laid out in a hospital bed, my eighty-thousand-dollar pile of twisted steel and imported leather in somebody's tow yard. Actually, it's after four a.m., so technically tomorrow *was* today.

While Peter was parking the car, I did my best balancing act up the front steps, fumbling for my key. Thank God my condo was on the first floor. I was pissed because I was exhausted, getting sober, and very very horny. But have no fear, Peter Peter Pussy Eater will be parked and in my bed momentarily.

Just as I was about to open my apartment door, I remembered Izzy. I forgot to call and let her know ahead of time that I was bringing Peter home, and more importantly to make sure she didn't have that Negro D-Roc up in my house. All I needed was to come in and catch them sexing each other down like wild animals.

My place was spacious, but the loft area she slept in offered no real privacy. I was ready to get buck wild with Peter and I was not about to limit us to the bedroom.

"Yooohooo, Iz, it's me and I've got company, are you home?" I tapped on the door lightly as I unlocked it, still tipsy. No answer. I tiptoed in noisily and tripped up the loft steps, making another announcement. Her bed was empty. Yes! It was on!

I left the apartment door unlocked for Peter, and by 4:45 a.m. I'd stripped down to all my glory and climbed into bed, and he was sliding in next to me. *Ahhhh, my old reliable.* What would a girl do without one? He lightly ran his fingers over my face and lips, and then began to kiss me. He was a good kisser and quickly turned me on. "You are so amazing, Destiny," Peter whispered.

Okay, bad move. Don't talk, just go to work, man! I'm sorry, but I'm not interested in all the lip service. It's almost five. If he wanted a lady tonight (sorry, this morning), I was *not* the answer. I put my hand over his mouth and pushed his head down under the covers. Peter parked his mouth between my legs and began to do what he was best at doing, that swirly thing with his tongue. *Oh, yeah, that's it, right there.*

I was starting to work up to a nice warming body temperature when all of a sudden he stopped! "Destiny, I'm glad you wanted to be with me tonight. I've really missed you." His sweet voice was muffled.

Huh? I know I'm not hearing voices from beneath the sheets. Did this fool just speak?

111

"Peter, baby, you're blowing the mood," I said, sounding whiny and agitated (both of which I was). Totally un-Destiny, but a girl's desperate here. I needed some major sexual healing.

"I know it's just been a minute."

"Right, for me too, but don't stop, and please, baby, make good use of this," I said, handing him a condom.

"You know I been feelin' you for a while. Wassup wit us? Is this ever going to go anywhere? I'm lookin' for that next-level shit, D."

Okay, this was not the time for Peter to go into wimpy-guy mode. He knows my get-down! It's about having fun. When you start bringing that relationship rah-rah my way, you gots ta go! I quickly decided I was no longer in the mood. He was more interested in lollygagging than living up to his name. I know he *really* likes me, but I unfortunately just wanted to get laid.

"Oh, hell no! End the jibber-jabber already! Baby, you're the sweetest and I love you like cooked food, but all that talkin' gots ta go!" I handed Peter his clothes and escorted him to the front door. The poor boy was begging for another chance the whole way there, but I'd heard enough.

Good riddance!

After dead-bolting the door, I was sober and *still* horny. I climbed back into bed and reached for the bottle of Merlot and the wineglass that I kept handy on the nightstand.

Putting a man out just like that doesn't mean a thing to me, probably because I used to see Juanita do it all the time. She didn't even blink about it. She was always throwing Carlton out. Even though she and my father were together, she'd put his ass out anytime she felt like going back with her old man, Teddy. Teddy was a big spender, and Juanita threw that in Carlton's face every opportunity she got.

She'd put Carlton out for two or three days, and he'd have to go stay with one of his buddies or at a hotel. But Carlton would still come by the Belly Room to make sure Juanita was okay. Eventually, she'd feel bad, say yes, and he'd run right back to her. She liked living on a seesaw.

I drained my glass and dialed Malik's cell phone. It rang, and rang, and rang, until the voicemail message came on. "What happened to you tonight?" I slurred. "You are so wack, wack, wack, wack, *wack*!" I hung up and pressed REDIAL. It rang, and rang, and rang some more. His voice message came on again. "In case you didn't hear me, I said you were W-A-C-K, *WACK*!"

I hung up and poured myself another glass of wine. Okay, I probably shouldn't have called. He's going to think I'm crazy. He probably already does. I AM NOT NEUROTIC! I suddenly felt the urgency to call Curtis. I got his voicemail. "Where the hell are you!" I hung up quickly. Was I cracking up? This behavior is very UN-Destiny Day.

I know I'll regret everything tomorrow. No I won't, I'll just do like men do and act like none of this ever happened. In the meantime, my electric boyfriend (a gift from Izzy) was peeking out of the drawer. Hello, *baby*! (Diamonds and dildos are a girl's best friend, please believe it!)

Ahhh, mmmmmm, unhuh, right, ri . . . mmmmmmm, riiiiiiiight theeeeeeere . . . unhuh . . . mmmmmmmmmmm! Thaaaa aaaaaaaaas it! It's the best remedy to battle insomnia, that Ah-Me-So-Horny demon, and the perfect replacement for Peter, Malik, *and* Curtis. I don't need any of them. I'll just lie here sprawled out and spreadeagled, my one glass of Merlot deep, and let myself get (literally) buzzed away into sweet dreams.

Disco Inferno

Izzy was still dragging out her commentary about my rift with Jenna *days* ago. "You know you wrong how you do that girl, right? You don't even *want* Peter."

I did my best to ignore her and concentrated on shopping for jeans at my favorite SoHo shop for funky fun apparel, Big Drop.

"Izzy, let it go. Jenna is so over it. She's fine now. I just have to let her know who's in charge every now and then."

"Tha's right, Mama, show her who's the head bitch *in* charge and *in* control, right? You're gonna miss that girl when she quits."

"I guess I'll never know, 'cause she ain't never quittin'," I snidely shot back, and I stuck my tongue out.

Izzy decided to try on a pair of jeans for herself. "Ooh, Mami, look how they fit my ass. D-Roc would like these, right?"

"No comment."

"You're so wrong. Well you'd better be nice, 'cause he's meeting us here in about ten minutes. C'mon, loan me the money for them and I'll give it back in a coupla weeks. I'm up for a soap opera."

"That's awesome, Iz! Which one?"

"It's Spanish, and yeah, I know I don't speak Spanish, but my agent says I'm a shoo-in. Anyway, why don't you ever want to hear about D-Roc?"

"I just get weird vibes about him."

"You've been around Josephine too long, Mami!"

My cell rang.

"Yo, I'm rollin' to the Coffee Shop. Meet me in fifteen." Malik didn't even bother to say hello. I hadn't heard from him in four days and now he just wants me to drop what I'm doing and come see him.

"Uh, hello? How about a 'Hey, how you doin' or somethin'? You didn't show up at my party the other night. You've been MIA. What's up with you?" I was perturbed by his rudeness.

"You're killing me, D. I know how you feel, but it's been hectic. I've got a lot of irons in the fire. This Freedom record is bananas. I gotta bounce, see you in a minute! Oh, and don't be wack!" Malik chuckled and hung up. He busted me, so what?

I twisted my mouth and looked at my watch. It was six-thirty. I hated when Malik pulled this crap and didn't give me warning. Lucky for him, Izzy and I were getting hungry and our next quest was a good meal.

We are firm supporters of Gold-Diggers' Amendment Number Twenty-Five: Free food is the best food. Malik won't mind me bringing Izzy, however he might look at me half-crazy for bringing D-Roc along. But the last thing I'm going to do is tell Izzy her man can't come. Malik just better be glad the Coffee Shop is only about a ten-minute drive away. Otherwise, I would *not* be showing up.

115

The Coffee Shop at Union Square is still the "in" spot after all these years. When I dropped out of NYU to start throwing parties full-time, it was the place where all the aspiring models worked. In the early nineties, music-industry honchos like Russell Simmons and Andre Harrell were always hanging out here, not only for the good food, but to scope out long-legged beauties.

"There's your man." I pointed out D-Roc standing in the Coffee Shop doorway. She'd decided that it made more sense for him to meet us here. The man has a permanent scowl on his face. I don't know whether he picked it up in the joint and decided to keep it or what, but the brotha always looks like he's about to rob somebody.

" 'Sup, Destiny." D-Roc wasn't much for words. Izzy and D-Roc were immediately all over each other. She towered above him by a good two inches. D-Roc was still as fine as he was back in the day when they had him on the cover of *Right On* magazine.

I still remember his entire outfit: red parachute pants, a tuxedo shirt, and his hair in a long, curly shag, *au naturel,* no jheri juice up in there. I used to have his poster on my wall. He still has those boyish looks, but he's replaced the shag look with a close haircut and a goatee.

"And there's your boo right there," Izzy snickered, pointing to a group of about five brothas dressed like overaged rappers, huddled at a corner table. "Don't be sayin' that out in public," I said, shoving her. "That's just what I call him when we're in the passionate throes of lovemaking." We laughed. "Malik's with all his boys as usual," Izzy said sarcastically.

"I hate that he has to have an entourage everywhere he goes." Malik's crew was broke and not one of them owned a car. They were always driving one of his.

We made our way over to the table. Malik had a distressed look on his face. I think it's that thug thang (not to be confused with D-Roc's prison thang). You know brotha be having issues on the brain, like how to get more paper, and baby mama drama. But Malik didn't have too much of the latter.

Malik believed the best way to steer clear of that headache was to make sure baby and mama had all the amenities they needed: car, house, plenty of money, and a child-sized designer wardrobe that consisted of nothing less than the finest in infant hip-hop gear from Roca Wear to Sean John.

It's almost sickening that some of these kids can barely speak proper English or spell "Roca Wear," but are wearing it and can tell you exactly how much it cost. But somebody answer one question for me: Why does Malik's oldest son have a platinum chain, with a tiny dog-tag hanging from it that spells out LIL MALIK, in diamonds, hanging from his neck?

I'll keep my opinion to myself. People get funny when it comes to their kids. I'm just happy Malik has his situation under control and Baby Mama is cooperative. If I had a Benz I'd be cooperative too.

"Wassup, Talib," I said leaning in, giving him a halfhearted hug. " 'Sup, Amaru." I did the same. I waved to the others. I disdained his crew mainly because I got sick of them always trying to play gatekeeper when it came to me and Malik.

After our food arrived, D-Roc was the first to clean his plate, but not before singing an awesomely bad *a cappella* version of R. Kelly's "In the Closet." So terrible it wouldn't even make the *American Idol* blooper reel. I just shook my head as I watched this man shovel forkful after forkful of food into his mouth without even coming up for air. Even Malik and all his boys noticed. He sucks as a singer, big time, and the only "comeback" performance he's going to be doing is in the San Quentin production of "Jailhouse Rock."

I excused myself from the table and yanked Izzy by the arm, forcing her to join me. Once we were inside the ladies' room, I braced myself against the door.

"Ma, I don't have to go to the bathroom," she said, with a baffled look on her face.

"Girl, we need to talk. What's your man doing out there?"

"Wha?"

"Izzy, D-Roc just ate his dinner like it was about to be lights-out, and he keeps talking about goin' back to hustlin' if his record doesn't sell. And what's up with the impromptu performance?"

"Oh, he didn't practice that."

"Look, Iz, I think you need to *rethink* this D-Roc situation," I let out a sigh. "He has a lot to get together first before you should even consider getting serious with him. Did you forget the brotha spent nine years in jail?"

"First off, that was a decade ago, Ma! I can't believe you're holding it against him that he was locked up! I know he's had a hard time getting it together since then, but with his new record deal he's gonna blow up. An', he's jus' jokin' about goin' back to hustlin'." There was an edge of anger to her tone.

"Izzy, the last thing I would ever do is judge a man because of his past. I know people get caught in the wrong situations at the wrong time, *most* of the time. I just question if the brotha is emotionally healthy."

"He can't help that he got a bad hand of cards in life!"

"Iz, you're missing the point. He learned how to be a man in *jail*. Unless he met some older guy in the joint who was in the Nation of Islam—and you ain't never told me his name was D-Roc X—for a black man, jail ain't no place to spend the most crucial years of your development."

"I'm droppin' the subject." Izzy definitely had an attitude. We rejoined our party as Malik was settling the bill. Izzy purposely avoided all eye contact with me. She'll get over it. Tough love is long overdue in this situation.

"What's the spot tonight, Mama?" Malik called out from the other end of the table, and he blew me a kiss. I blushed.

"Jenna is doing Joe's Pub." One night a week Jenna helped out her girl DJ Monica at Joe's Pub in the Village. It gave her a chance to make some extra cash. I didn't mind her moonlighting as long as it didn't run in competition with my parties. DJ Monica specialized in Brazilian/Afro beat, house, and rare grooves.

"Let's roll!"

I smiled. I always liked partying with Malik. He was good for buying the bar out, and unlike a lot of guys, he could dance well. His rough-and-rugged two-step move was a major turn-on.

When we arrived at the club, Rico and Jorge were waiting in front for us. Our posse was ten deep. I made note of Jorge's new wardrobe. Since when did being an exotic dancer keep you paid enough to wear Versace Couture? Izzy wasn't quite as tactful.

"Jorge, damn, you wearin' the new line that's in the magazines?" She gave me a sly wink.

"I'm workin' it right, Mami?" Jorge spoke in a heavy accent like Izzy. He showed off his ensemble, doing an elaborate twirl. "My Papi takes care of me," he said, pointing to a beaming Rico, whose nose is so open he can't see the imminent train wreck. I had already gotten in one friend's business tonight, so why not make the rounds? I pulled Rico to the side before doing a quick check-in with Jenna.

"Rico, what are you *thinking* buying that boy an outfit like that?"

"Destiny, look at it like this, you like for your men to buy you nice things, right?"

"Of course, but my men have the money to make those kinds of purchases. Plus, aren't you supposed to be saving up to get your book done professionally?"

"Girl, I got my book under control! Anyway, ain't you ever heard of credit at Jeffrey New York?"

"I thought they closed your account," I asked.

"Not anymore! I got the hookup." I threw up my hands. Rico thought he had it all figured out.

Inside Joe's Pub, the open floor plan brought back memories of my early club-promoter days. Joe's Pub was a great place to throw a party, because you can see everyone in the entire room from every vantage point. The large bar area lining the far side of the club is great because you never have to wait long for a drink. When you're in the festive spirit, you want your drink "right here, right now!" Every promoter's nightmare is having a bar that can't accommodate all the guests.

I spotted DJ Monica across the room behind the turntables as we entered, and I waved. The crowd tonight was different than my typical sets. There was more of a bohemian, Downtown vibe, infused with an international flair, but still sexy and glamorous. A few dreads were sprinkled throughout the room, too. Jenna set up a VIP table for us in the small balcony area. Malik passed her his credit card, to get the Cristal flowing.

DJ Monica, representing for the ladies, gave me a shout-out and proceeded to pump up the volume, mixing in River Ocean's "Love And Happiness," featuring the superhuman vocals of La India. This *chica* has some lungs on her, and can blow. I call her the Puerto Rican Patti.

You could feel the electricity building in the room as La India's voice morphed into the pounding, pulsating, passion-filled bass. DJ Monica carried me back to my roots. I imagined being deep in the African bush in the middle of an ancient tribal ritual, the music sending out a drum call to the gods of love and happiness . . .

Bodies swaying, thrashing, and jerking rhythmically to the congas, timbales, jimbes, and bongos . . . *cackcuncackcakcackcuncuckcakbrrrrackcacacuncak* . . .

. . . taking me on an ethereal head trip with hypnotic, driving sounds, unleashing, unbridled, unbounded feel-good spirits. I was in a zone, one with the music.

We had already polished off two bottles of Cristal. Izzy had forgotten all about being mad at me for blasting her with my opinion of D-Roc. I climbed up on top of the table to join her. She was rolling her body like she was in a trance. The girl still had it! In all my tipsiness, I made a poor attempt at doing that booty-clap dance the girls in the Lil Jon video do. Izzy cheered, joining in. The two of us teetered sloppily. If it were 1985 we would've been giving two-thirds of Vanity Six a run for their money. Truthfully, we looked like a broken-down Vanity One-and-a-Half.

Snap! went the heel of one of my Gucci slingbacks.

I clumsily climbed down from the table to recover from this catastrophe. In my drunken state, I tried putting the heel back in place on the shoe and giving it a hard whack. No luck.

I decided to just wing it with one shoe on, one shoe off. I was just about to go back to practicing the "drop it like it's hot" booty-bounce clap thing when I saw D-Roc arguing with a barely-twenty-something woman in the corner of the VIP area. Three other women were huddled around them.

Too late, Izzy spotted the spat before I could block her view. "*Hijo de puta!*" Izzy shouted, stumbling and pointing at D-Roc. She must've really been angry to call him a *son of a bitch* in Spanish. She didn't know many words, but she knew the bad ones.

"Izzy, this ain't worth it, baby," Rico said trying unsuccessfully to calm her down.

"Who is this *puta* and her roached-out, hoodrat crew?" Izzy was wasted. Her words were slurred and she was making threatening gestures to the group of girls with D-Roc. Before D-Roc could respond, the woman he was arguing with did.

"Who the hell are you?"

"Shut up and go over there!" D-Roc shouted at the woman.

121

"Izzy, stop buggin'! She's an old friend, going through some stuff, and my manager told her where I was."

"You're lying, D, and this trick *puta* could get beat down!" Izzy's adrenaline was pumping.

Meanwhile, the woman, having had about enough of being called a whore, called on her girls for backup.

"What did you say?" the woman said, standing up to Izzy.

"You heard me!"

D-Roc was excited by the imminent girl fight, and Jorge was jumping around acting as though this was about to be bigger than the Thrilla in Manila.

"Get him!" I yelled. Rico was embarrassed and knew he'd better get his boyfriend in check fast before I laid Jorge out personally.

Izzy lurched toward her shouting-match opponent. The woman was hanging onto D-Roc. Izzy threw a punch and missed. I tried to pull her back, but Izzy was too fast for my liquored-up reflexes. She wiggled loose and slapped the girl in the face with a strong right hand, knocking her backward. The rough-and-ready hoochie crew was stunned, and a mêlée ensued. The force of Izzy's own swing caused her to topple over. I fell on top of her. I felt Malik pull me out of the confusion. Rico scooped Izzy up and tossed her over his shoulder.

The wheels of Malik's black-on-black, tinted-out Denali screeched away from the club in a fury. And now there we all sat . . .

Me disgusted, half-drunk, minus one Gucci shoe. Izzy in the backseat crying hysterically in Rico's arms. Jorge running off at the mouth: "You was like Tito Trinidad up in there, Mami!"

At that moment, I wondered: Could my life ever be normal?

"I can't believe he did this to me!" Izzy kept repeating over and over as she wept.

"I can't believe you're fighting over that jerk!" I said, ready to reach back and slap her for ruining the night.

"I can't believe four bottles of Cristal are wasted!"

"Shut up, Malik!" Izzy bawled harder.

Some women will never learn. That's exactly the reason why I'm not crazy about hanging out with women. Izzy and I were brought together by fate. I don't get it when women start tripping and getting jealous. The sad part is that most of the time it's over a man.

Izzy's biggest problem is that she's always ready to jump on the other woman if something funky goes down between her and D-Roc. She always seems to get involved with men who tell her a bunch of lies, and when all hell breaks loose, and she's ready to beef, I'm the one left to back her up at the showdown. And when the dust settles, mine is the shoulder she cries on.

I love Izzy, but she needs to realize that showing out over a two-dollar romance-novel line is worthless! Who cares if a man's faithful or not? I don't have the desire or time to regulate someone else's behavior. I wish a man would step to me on a "where have you been" power trip. That brotha betta check himself and read my lips: Don't ask me. I won't ask you.

Love Rollercoaster

YOU HAVE ONE NEW MESSAGE . . .

Malik: Hey, Mama, I want you to roll with me today!

MESSAGE DELETED.

Maybe Malik *is* finally starting to act right. He's called me almost every day this week. I think I'm gaining in the control department. Malik's just a tougher nut to crack open, but eventually they all do.

I called him back right away, and to my surprise he asked me to join him for his Saturday-afternoon ritual. In all the time I've known him, we've *never* done his "Saturday thing" together. I don't even know if I'm sure what the Saturday thing *is*, but I'm down. As strange as our relationship is, I feel like we're getting closer.

Breakfast at Jeys (pronounced "Jays") in Newark was our first stop. I ordered: fried hot links, grits, scrambled eggs and cheese, and wheat toast. Malik opted for the steak and eggs. As he scrolled through his BlackBerry, I made a few calls. We looked like an advertisement for hip-hop power couples.

"That new Garcel joint is bangin'!" I said, taking a hearty mouthful of grits and eggs.

"She aiight, but I think she's overexposed."

"Stop! I'm giving her a party in the Hamptons on Labor Day weekend. I really want you to be there with me. MTV is taping the whole thing."

"Word? That's dope. I'm proud of you, Mama."

"Thank you, sweetie," I said, smiling. That was another reason I was crazy about my Malik. He was supportive of what I was doing. A lot of guys would be intimidated and hatin' on a woman who had her career together and the balls to match.

"When Freedom's album is released, I wanna do something like that on BET."

I smiled. That's what I liked. A brotha lookin' out for me and I could look out for him, too. We could both get all the paper.

After breakfast, Malik asked me to tag along with him for "therapy." Part Two of his "Saturday thing." It turns out going to the laundromat was Brothaman's therapy. I didn't get it. He made all that money, had all these jewels, and didn't even own a washer and dryer. I never even knew that before today. I was glad I had stuffed plenty of magazines in my bag for the trip. The wash-and-fold was deep in the 'hood in Newark.

"Malik, baby, why don't you just buy a washer and dryer?" I said as we pulled into a parking spot in a tiny, slightly dilapidated strip mall.

"Comin' to the Laundromat keeps me connected to the realness of the 'hood."

I was speechless. Now that's something I will never agree about with Negroes in the music business, who are rappers or producers from the inner cities and the projects, and who won't let go of that life. If you've been blessed with a way to get out, and make your life better, why are you trying to keep *living* that life?

"Malik, I'm sorry, honey, but you don't have to forget where you came from. But damn, you rockin' fresh gear, hundreds of thousands of dollars worth of ice and platinum, you driving a car that cost more than what most people make in a lifetime, and your ass can't go to Sears and invest in a Kenmore. I mean, damn, at least find yourself a fluff-and-fold and pay somebody to wash your drawers. But what the hell do I know—I'm just using common sense."

"Yo, D, being here calms my nerves. I love being around my peoples in the 'hood. C'mon, we gotta go before all the good machines are taken!"

Hello? Something was very wrong with this picture. Didn't his "peoples in the 'hood" look at him cross-eyed when he rolled up to the suds spot in an eighty-thousand-dollar ride? I was stunned, winded, befuddled, shocked, and stupefied by the entire moment. Malik went right on about the business at hand, grabbing two large bags of dirty clothes out of the trunk and heading inside. I guess he *was* serious about getting one of the good machines.

I hopped onto a long table used for folding and sat quietly, Indian-style, flipping through the latest *Us Weekly* and *In Touch*, catching up on all my Hollywood gossip. Malik had his back to me, loading clothes into the washing machine. A thick sista with her hair wrapped in a doobie, wearing a Roca Wear velour two-piece that showed off a very unappealing gut, stomped in with a bad attitude and three bad-ass kids running behind her. Then she got mad because all the washers except one were in use.

She dropped her basket and rolled her eyes. "Daquan, Jaheim, and Shawn, get yo asses over here!" she shouted, with a heavy Jersey-girl accent. Then she looked over and gave me an icy stare. I curled up my lip and put down my magazine. This chickenhead clearly didn't recognize that I was a ghetto princess and, in accord with Kimora Lee Simmons's School Of Etiquette, "*I will whup a bitch's ass!*"

Malik arrived just in time. "Wassup, Ma?"

"Hey, Malik," she said, smiling. "I ain't seen you in a minute. Where you been at?" She patted her hair self-consciously.

"On the grind, Ma." He slid his arm around me. Her smile slowly began to fade into a look of disgust. "I'm done with those three over there."

"Thanks," she said glaring at me again. "Daquan, Jaheim, and Shawn! Come get these bags!" She instructed her three crumb-snatchers to drag the bags of laundry to the other side of the room.

"See, this is why I don't understand why you come down here to wash your clothes," I said agitated by the laundry hoochie.

"I told you I need to be with my peoples," he said, kissing me on the lips.

"Malik! My man!" It was a brotha with cornrows, clearly in need of a re-braiding and some oil sheen. He had on a Sean John sweat-suit and old Air Force Ones.

"Wha's good, baby!" The two men gave each other street-soldier pounds. "Oh, Boo, this is Destiny."

"How you, Ma?" Mr. Boo said to me.

I just nodded. Somehow I felt out of place. Seeing Malik and Mr. Boo congregate and pontificate in the middle of the Sudz and Spin suddenly brought another realization to me: People can sit up and talk all day about how they know hip-hop and are keepin' it real. But Malik and what he represents is that *real* hip-hop. I've been hood-winked and bamboozled.

What I thought I knew was just some homogenized version of the truth. Malik and Mr. Boo represented life uncut and uncensored.

"Jus' been in the studio since I got home."

"Wassup wit Dot and Woo?" Malik asked. I suddenly thought my man was speaking a foreign language. What followed was even more bizarre and surreal. It was like I was in the middle of a Nas song.

"Yo, son, Dot I know is havin' it rough doin' a bid, Woo jus' be chillin' back at the crib, and that nigga Black just had a kid, fuck it! Premiere took the wrap on some shit from way back. It all went down wit him and Rob Uptown! Loon's baby mama and him ain't togetha, but whateva.

"Shorty tried to set him up wit that fake crew from Queens, but it's all good, na'mean? Since I'm on the streets I put it to a cease. I'm glad to be back, I'm jus' keepin' it real, you know the deal. Same-o, same-o. Chickens is stalkin' and loudmouths still be talkin', so I just keep my head up, gotta get that paper. I'm jus' tryin' to rise above, so keep a eye out for that demo, yo!"

"Word! Holla at Talib when you got some tracks for me to listen to," Malik said, nodding his head.

"Word! Let me grab this washer real fast. You know they be snatchin' 'em like welfare cheese around here! It's nice to meet you, Ma. One!"

They gave each other dap and sealed it with another street-soldier pound. Then Mr. Boo picked up his bag of dirty laundry and walked away. I examined Malik more closely—his street-corner stance; his signature sag; a hot, fresh pair of sneaks; hat to the back. It used to be sexy. It wasn't looking so sexy anymore. I thought about how he had communicated with everyone in the Sudz and Spin on this quite enlightening Saturday afternoon. This was the world he felt comfortable in.

The laundromat summed up everything about Malik. He was

just a brotha from the 'hood who had become a ghetto superstar. Keepin' it real, keepin' it gully, trying to hustle and earn his way day to day. I was the phony. We were from two different worlds and I didn't belong in his. So, I guess it's like Nas said, life is about "clothes, bankrolls, and ho's" and maybe this really wasn't my element.

Love Hangover

I need to think. A walk would be good for my mind. What I was really itching for was an oldie-but-goodie. Music always helps me sort things out. Bobby's Happy House on Eighth Avenue and 125th Street was definitely the remedy. Bobby Robinson, the one-eyed shop owner, specialized in golden oldies.

"Baby girl! I got just the thing for you!" he said, gently pulling an LP, wrapped in what looked like a plastic baggie, out from behind the glass counter. A rare copy of Aretha Franklin Live at Fillmore West. "This here is like one of a kind." Now, I'm sure I could go to Tower and find five or six copies of this same record on CD, but it's not the same. Bobby's Happy House *is* Harlem, and I'd rather give my dollars to a black-owned business any day.

I thought I had made it out safely, but one of Bobby's buddies who's always hanging out with him at the shop stopped me to give me his two cents on what he called the *new* Harlem. "You seen all these white folks, Destiny? They tryin' to take over Harlem, jogging and walking their dogs like it belongs to them." I just nodded in agreement. "Yeah, you watch yourself, baby girl. Harlem is starting to turn into one of those science-fiction movies. I call it Invasion of the Negro-Snatchers!"

We all got a good laugh out of that. I made a quick and courteous exit, and just in time: more of his friends—a group of about three old-school sistas—were just walking into the store, and those ladies can really talk.

I was so distracted I looked up and saw that I had walked all the way to Josephine's cafe. She was headed out to the market and insisted I tag along. Fairway at the edge of 125th Street and the Hudson River was what Josephine called *her* "therapy." Okay, first the laundromat with Malik, and now this. I guess everybody's got their own special something. At this rate, I'd better get me something soon, too.

Josephine could be quite eccentric at times, so I just figured it was one of her weird ways. I mean, who actually gets therapy in a grocery store? Plus when I joked about it once, she got mad and told me I'd never be invited to go. She must've really sensed I needed some kind of therapy today to let me tag along.

"I can't believe I've been living in Harlem all this time and have never come to this Fairway," I said in amazement, getting out of the gypsy cab.

"I told you it was something to behold."

She was right. Outside there were fresh fruit and vegetables that lined the entryway. For a moment I thought I was at a country market, not in Manhattan.

Inside, more fresh fruit and veggies lined the walls. I could smell the aroma of spices, fresh ground coffee brewing, and delicious roasted chicken. Josephine was right at home.

"Sometimes I just come here to walk around. I take my time going up and down each aisle."

I saw that everyone seemed to be operating at an easygoing pace, none of that frantic New York energy. People were pleasant and relaxed. It put me in the mood to talk.

"Why do I feel like maybe something I'm doing in life isn't working?"

"When we get that uneasiness with ourselves, that's what it is. Something isn't working right."

I stared in bewilderment at Josephine, who had just poured us two cups of hazelnut coffee from the self-service stand.

"Destiny, you're always the big talker, the one who has all the answers, Miss Bad-Mutha-Shut-Yo-Mouth," Josephine said, giving her best Isaac Hayes "Theme from *Shaft*" impersonation. I couldn't help laughing. "I saw through you the first day I met you back in ninety-two when you came into my old café with Izzy, who was sweet as pie back then, but just as simple. She listened to everything you told her to do. Both of you were so green. The difference was that you were a go-getter, a leader. You weren't going to let anything stop you in life.

"And when you told me you had withdrawn from NYU, I didn't say much. It wasn't my place. I just listened. I can tell you now that I agreed with your aunt, but I also had a mind of my own when I was your age. Nobody could tell me anything, like every time I said 'I do' and married another fool. But I have no regrets. And neither should you. Life is about living!

"Destiny, what you're feeling right now shouldn't make you nervous or upset. It should make you feel excited that your soul's been awakened. Your heart's trying to tell you that it's time for something new."

"But what's the something new?" I asked.

"That's your problem, Destiny. You always have to be in control.

In control of business, your friends, your feelings. You've got to know *right now*! It's got to be done *right now*! I'm telling you to release all that *energy* right now!" Josephine's eyes narrowed and her jaw tightened. She placed her hands on my shoulders, "You've had to bear the burden of a lot of crap. Losing your first connections to life, before you could even understand, is the reason why you do and feel the way you do about a lot of things.

"You've never healed properly because you had to keep moving with time. Right now the Spirit may not be ready to reveal what exactly that 'something new' is, but I guarantee, if you allow Destiny to be quiet for a change, this world may just open up and give her something shiny and sweet."

We didn't do much more talking after that. Just kinda chit-chatted about the weather, ate some free samples of international cheeses and olives on display. As a matter of fact, Josephine didn't buy very many groceries—just some nuts, dried cranberries, and pita chips.

I felt different walking out of Fairway than I did walking in. Hmmm, maybe this so-called Spirit *was* in fact preparing me for something "shiny and sweet." I kind of liked what Josephine was saying.

I Will Survive

"Rico, it's Destiny and Izzy. Let us in," I said, banging on his apartment door. There was silence. Izzy motioned for me to try the handle. The door was unlocked. I slowly opened it, and there he was, curled up in a ball on the lounger, crying like a two-year-old.

"Oh my God, Rico, wha's goin' on, baby?" Izzy rushed over and put her arms around him.

"It's Jorge," he said weakly.

"I knew it! Tell us what happened!" I said.

"He ran my phone bill up to two thousand dollars calling Puerto Rico. He said he needed to call back home to his best friend who was having some legal problems. And then he convinced me to buy his friend a ticket to come here, and . . . and . . ." Rico was building up to an outburst. ". . . and I caught them in bed together." He burst into tears.

"Wha?! Bitch, you better pull it together! It's time to kick his ass!" Izzy wasn't known for her tact. I shot her a look.

"I'm an idiot, I know," Rico lowered his head.

"You used poor judgment, but the last thing we think is that you're an idiot." I tried to sound encouraging. Izzy made a smirk. I elbowed her hard.

"We jus' need to beat Jorge down!" Izzy was fuming and ready to go upside Jorge's head.

"We don't need to do anything but calm down," I said. Somebody had to be the voice of reason. I had two head-cases on my hands, and I was barely hanging on to my own sanity.

Three the Hard Way (that would be us) sat for an hour and a half, waiting for Jorge to return. As soon as we heard the door open, we jumped up and got into our best *Charlie's Angels* poses. Jorge strolled through the front door in sunglasses and Rico's best clothes from head to toe. Enrique, the unwanted houseguest-slash-boytoy from Puerto Rico, followed him in holding a bottle of wine.

I walked up to Enrique and snatched the bottle out of his hand. "Baby, you gots ta go!" I said. Meanwhile, Izzy had already yanked Jorge's five-foot-six waif frame by the collar.

"That's my Armani!" Rico shouted, and he pulled off the jacket Jorge was wearing. Then he made him give up the shirt under it, too.

After we escorted the half-naked Jorge and Enrique out of the apartment and to the curb, we decided to celebrate the Emancipation of Rico at his kitchen table over three glasses of wine.

"I have an announcement to make!" Rico stood up tapping his glass. "Here's to cutting all the crap out of my life. It's official, no more Jorge, José, Antonio, Javier . . ."

". . . Ronnie, Bobby, Ricky, and Mike!" Izzy added, to the tune of New Edition's classic line.

"Rico, let this be a lesson that you need to get focused," I said.

"I know I'm doin' it for real now. I haven't had my professional life in order, but I'm making a commitment. I'm turning in my player's card, and I've decided that I'm going to practice celibacy."

"You lie!" Izzy shouted. "Honey, you are worse than Destiny when it comes to that revolving bedroom door!"

"No, I'm doing it! I'm about to be committed to *me*, and when Mr. Right comes along, I'll know it's for real. I'm too old and too tired to keep wasting my time with relationships going nowhere. I'm almost forty, and I need to get my life in order. I want a man who's got something going for himself. I say we *all* need to think about settling down."

"Speak for yourself, Rico," I said. "I know the Jorge situation was bad, but don't you think you're making some big statements kind of soon?"

"I told you I'm done with playin'! I've had enough action for two lifetimes. I can hold out for Mr. Right."

"Or Mr. Ay Papi," Izzy had managed to crack herself up once again. "No, I believe you, Rico. A good man is hard to find."

"But a hard man is good to find!" I added. Rico lightly whacked us both.

"On a serious note," I went on, "I'm glad you're done with that craziness, Rico, because we're too old to be beating folks up and throwing 'em out."

"Pu*leeze*, Ma, you snatched the bottle out of that boytoy's hand first!"

"I'm ashamed of myself, too. That's why neither one of you better pull me into your drama again. No more love-gone-bad rescue missions. And, Izzy, I *really* hope you're through with D-Roc and your fighting-women-over-men days."

"Mami, I'm so ovah him! I found out that girl at the club is his wife, *and* the mother of his one-month-old twin boys. I'm officially retirin' my belt."

"I hate to break it to you on the *arroz con pollo* tip, but Miss Thing, he didn't have nothin' to offer you except bubble gum and dick!"

"High-five on that one, Rico," I said.

Who knows, maybe Rico and Izzy *had* learned their lessons and were ready to make changes in their lives?

My cell rang.

"Hotline!" Rico shouted.

I was still laughing when I answered it.

"I just needed to hear your voice," the unknown caller muddled.

"Curtis?"

"God, I miss you. I miss hearing your voice and seeing those pretty breasts of yours."

"Oh, so you decided to think about me."

"Where's the sweet Destiny Day I know?"

"She left the country!"

"Where are you?"

"Out!"

"Quit being a smart-ass, Destiny. I need to see you."

"You want things when they're convenient for you, Curtis."

"Where are you?"

"At my friend Rico's. You're more than welcome to join us."

"You know I don't do that crowd thing. I wanna see *you*."

"Too bad. I'm drinking and carrying on," I said flatly.

"I'll be there in ten minutes to suck your pretty toes."

"Whatever! You'll have to wait." I pressed END.

Rico and Izzy were both looking at me like I had just sprouted a second head.

"Why the looks?"

"Alls I'm gonna say, Ma, is you might need to make a pledge today, too."

"Oh, I'm not like you and Rico. I have my various situations under control. I'm not even really diggin' Curtis anymore. I'm just going to hang out with him for a bit. I mean he *did* hook the Garcel deal up for me."

"So you owe him some extra pussy for that?" Rico smarted.

"Don't even try to make my situation sound cheap!" I was offended. "Hello, I'm *not* the one who just got bamboozled by Papi Chulo!"

"Practice what you preach, Mami, tha's all." Izzy and Rico had no idea what they were talking about. I wouldn't want to hurt their feelings, but their disastrous personal lives could never be compared to mine.

Curtis was parked in front of Rico's building and had been sitting there for a whole hour. "I take it I was worth the wait!" I said, getting into the passenger side of his car.

Five minutes later he was doing just what he promised—sucking my toes, as I lay on the seat and he kept an eye on the road. He took the long way to my place, cutting all the way across town. I was getting hot and bothered and couldn't resist the growing bulge in his pants. I pulled my shirt off, then leaned over and unbuckled his pants (God bless tinted windows). He exited the West Side Highway at 125th Street and rolled to a stop.

"I can't wait to get inside you."

I suddenly remembered that Jenna was working from my place. "We can't, baby—" *Kiss.* "—my assistant—" *Kiss.* "—is—" *Kiss.* "—working—" *Kiss, kiss.* Oh, well, forget logistics. I pressed the HAZARD button. We had our very own love shack on wheels. I reached into his pants. He was eager, and excited to see me again.

"Kiss it, baby," he moaned leaning his head back on the headrest. I gave him one of those famous black-girl, I-know-you-must-be-trippin' looks. "C'mon, Destiny, just a tiny kiss, please?" Now, I might like to get freaky, but I'm very particular about what I put in my mouth. First off, you have to be one of the few, the proud, and the chosen to earn the opportunity for Destiny Day to bless the magic stick. And in his defense, he's earned it.

However, Curtis ought to know better by now. If a sista can't stand lying in the afterglow of sex, you know she's not trying to taste some clammy and crusty *thing* that's been trapped in a pair of boxers half the day. Not to totally gross you out, but think about it. You're walking from meeting to meeting, in and out of the car, the New York elements. Chile, that kind of constant friction generates heat. And there's nothing worse than warmed-over, salty balls. I checked my purse: I was all out of baby wipes. There was nothing more to discuss.

"Then if you're not gonna lick it, get on top!" Curtis pleaded like some desperate soul. Okay, so I'm game. He's undressing, I'm undressing. I ask for the condom, and he twists his face up like I just spoke alien talk or something.

"Excuse me? You don't have a condom? Negro, if you comin' to play ball, you have to have your uniform on!" His face dropped. "You'd better hope . . ." I said, sifting through my purse, only to find an empty trial-sized condom box. "You're out of luck, Curtis!"

So, now I'm putting my clothes back on and he really starts begging for the ass. I'm still looking at him like he's lost his mind. Curtis is pleading his case with his best litigation act yet, saying things like, "Baby, forget about the condom. You know me. I'm clean!" and "I'm hurt that you don't trust me!" and "You need to think about what you're doing!"

Oh, but the best part was when he started scraping the bottom of the desperate-for-pussy barrel, "I need to feel you." His face was contorted, as he sat half-dressed, hanging out of his underwear in a very unflattering slump. I waited until he was completely done with the need-some-booty-bad antics. I began to speak in a very clear and controlled tone.

"You're right, Curtis, I do know you. I know you well enough to know that I'm probably not the only extracurricular piece you're hitting. Now, I like being with you, but you know the rules. When you get your game in order and come correct, then we can screw sideways and upside down until your thing falls off! Until then, drop me off at home." I folded my arms and didn't think twice. I was furious thinking about the cocktails I could be having right now.

"And you need to get us a hotel!" I shouted. "Cheap-ass motherfucker! I'm not some two-dollar ho!" I slammed the car door and stormed off. This whole situation with Hot-Shot-Cheatin'-in-the-Next-Room-Lawyer has run its course and is just . . . just . . . WACK! I guess I *will* be making a pledge today—one to cut this brotha from the squad, effective, as Rico would say . . . im-mee-chit-ly!

{1} TIRED OF BEING ALONE

{2} TELL ME SOMETHING GOOD

{3} YOU DROPPED A BOMB ON ME

{4} PART TIME LOVE

Tired of Being Alone

Malik's text message was sweet, even if it was two and a half weeks late:

Yo, D, I know it's been a while. I guess a long while. I just kinda had to dip for a minute. I went back to Philly to spend time with my family. My sons are gettin' big. I took them with me. I'm really frustrated with the music game. Freedom started wildin' out. But it's all good, the album's back on track and almost done.

We only need one or two more songs. I got one comin' from Mike City and another one from Timbaland. Ummm, anyway, you probably don't wanna see me, but I reaaaally wanna see you. Maybe we can try to get things back like we used to. Hit me.

Ten minutes ago, he called promising to stop by on his way to the studio. I said okay. Was I supposed to flip out on him or something? Trial and error has proven, irate-black-woman tactics don't work on Malik.

At this point, I'm immune to it all. The way I see it, I've got two choices, say no and don't see him, or do exactly what I'm doing right now, a quick tidy-up and shower, and look like a million bucks when he gets here. The goal is to win the war, screw the battle!

I had just stepped out of the shower and gotten dressed when the door buzzer rang. It was Rico. Bad timing.

"Please don't tell me it's Jorge again, because I'm not available," I said, letting him in.

"It's not Jorge, it's me!"

"What's going on with you, honey?" I said, fluffing the pillows arranged on the couch.

"I'm just stressed right now. I'm not sure I'm strong enough to do this celibacy thing."

"Rico, you can do it! Plus you've got plenty of things to occupy your time, like concentrating on your career. You can't expect for stuff to just drop in your lap." By this time we had moved into the kitchen. I decided to whip up some vittles for my man, who would be here any moment. "Baby, you've had your priorities mixed up," I said rinsing two pounds of chicken wings and dumping them into a large pan.

"Well, maybe if someone would invest in my dreams, I could get a book done!"

"If *someone* showed they were serious then *someone* might consider investing." I cut my eyes at him. Rico was always looking for everybody else to bail him out, pick up the slack, and take responsibility for what he needed to be doing. I reached for the adobo seasoning.

"Rico, I love you and I know how talented you are, and I hate to

144

say it, but you tend not to finish what you start. I'm not trying to see my money get flushed down the toilet!" I slid the pan of now-seasoned chicken wings into the oven, set the timer for thirty minutes, pulled out various ingredients for a salad, and started chopping away. Rico poured us each a glass of wine.

"Go ahead, Destiny, you can be honest. You don't believe in me." Rico can be so dramatic.

"Don't you dare say that! I'm one of your biggest fans, but you need to stop being so down on everyone else. Stop comparing what you do to what the next person's doing. You're way too negative, and you just need to concentrate on being the best for you. But the first step is *taking* a step!"

We sat down on the sofa and I took Rico's hand in mine. "The only person you have to compete with is yourself. I'm down for you, but you have to be down for you, too! When you show me that you're really ready to do this, I got your back and I'll put my money where my mouth is."

"Then I'm gonna show you!" We toasted and drained our glasses. "Speaking of putting something where your mouth is," he gave a devilish grin. "Wassup with the Ghetto God coming over and all the cooking? A bitch can throw down, but the last time you cooked was Christmas!"

"Stop it! You're such a liar. I don't mind cooking for some good lovin'!" We high-fived.

"But seriously, could this be love?" Rico asked with genuine sincerity.

"Don't you dare form your mouth!" I said.

"I live for Mr. Malik! I mean who else can handle the legendary Destiny Day?" Rico said.

"True! I dig how I have the freedom to live my life. But the last thing I'm looking for is love. Love is a fairy tale. A fantasy that doesn't exist. When are you, Izzy, and Josephine going to get that through your heads? What Malik and I have is chemistry. He's a great maintenance man, when he acts right. Damn, if I can just get him on a regular schedule."

"I think deep down you really do want commitment. You can't tell me that if Malik asked you to be with him today forever, you'd say no?"

"Malik would never do that."

"You's a control freak and Malik's done thrown a snafu in your system. You haven't quite figured out how to control him yet. But you will, and when you do, I feel sorry for him." He took a sip from his glass. "But hey, what do I know, you might be in love. Making your famous chicken wings and lighting all these candles and smellin' all fabulous and thangs."

"Rico, you sound ridiculous! Don't try to psychoanalyze me!"

"Lawdy, the Legendary might be falling in love!"

"On that note, it's getting late, and you've crossed the line." I took his glass from his hand. "Malik will be here soon." I handed Rico his jacket and took him by the hand, leading him to the front door. "And you need to go home and think about what I said and get focused!" I opened the door and rudely pushed him into the hallway.

"Damn! I've been thrown out of better places!" We shared a laugh. Rico kissed me on both cheeks and I closed the door.

● ● ●

By one a.m. the television was watching me, the candles had burned down, and the phone was ringing off the hook.

"Hello," I answered, half-asleep.

"Wassup, Mama." Malik's voice was low and raspy.

"What the hell happened to you?" I said, drowsily, checking the clock on the television.

"Shit's hectic and I got caught up with Freedom."

"So, what, your phone just started working again?" I was livid, looking around the room at the table that had been set hours ago and the wilted salad and cold chicken wings.

"Baby, I'm sorry. I still wanna see you tonight."

"Whatever, Malik! It's tomorrow now, and last night was my night off and I could've made other plans. I fuckin' cooked!"

"You made chicken wings?"

"So, what if I did?" I snapped.

"That's my favorite! I'm headed uptown now. Can I come through?"

Twenty minutes later, chicken bones were scattered all over the coffee table and clothes were strewn about the living room. Malik and I were in the middle of a serious body lock on the floor, my legs strapped around his back. I let out a moan on his down stroke. "I'm not some hoodrat booty call," I said, breathing hard, making sure to thrust all I could muster at him. I wanted to punctuate my words.

He took a deep breath and pushed himself deeper inside me. I did my best to continue stressing my point under the extremely challenging circumstances. "I'm not dealing . . . *unh* . . . with . . . *ahh* . . . your drama anymore. When you tell me you're . . . *aaaah, mmmmm* . . . comin' over . . . *aaaah, oh yes!* Then you better show up at that time!"

"Shut up and turn over!" Malik ordered, flipping me over on all fours. He pushed himself deep inside me again, but from behind. "Whose is it?"

"Mine!" I moaned through gritted teeth.

Smack! He smacked me on my bare butt with an open palm. "You know I'm crazy about you . . . *ahh!* . . . but you gotta understand a brotha is workin' . . . *uhh, uhnnnn!*"

147

Smack! on my right butt-cheek again. This time harder. I felt the sting. It turned me on more.

"That's it!" I whispered.

"Whose is it, D?" A few more strokes and I was almost . . . just about . . . just about . . . right . . . THEEEERRRE!

"Yours!" I screamed in ecstasy.

"*Ahhhhhh!*" Malik gripped both my butt cheeks, and echoed my sentiments.

After I washed up, I tossed him a towel to wipe off. Malik was stretched out on the couch. I climbed on top of him, pulling a cashmere Ralph Lauren throw over our naked bodies, resting my head on his chest.

"I'm sorry I didn't call."

"What's the excuse now?"

"Shit was just crazy at the studio."

"It's always crazy at the studio," I replied coldly. I was really getting tired of hearing that same old line.

"You're right."

"You still should have called," I said.

"I'll never do that again."

"Whatever."

"It's the last time." Malik lifted my head with his hand, pulling me close to his face. "I promise," he said softly, kissing me. "D, I'm having more problems at Freedom's label and I'm gonna have to make a move sooner than I thought."

"Are you still thinking about doing the record independently?"

"Absolutely! I've got a hundred-fifty G's and I need another fifty."

I knew what Malik was asking without asking.

"Malik, I'm just uncomfortable with loaning money to friends."

"What the fuck . . ." He jumped up in a huff. "This isn't a loan to one of your girlfriends, D. It's me. This is business. You could've had points on the album. But you know what, fuck it, D! I got enough battles out here to fight, and cats trying to take what's mine. I need a woman who's ready to build with me, not against me."

Malik started to dress. I felt confused and angry and crappy all at once. I have a rule about loaning money to people. The rule is *don't*. Giving Rico a couple hundred dollars here or there is nothing. This is fifty thousand dollars and far more than helping Izzy out with her rent.

At the same time, I'm pissed off because this brotha insulted me by implying I'm against him. The last thing Destiny Day would ever do is kick a brotha when he's down.

"Malik," I took a deep breath and grabbed his arm. "I'm not against you."

"I'm out here with my ass hangin' in the wind, D," Malik's voice cracked and for the first time I saw fear in his eyes. "I gotta win with Freedom, or this shit is over for me," he buried his face in his hands. "I just don't know anymore. Maybe I just need to give up on my dream. I thought I could single-handedly save black music. These fools are makin' garbage out here. I was talkin' to my father and I see how an old dude who dedicated his life to makin' great music is sad over this shit out here."

"Malik, you're not out here alone. I want to build with you. I've got your back, baby. I'm not going to let you give up on your dream. It ain't over, and whatever we gotta do, we'll do it together."

Malik looked me in my eyes, and put his arms around me.

"I'm crazy about you, Destiny, and we could really do this."

The thought of Malik and me hand in hand taking on this "thing," the business and life, and getting the best of the naysayers, made me feel empowered, and it crystallized my feelings for him. What happened next was a sequence of events of such magnitude, those who know me would say, that it was bigger than an Elvis sighting: I got up, opened my purse, pulled out my checkbook, and wrote out a check payable to Malik Jaru in the amount of fifty thousand dollars. I swallowed hard.

Usually, when it came to me and a series of zeros, it had to be for property or some sure-fire investment opportunity. On top of that, all the financial aspects had to be outlined in a document that at least *one* of my two lawyers had previously reviewed and red-lined before I handed over a dime. Hell, I had never taken a risk this big for anyone, or anything, not even God.

When I returned to the bedroom, Malik was still sitting where I'd left him.

"This is for you," I said softly, handing the check to him.

"D, I don't know what to say."

"Just say thank you."

"Baby, thank you for holding me down." He smiled. "Come here." He leaned in, kissing me on the lips. "You know you're the best, right?" He held me close and I melted into his arms again.

"Yeah, and you'd better know it, too," I teased.

"You are *so* crazy. I love you, Mama," Malik said, pulling back, looking me deep in the eyes.

"For real?" I never imagined *any* man saying those words to me. "Malik, I'm not really into all that sentimental stuff, but you're my heart and . . ." I smiled coyly. "I love you, too." I placed my hand over his. "Wow, that doesn't even sound like something Destiny Day should be sayin'." We shared a laugh.

"I got you forever, D. That's my word." He pulled me close and held me for what seemed like *forever*.

Perhaps it *was* time to put all my energies into one place, one man. I don't want to call it settling down or a commitment, but we could kind of have that Kurt Russell, Goldie Hawn love thang. My boo, my baby, my warrior was contemplating his next big move and I had to be there for him. All was well in gangsta's paradise again.

Tell Me Something Good

"I've never felt like I wanted to be in anybody's corner or that I was even that type of person before Malik," I said, looking intently at Josephine. I couldn't wait to get to the Tea Café this morning to tell her about my feelings for Malik.

"Well, I'm not here to discourage any woman in love, especially one named Destiny Day. It must be real, because I don't think you've seen anything this side of noon since you were a student at NYU. I know when you've got your mind made up about something, there's usually no turning back."

"Josephine, do you think this is love?"

"You don't know? Wasn't it you who said that love was 'fairy tale, fantasy crap,' or something like that?"

"Okay, go ahead, throw my words back at me."

"No, I'm just saying them to make a point. Love is very powerful, and we can't dictate when it's going to happen. The only thing I'm concerned about is right here." Josephine placed the palm of her hand lightly over my heart.

"I guess the power of love beat me down, Josephine. Call up all the tabloids." I smiled. "I know it's real, because there was a time when if a man came off weak to me, I'd throw him out like old garbage. If I sensed a man was getting too clingy, and wanted to be with me on a serious level, I'd cut him off so fast the brotha wouldn't know what hit him. Hey, Rick James said it best: 'I was cold as ice long ago.' Malik is *it* for me, Josephine."

"I believe you, Destiny. Maybe love and the whole marriage-and-a-baby-carriage thing *is* for you!"

"Whoa, Nellie! You're being overzealous. Let's just take it one step at a time. Malik and I have a lot to do before all that. Hell, I don't even know if all that is in the stars. We might just end up *together* until we die. Why do you need all that ceremonial crap? I just want to help him get through this situation with his artist and then we'll see."

"What situation?"

"Freedom lost his deal and the world is against this brotha. I need to be by his side. If I were in the same situation, he'd do it for me. He's decided to put the record out independently, and I invested in the deal."

"Wow." Josephine's eyes went wide. "How many investors?"

"Just me."

"Did you get it all in writing?"

"I didn't need to. I've got the man *and* his word."

Josephine gave me a doubtful look.

"Are you insinuating that Malik would try to take me?" I asked defensively. She didn't respond. "Whatever it is, Josephine, just say it. You sure have an opinion about everything else!" My tone was sharp and agitated.

"Back up, Destiny. I'm not saying a word. What you do with your business is *your* business, and I think this is my cue to step away."

"Oh, it's *definitely* your cue and this *is* my business!"

"I told you, when it comes to you, I'm only concerned with what's right here," she said, this time placing her hand over her own heart. "I've got customers." Josephine got up and walked back to the counter, where a small line of people had begun to form. I had never raised my voice at her, but nobody ever questioned Destiny Day. Conversation over.

● ● ●

I let a week pass, hoping that tensions between me and Josephine had settled. Izzy and Rico were meeting me at the café for lunch after Izzy's big Spanish-soap-opera audition. I was feeling even more out of sorts about Malik. I'd left messages every day and gotten no return calls. But what the hell, I figured it wouldn't hurt to try him again. This time I got wise and blocked my number. *Maybe I can catch him off guard and he'll answer*, I thought. By the fifth ring his voicemail hadn't answered, so I hung up, dejected.

The last thing I want to do is stress him about hooking up. I'm only calling because I need to make sure he got Freedom's project rolling again. Damn! Who am I fooling? I really want to hear his voice. Why am I going through all the dramatics and playing games? I want him to see my number! He needs to see that I'm calling! Fuck it! I unblocked my number and dialed again.

By the sixth ring his voicemail picked up: *You know what to do. Peace!* I closed my eyes, picturing his soft lips mouthing the words. Oddly, I felt a moment of sweet relief, letting out a harbored breath at the sound of his smooth, laid-back baritone. At least the message wasn't saying, "Malik's dead!" or "If this is Destiny, don't call back!"

And it was all good until the message prompt beeped and the Nextel lady's voice came on: *The mailbox you are calling is full.*

Bitch!

I shook it off before reaching the Tea Café. When I entered, Josephine was busy cleaning off tables. Without saying a word, I picked up a rag and joined in.

"You know you need to get yourself a staff," I said.

"Nope, don't like a lot of *people* in my business. You know what I'm talkin' 'bout, don't you?" She didn't even look up at me.

"Touché!"

"Aw, baby you ain't seen nothin'. I can get *all* the way gone outta folks' *business*." Josephine reached for the last saucer. I blocked her hand, gripping it in mine.

"I'm sorry, Josephine. I was out of line snapping at you the other day and saying hurtful things."

"Apology accepted. Destiny, I wasn't angry with you. Life's too short, and I love you. I was just disappointed that you would take that type of tone, knowing how much I care about you. Love is a great thing, just don't let it take your sweetness, make you get ugly with people who mean you some good. We're like family, and family doesn't just give up on you like that, okay?" We hugged and quickly moved on like there had never been a rift.

By the time Izzy and Rico arrived I was on my second cup of green tea.

"Sorry we're late, but the Puerto Rican Princess here has good news," Rico said, sitting down.

"Girl, I booked the soap opera!" Izzy squealed. "I start working tomorrow!" Her hair was a curly ball of frizz, bouncing all over the place with her excitement, and she was glowing and as gorgeous as ever. "I'm gonna be on *La Familia*!" Izzy pulled up a chair between me and Rico.

"Girl, you are in a world of trouble if they need you to speak Spanish," I said.

"She'd better learn if she gonna eat tomorrow!" Rico gave her a playful shove. "Chile, I'm happy, 'cause I was about to tell you to forget about trying to act and ask you how many words you typed per minute!" Rico let out an overdramatic sigh.

"Did it really have to take all that?" I teased.

"No, he's right, Des. I was like, damn, maybe I can't make it. But my *abuela* told me to just pray, and she lit a candle for me at Mass on Sunday. I know her prayers worked."

"Speaking of your grandmother, what's up with Carmen?" I asked.

"Why you gotta fuck up the mood?" Izzy turned sour. "She's still livin', if that's whatchu wanna know, but I don't really care wha's up wit her."

"Izzy, you don't really mean that."

"Yes I do, Des!"

"Are you sayin' that if yo mama was to die today or tomorrow you wouldn't care?" Rico asked.

"Tha's exactly what I'm sayin'!" Izzy was getting uptight. "To me, Carmen is dead already."

"Let's change the subject," I said. We all shifted uncomfortably.

"Well, I know one thing: A bitch is possessed walking around here with that little bitty coat and outfit on," Rico said, checking out Izzy's attire. As usual, he had done a brilliant job of lightening the mood.

"If you got it, flaunt all of it! Baby, it's May and summer's on the way," I said. Izzy was wearing a miniskirt, motorcycle boots, one of my cashmere T-shirts and a lightweight Juicy Couture jacket. "Hey, is that my jacket?"

"Mami, it brought me luck!"

"I'm glad somebody has some good news, considering I haven't heard from Malik."

"I ain't surprised, Legendary. He just can't get it right."

"Yeah, but we decided to take things to the next level, and now he's gone MIA again."

"Honey, you know yo man," Rico said. "You just need to give it up, and turn it loose. He gon' come back in a few days or a coupla weeks like he always do. You know he's a busy man."

"I don't know, Des. Is like, now that he knows he's got your heart he's shittin' on it."

"Izzy, you sure have a twisted way of encouraging a sista!" I said.

"I'm jus' keepin' it real, Ma!"

Izzy's phone rang. I don't know why, but my heart jumped.

"Ooh, that better not be D-Block!" Rico's cheeks puffed up.

"No, for your information, it's my cousin from St. Louis that I was telling you about, Des. Remember she e-mailed me two weeks ago? Her name is Jewel and she's visiting the East Coast for the first time." Izzy answered and put the call on hold. "Hey, maybe you all know some of the same people."

"First off, I was born in East St. Louis, and I don't know any Puerto Ricans there. Secondly, Markum is really my home, so I doubt it!"

"She's not Puerto Rican. She's on my daddy's side, an' my bad, I thought all you *country* people knew each other." Izzy let out a deep belly laugh. "Now, shhh," she answered her phone. "Hi, Mami! I'm glad you called me back, I loss your number. I've been so hectic. I just booked a job on a soap opera, but why don't you hang out with me sometime? My girl Destiny I was tellin' you about has a big party at this place called Cipriani and you should come wit' us!"

I started shaking my head. Iz and her big mouth. The Cipriani party was not the place or the night for Izzy to be bringing her country-bumpkin cousin.

156

"The party's gonna be hot. Oh, what to wear? Jus' throw on a sexy dress, and some strappy stilettos . . . Oh, you don't have a car? Well, you could take the bus over from Jersey and I'll drive you back."

I looked at her like she was crazy. Drive her back in what? Izzy doesn't have a car. I know what's coming next . . .

Izzy hung up the phone.

"Can I please borrow your car after the par—" I gave her the hand, cutting her off. "Thanks, Des, I haven't seen my cousin in like twenty-five years. She called my *abuela* and got my cell number. I can't diss her. She's jus' visiting some family friends in Jersey and they're like real old an' shit."

I began to rub my forefinger and thumb together and put on a really sad and pitying face. "You know what this is? It's the world's smallest violin, playing for you and your sorry cousin!"

She balled up a napkin and tossed it at me. "I'm serious! Stop playin', alright? Jewel is really sweet. She's a schoolteacha and she's been here for a few weeks. I feel bad fa her. She sounded so down . . ."

"You don't even know her, she could be crazy."

"Yo, if she walk all up in there crazy-like an' stuff, I'm outta there!"

Scenes from the Velvet Rope

The crowd was starting to thicken in front of the club, but it was still early; by midnight it'll be pure insanity, trust me. Tonight is my weekly party at the Club P.M., a chic spot also in the revived meatpacking district. A sexy blouse and the right designer shoes and jeans will do you right every time.

However, as fabulous as all that sounds, the last thing I'm interested in doing tonight is partying. I've been trying to reach Malik for the past week and both his cell and BlackBerry are disconnected, and I'm beginning to feel a bit panicked. I'm trying my best not to think about it, especially with four more hours still left to work.

"Destiny!" I heard a bubbly, cutesy voice call my name from a taxi that was pulling up. It was BJ Friday, editor-in-chief of the hip-hop magazine *Blazin'*, and she was tonight's guest of honor. She looked like she'd been kissed by St. Tropez's rays. The color of her short, sandy, curly frock matched her skin and eyes.

Her girl Capri, New York's most in-demand wardrobe stylist, was with her. Everything Capri does is big, loud, and borderline obnoxious. She's always talking about her latest escapades in Paris or Miami with Beyoncé, Paris Hilton, or even Madonna, or her twenty-thousand-dollar shopping sprees in Milan.

"Destiny, you look amazing. I took BJ to Naples for her birth-day," Capri said, dramatically removing her large, dark, shades.

"I'm *fantastic*, Capri." I played right along with her grandiosity. I was not in the mood to socialize. "Champagne's chilling inside, birthday girl!" I gave BJ a hug and sent them on their way.

You Dropped a Bomb on Me

Entering the club, I briefly greeted party guests loung-
ing on the long sofas inside P.M.'s dimly lit main bar
area. Since I wasn't my usual diva-of-the-party self, I
decided it was best to keep my schmoozing to a mini-
mum. All I was focused on was getting a good, stiff drink and finding Jenna.

Tonight's party was intimate. I'd only requested that Chryssa
come in to work with Jenna. However, *I* seemed to be doing most of
Jenna's work tonight, which only made my sourpuss attitude worse.

Yes! There is a God, and *She* is all-knowing!

Chryssa had a freshly poured drink waiting for me as I approached the bar. With stunning alacrity, I removed the drink from
her hand, careful not to spill a drop, plucked the peach garnish out

of the glass, and tossed the chilled, frothy liquid down the hatch. "Get me another CR Lust, *please*." Chryssa hurried off.

That drink had done a poor job of washing down the anxiety I felt over Malik. Had he really been that dirty, pretending to care and love me, just to stiff me for some money? Why didn't I see it coming? Destiny Day is smarter than this.

Chryssa returned with another CR Lust as instructed, and I gave her a repeat performance. "Where is she, Chryssa?" I snapped, realizing I hadn't seen Jenna in over an hour.

"She's with Peter," she hesitantly answered. I was enraged and went on the warpath. Since Malik was nowhere to be found, Jenna was about to catch the fury. I was trying my best not to lose my temper in front of my partygoers, but it was time to deal with Jenna once and for all about Peter, woman to woman. I headed for the dj booth where Peter was spinning.

"Jenna! Why have I been working this party, outside and inside, doing your job, while you're in here pushing up on Peter?" I cut into her with no warning. Peter looked stunned.

"What the hell is going on?"

"Nothing. Destiny—we were just talking about some stuff."

"Yo, Des, why you buggin'?" Peter said.

"Excuse me, Peter, but this is between *me* and *my* assistant!" Jenna followed me out of the dj booth.

"When did you start discussing business with my client?" Jenna looked like a cat who'd just burped up a feather.

"I hope this isn't what I think it is. I told you from Day One, Jenna, that going after any of my men is a no-no."

"Destiny, I know the deal with you and Peter, and I would never step to him, but he needed to talk, and . . ."

"And what? You had to be a sympathetic ear, on my dime and my clock! Look, me and backstabbers don't get along. I'll put it plain and simple for you: One of us isn't going to win, and I don't lose! Watch yourself." I stormed off.

I wanted to make sure Jenna felt the impact of my words. I motioned for the bartender to bring me a round of Patrón shots. Oh yeah, I was goin' there tonight! Jenna was way out of her league. I sauntered up to Peter and planted a full open-mouthed kiss on him right in front of her. We took our shots and I parked myself right next to him for the entire night. Peter put on his most seductive beats and I began shimmying and grinding him from behind. Jenna caught a full view. I could see the anger swelling in her eyes. Girlfriend has no idea. If she wants to rumble with the bee, she'll get stung real quick.

Part Time Love

I had a dream last night. Actually, it was at around five this morning . . .

Juanita was in it, and it was just the two of us, and I was all grown up like I am now. I walked into the Belly Room, a smokey after-hours joint, and Juanita greeted me with a smile from behind the bar. She looked even prettier than what I remember. The club was empty, and she was playing that same, sad, soulful music she liked to play when she was depressed or drunk, or both.

Al Green was wailing in the background. Juanita opened a bottle of Crown Royal and poured herself a drink, then slid me one.

"I remember you used to drink this stuff when I was little. Carlton would keep the purple and gold felt bags the bottles came in and let me save my pennies in them." I smiled to myself at the sentimental thought that felt like lifetimes ago.

"Girl, you got a memory just like your daddy! C'mon drink up, the ice is meltin'." She took a sip from her glass. " 'Round here I like my liquor smooth and dark like my men." We toasted. "So, you done went and did it, didn't you?" She said, leaning close to me.

"Juanita, what are you talkin' about?" I frowned. The drink was so strong my chest burned and felt as though it was about to sprout a patch of hair.

"You went and gave your heart away. I told you not to do that shit, but you know you soft like your daddy."

"Don't talk about my father. He's good to you, but you don't appreciate him. Ain't nothin' wrong with giving your heart away to a good man." I took another swig of the hot liquor. "I usually like to mix mine."

"Nah, I likes mine straight no chaser, but trust me, it gets better by the second glass." She polished off her drink and poured herself another. "At least Malik's got some money in his pocket."

"Yeah, well, I haven't met too many men who don't. But is that all you care about?"

"That's all any woman with good sense should care about. Money can make you happy when a man ain't around," she said in a somber tone.

"Do you really believe that, Juanita?"

"And if I don't, still don't change the fact that every time I open my eyes it's rainin', even when the sun's out. Shit, the pain meets me at the door with a big shit-eatin' grin. Whatchu know about that?" She laughed. "Yeah, that's what I thought. Go on, get outta here. I gots ta set up for tonight." I reached into my purse and pulled out a twenty. "What's that for?" she asked.

"For the drinks."

"It's on me."

I woke up around nine a.m. with an eerie feeling, and all I could think about was finding Malik. I remembered I had numbers for Talib and Amaru in an old cell phone. The quest became finding it. I raced up the loft steps and started rummaging through stacks of boxes filled with office files. Izzy was dead to the world and oblivious to the loud racket I was making. I found it!

I turned it on, praying I had juice left in this sucker. Yessss! A half bar of battery power was good enough. I jotted down both Talib and Amaru's numbers. As soon as the clock struck a decent hour, I was going to be on the horn.

By noon I was dialing Amaru. His number was disconnected. Then I dialed Talib but made sure to block my number in case he was with Malik. It started to ring, and ring, and ring, and ring—no voicemail, no nothing. I must've tried a hundred more times. At about three o'clock I got lucky. Talib picked up.

He was stumbling and stuttering, shocked to be hearing from me, of all people. Before he could catch himself, he was offering up directions to Malik's house. Okay, the truth: I threatened to get my girl Iz and go up to every studio in Manhattan and raise hell if he didn't tell me where Malik was. Everybody knows Izzy can act a fool.

Which brings me to my current state of affairs . . .

I'm doing seventy-five on the New Jersey Turnpike, headed to Malik's apartment in Jersey as we speak. I felt foolish demanding Malik's address. In the entire year that we've been messing around, I've never been to his house, never even been invited, and stupid me, never asked for an invitation.

I pulled up to Malik's prewar building, surprised by how average the place looked. I guess I was expecting some luxury penthouse setup, not a working-class neighborhood in Elizabeth, New Jersey. No diss to Elizabeth, but this man could afford to be in some plush Manhattan high-rise. I'd only seen signs pointing in the direction of here, on my way to catch a flight out of Newark International.

Talib was standing outside waiting for me with a big stupid grin plastered on his face. I parked my car on the street and rushed over to him.

"What's up, Talib?" I asked. I lit up a cigarette. Malik had me chain-smoking over his ass.

"Hey, Ma, I still haven't heard back from Malik, but he won't mind me letting you into his place. He's flying back tonight from Miami."

"Miami? When did he go there?" A row of wrinkles had formed across my forehead.

"I'm not sure."

We entered the building and stepped onto the elevator.

"How long has he been gone?"

"I don't know."

"Well, what did he go there for?"

"I don't know."

We exited on the fifth floor. Malik's condo apartment was at the end of the hall.

"Was it about Freedom's record?"

"I don't know, really. I heard Lil Jon has a studio down there."

"Well, what the hell *do* you know?" I was beyond frustrated by this entire exchange. Either Talib *was* that dumb, or Malik had his boys trained like show dogs. They knew better than to go off script or there would be hell to pay and no Scoobie Snacks.

When he opened the door, I looked around in amazement.

"Malik's flight should be in at about seven."

I couldn't speak. Were my eyes playing tricks on me? Malik's apartment was practically empty. The hardwood floors were immaculate, the walls freshly painted white throughout. The long foyer leading into a large room was probably big enough to fit two of my living rooms in it. Talib kept babbling about stuff to drink being in the fridge, to make myself comfortable, and that the television was in the bedroom, but it all sounded like mish-mosh. When he left I heard the door click, and that snapped me out of my daze.

I walked through the enormous apartment. There were no blinds on the windows, one room contained a brand-new computer still in the box and a few other smaller boxes with office supplies in them; there were about four other rooms near that one, each as empty as the one before it.

The clatter of my heels hitting the floor echoed throughout the entire apartment. I walked back into the foyer and slowly opened another door. A massive bed, big-screen television, and stereo system were inside. It was the first sign of life in the whole apartment. I figured it must be Malik's room and sat down on the bed in awe.

I had just entered the Twilight Zone and Rod Serling was making an announcement over the loudspeaker: *Imagine if you will, thinking that a man exists, but he really does not.* Perhaps Malik's been abducted by alien invaders? What is really going on? Does this brotha live here, or with his BM (baby mama)? I chalked it up as one big twisted and deceptive tale.

I looked at my watch. It was six o'clock. I decided to do like Talib said and make myself comfortable in front of the television. I took off my shoes and crawled into the huge bed. I was nervous, like I needed to keep my keys and purse next to me in case I had to make a fast exit. I didn't even take off my coat. I left the hall light on and turned the television up loud, letting the Evans family keep me company during Nick at Nite's *Good Times* marathon. Hell, I'm not going to lie, I was scared.

I must've missed Malik's homecoming. When I woke up it was the next morning. The sun was blasting directly in my face from the large window next to the bed. It was nine o'clock. I had to get my ass back to the city by ten for a meeting with the MTV folks about

Garcel's party. Either I'd better grow some wings or hurry my behind up.

I opened the closet door and found five shirts hanging sadly on the rack. They looked like they were wondering where Malik was, too. I shook my head in further disgust, grabbed a towel from the shelf, and dashed into the bathroom. After I showered and redressed, I smoothed the covers on the bed, straightened up the bathroom, turned off all the lights, made sure the door was locked, and got the hell out of Dodge.

I contemplated calling Malik one more time to ask where he was, what he'd been doing, what's going on with Freedom, the album, my motherfuckin' money . . . but to hell with it, there were just too many unanswered questions and secrets for me to deal with in this situation. As a matter of fact, I don't think I even want to know. It's time for me to go MIA for a while.

Disk Five

Funkdafied

{1} GOT TO GET YOU INTO MY LIFE

{2} NO PARKING ON THE DANCE FLOOR

{3} SQUARE BIZ

{4} DO YA WANNA GET FUNKY WITH ME?

{5} THANK YOU (FALETTINME BE MICE ELF AGIN)

{6} SUPER FREAK

{7} QUE SERA, SERA (WHATEVER WILL BE, WILL BE)—

SLY AND THE FAMILY STONE VERSION

Scenes from the Velvet Rope

INTERIOR/EXTERIOR: CIPRIANI
9:00 P.M.

I'm completely furious! Several key names and VIPs have been left off the guest list. Somebody screwed up and is sooooo fired! Tonight is so important even *I'm* wearing a headset. *Hollywood Weekly* and MediaMax came to New York's hottest partygirl—me, of course—to throw a five-hundred-thousand-dollar exclusive bash honoring *HW*'s latest issue, "Hot Hollywood," that features forty female power players under forty in the entertainment business.

Number twenty-five, and the only African American listed, my girl, Lindsay Bradley. This was huge for an African-American woman; she was sure to go down in history. New York's premiere Cosmopolitan Girl has been coming to my parties for years, showing me love. She hooked the whole deal up.

Buzz! Buzz!

My Nextel walkie sounded off.

"Destiny, hi, this is Heather and there are people at the door who aren't on the list, and um . . . someone who's the editor of *Core* magazine and ummmmm . . . Mr. Watson, and ummmm . . ."

Buzz! Buzz!

"What the hell is going on? Jenna, you know I'm about to go there. You'd better handle this. Where's Nikki? Get her over to VIP!" We were short Chryssa tonight. I was doing a gig at Club Bed downtown and she was running that party. Jenna and I went back and forth like madwomen on our walkies.

"I just sent Nikki over to VIP and I'm right here at the door with Heather now, Des! It's Mimi Cole and Edward Watson and his wife . . ."

Before she could get another syllable out . . .

"Jenna! You know I can't have Mimi Cole and the Watsons standing outside one of my parties because somebody in my camp botched things up! Mimi *is Core* magazine," I shouted into my headset. "It's the biggest magazine for black women in the country. Watson is the president and CEO of MediaMax. Remember them, the good folks who are paying us tonight?"

Jenna was consoling a blubbering Heather, whose name would soon be erased from memory. "She's fired!" I shouted, *Apprentice*-style, breezing past Jenna and wimpy-girl Heather. "Send her ass home, Jenna! She's messin' with my money *and* my relationships!" Heather was boo-hooing a river at this point.

I stormed out through Cipriani's massive doors and Big Tom and Kwame, my bouncers, parted the crowd like I was Moses stepping through. I blazed up a fresh cancer-stick and puffed away like a madwoman. My flowing silk Armani slip-gown with delicate beading whipped and cut the air like a serpent. I spotted Mimi and took a deep leveling breath, tossing a half-smoked, perfectly good cigarette. Never let your guests see you stressed.

"Hi, Mimi," I said, gracing both her cheeks with kisses. *Mmmmmmwa, mmmmmwa!* She looked regal and fabulous as usual. That's one woman who can work some dreadlocks, and she hasn't aged in the two decades she's been at *Core*. It's so true that black never cracks. "I'm so sorry, I have a new, now-unemployed girl, and there was some confusion. Come, come! Enjoy the party." I then greeted MediaMax titan Edward Watson and his wife as well, and led them all inside.

172

Got to Get You into My Life

I seated Mimi and the Watsons at my table, which was elevated in the center of the room. Jenna knew the whole clean-up-a-screw-up drill: Cristal for all and a personal server for the rest of the evening. A tiny Chinese contortionist was balancing a small silver tray that held a freshly shaken, CR Lust, on his head. I smiled gently, grabbed my drink, took a big gulp, and surveyed the room as I bit into a juicy peach wedge. I had outdone my own self this time.

My Cirque du Soleil party theme at New York's famous Cipriani on Twenty-third Street was sure to be the talk of the town *and* the industry coast to coast for months. The ballroom was alive with fire-eaters, scantily clad trapeze artists swinging from the ceilings, and contortionists in glass boxes. My very own version of Zumanity.

Izzy stepped through the door wearing a white shimmery Dolce

& Gabbana frock and nothing but legs attached to a fierce pair of you-wish-you-could-think-about-gettin'-some Jimmy Choos. Rico looked as delicious as ever in a white Dolce suit.

"Y'all betta wear the hell outta those showroom loaners!" I said, throwing my arms around each of them.

"That's right, I turn back into a ghetto pumpkin at three a.m.!" Rico joked. I had passed on all my garment-district showroom hookups to Rico. He was not the least bit shy about schmoozing with the reps at Marc Jacobs, Roberto Cavalli, Dolce & Gabbana, and Armani. In fact, he got to do makeup during Fashion Week last year. He was one of several makeup artists, but not the head one; without that book it's hard to get the bigger gigs.

"Oh, my God, Izzy! You look exactly like you did in all those videos I used to watch!" a high-pitched, excited voice made a whispery-screeching sound. We all turned around to find it. Izzy was mortified. Never call a has-been a *has-been* like that. The voice belonged to one of the most perfectly wholesome and sweet faces I'd ever seen. Jewel—how fitting.

She wasn't as tall as Izzy, but she certainly had an inch or two on me. Her hair was all done up in Shirley Temple-ish curls, and she was wearing a conservative short black cocktail dress, a soft pashmina, and (good God) pantyhose, with a pair of sensible strappy Nine West high-heeled sandals. I can't describe it. She looked . . . well . . . absolutely . . . ummmmm . . . well . . . *sweet*. Poor baby.

She had good, conservative, Midwestern taste. I mean I think Ann Taylor is a swell designer, especially for business luncheons and such. But not for a Destiny Day party! Come on, people just don't wear pantyhose to one of my parties! I can't recall the last time I even owned a pair!

All I remember is Rico gagging, grabbing one of Jewel's arms, and Izzy grabbing her other one, and me grabbing another drink. They scooped that girl up with the swiftness of one giant eagle and within what seemed like seconds (I just know I hadn't finished half my drink), Miss Jewel was returned to the scene of the crime stockingless, pashmina-less, and her Miss Humble Ann updo had been set free to play out in the wild. Now she was ready to work the room.

Izzy, Jewel, and Rico sat down at my table and each scooped up a glass of bubbly. "Cheers! To a night Miss Jewel will never forget!" Rico toasted. I resumed working the room, spreading my magic.

At ten-thirty DJ Peter, the blue-eyed soul-child, took the party into overdrive with some Prince that led right into some classic Run-DMC. I had never seen so many rich, famous, and important white folks letting loose and shaking it up in one room; and you know I had all the black power players from film, television, music, sports, and Wall Street in the house, too.

Hollywood Weekly, of course, along with *Entertainment Weekly*, *Us Weekly*, *Jet*, *Ebony*, *Essence*, *Vibe*, *InStyle*, and more, were swarming all over the VIP area. I excused myself from a conversation with New York socialite, philanthropist, and all around bad-ass sista Sherry B. Bronfman. She brought black culture to the forefront of the wealthy inner circles of New York every chance she got.

We had been trying to get together for weeks to discuss doing a major event at MOMA. I was so busy admiring how Sherry was wearing the hell out her tangerine Elie Saab gown, I almost knocked the fresh CR Lust Nikki was holding for me right out of her hand.

"Just in time—I'm parched," I said, thanking her. I took a couple of big gulps and turned around to find myself face-to-face with a perky Lindsay Bradley.

"Girlie, the party is amazing!" We gave each other girlfriend smooches. I noticed an extremely handsome, six-foot, caramel-colored brotha, clean cut with freshly groomed soft waves, standing next to her. I could see an athletic build underneath his well-tailored Armani suit. I checked out his equally expensive Italian leather shoes. "Destiny, this is a good friend of mine, Taye Crawford. They did a big write-up on him in the *Wall Street Journal* last week!"

Lindsay had a tendency to give you that pep-rally cheerleader thing. I'm sure the Cosmopolitan in her hand had had some influence. She went on and on about how Mr. Taye Crawford was a former Wall Street wonderboy turned independent financial advisor and primary partner in Wealth Investment Group. "Did I mention Taye is putting a deal together with Russell Simmons and Trump?" Lindsay proudly advertised.

"Girl, all you need is a billboard in Times Square for a brotha," I politely teased. I wasn't impressed. Hell, everybody I meet *is* somebody. Taye was slightly embarrassed. What a shame. He didn't have enough game, and he had to put Lindsay up to making the introductions. Lindsay conveniently spotted a colleague across the room and sashayed away, leaving the two of us standing awkwardly in the middle of the room.

"Lindsay ought to be your publicist," I said.

"Sorry about that." He cleared his throat and tried to change the subject. "Destiny Day—that's a unique name," he said with a smile. Brothaman was not starting off with his best line.

"Let me help you out. Taye, right?" I reached for a fresh cocktail from a passing waiter. "I don't want to be rude, but I really have to check on some things, so thank you for coming and enjoy the rest of the party." I started away. He gently touched my hand stopping me.

"Look, I know it was kind of corny the way Lindsay introduced us, but I think you're . . ."

"Yeah, I know, brilliant, sexy, beautiful . . ." I smarted.

"You forgot arrogant!" His comment was biting. "Listen, I don't want to sweat you. I'm not staying long, and I just wanted to see if I could take you to dinner sometime."

"I'm pretty busy." I nonchalantly took another sip from my glass.

"Okay, what about coffee or milk and cookies?" I'll give him a point for his wit.

"I'm currently off caffeine, and I'm lactose intolerant."

"What about drinks? I see you've tossed back quite a few tonight."

"Good observation," I turned and looked him up and down. "Wednesday night I do Show." He was completely lost. This man was truly out of his league. "It's a club I give. Get there around eleven or twelve. I'll put you on the list." I smiled politely, giving the subtle hint that he should stop while he's still in play. "By the way, I meet a lot of men. Résumés don't do it for me."

"Good, because I don't need a job. Goodnight Destiny Day. See you at the Show," Taye said sharply, turning and walking away.

All I'll say is this: For a brotha to survive *that* encounter he must be about something. I smiled to myself and polished off my drink.

● ● ●

I got home around four a.m. My feet were aching and I was beat. I'd worked hard for my money tonight, and despite the Heather firing, the party was a success.

Before rolling over to sleep, I checked my messages. My heart stopped beating momentarily. What if one of them was from Malik? I cautiously pressed the ONE key.

YOU HAVE THREE NEW MESSAGES.

MESSAGE ONE:

Curtis: I know that we're not seeing each other anymore, but you can still call and check on a brotha.

Damn! Who wants to hear from him?

MESSAGE ERASED.

MESSAGE TWO:

Curtis: You sure you don't want to rethink this whole thing?

Urgh, he needs to get a life! The man is obsessed. I'll scream if the next one is from him again.

MESSAGE ERASED.

MESSAGE THREE:

Jacques: Destineee . . . this is Jacques Beauvais. My boy Clef [he was referring to Wyclef Jean] gave me your number. [I perked up!] He said he thought it would be a good idea if we hooked up and talked some business. I just got back from Miami opening a new spot. I'm comin' to Show Wednesday with Clef. I look forward to meeting you. Peace.

The Lowdown

IDENTITY: Jacques Beauvais, West Indian descent, smoldering looks and lots of bravado, a chocolate-colored Rick Fox, very Americanized. Successful restaurateur and former club promoter, owns the swank Patrois-Midtown and Patrois–Brooklyn Heights. One word: Dangerous. I hear he's buried a few bodies and I'm not about to ask questions.

Status: Recently divorced, a daughter, and New York's most talked-about and eligible bachelor.

Now, that was interesting. I hung up the receiver, turned the light out, and lay still on my back for a few minutes staring at the ceiling.

The room was thick with blackness. I'm excited thinking about Mr. Jacques and Mr. Taye. Maybe I can reinstate the "Maintenance Man" program. I remembered my last conversation with Josephine again. You know, about trying new things and all. I see that when one door closes, two more open, but I don't think I'm ready for anything too deep just yet. It's only been a month since I decided to let go of the Malik situation and, I admit, I need some more time.

There was a time when the old Destiny Day would hunt a man down who tried to dog her, but mug shots aren't becoming for thirty-five-year-olds. I'd say I'm making progress, and Malik is lucky. So, for now, until I can *completely* purge myself of the remnants of Malik, Mr. Taye Crawford has caught my curiosity the most. Besides, it's June, and everybody needs a summer sweetie. A date here or there may not be bad. Oops, I forgot to tell him Show was my hip-hop party. I hope he doesn't wear that suit. I closed my eyes.

Scenes from the Velvet Rope

Some crazy club kid with oversized aviator glasses, a spiked Mohawk, and a played-out Von Dutch T-shirt exited a yellow cab arm-in-arm with a washed-out fake fashionista with overdone weavalicious cascading curls.

"Yeah, I'm on the list?"

"What list?" I asked, taking a puff from my cigarette.

"Destiny's list."

"Oh, word? Well, let me check that out," I said playing along. I reached over and grabbed tonight's guest list that was attached to the clipboard Big Tom was holding. I licked my index finger and slowly began to flip through the pages. The kid was getting antsy and anxious. His two-dollar-video-girl-rip-off was fidgety.

"Yo, I *said* I'm on Destiny's list, what's the holdup?"

I looked at him and rolled my eyes.

"Who is this chick, baby?" Weavalicious chirped.

I took my time flipping through the rest of the guest-list pages, still pretending I wasn't me. A blacked-out Maybach rolled up, and Naomi and Diddy stepped out.

"Oh, yo—wassup, Diddy?" The kid's eyes lit up.

"What up, baby." Diddy gave the drooling boy a nonchalant pound.

"Destiny!" Naomi greeted me in her finest King's English and a round of smooches.

"Wassup, D." Diddy leaned in and gave me a kiss.

"I got y'all set up at my table," I said, unhooking the velvet rope, giving them room to enter the club.

"Oh, by the way," I said peering toward the obnoxious club kid. "Tell your friend here, *I'm* the chick with the list. The list yo ass ain't on! Get rid of this clown, Big Tom." I handed the clipboard back to Big Tom, took a final puff of my cigarette, flicked it into the gutter, twirled on my heels, and headed inside the club, leaving the dumbstruck poser club kid and his weavalicious sidekick with a fabulous rear view shot of yours truly.

No Parking
on the Dance Floor

The hip-hop was banging, the crowd sprinkled with just enough celeb faces.

"Wassup, Clef?" I give Wyclef Jean a haven't-seen-you-in-a-lifetime hug. "Marie!" I gave her an equally warm hug. I considered Wyclef and his wife, Marie Claudinette Jean, the fashion industry's newest and most talked about designer, to be Haitian hip-hop royalty. I was glad I was wearing the outfit she sent over from her Fusha collection. She normally designed for girls who were tall like Izzy and grazed on birdseed and wheatgrass, but she'd sent me over a Destiny Day exclusive: a floor-length fitted leather skirt and matching leather shrug. I'd decided to rock it with a simple pair of Gucci sandals and a wife-beater.

"Where's Jacques?" I asked.

"He's coming later, and he's looking forward to meeting you, sis," Wyclef said with a wink.

There were a few nondescript rappers in the club, but mostly model-types, hip-hop heads, and music-industry execs trying to keep their fingers on the pulse. Taye entered. He'd taken me up on my offer after all, and—yes!—no suit. He was tastefully dressed in jeans, Ferragamo loafers, and a tailored shirt. I greeted him with a friendly hug, like the rest of my personally invited guests, peeping his sterling cufflinks and Cartier timepiece.

"Classic dresser—a little conservative, though," I teased.

"I'm glad I'm an educated brotha, because you didn't give me an address."

"Good, you passed the test!" I said.

"Nice party, a few hoodrats, but the music's good." Touché. Taye Crawford wasn't a pushover after all.

"Thanks, VIP is better, unless of course you and your comments would like to stay down here with the hoodrats."

I took his hand and led him to my table, where he could catch all the action: the light-projected graphics with the "DD" logo flashing on the walls; hip-hop go-go dancers, dressed in lingerie, in cages. I left him with stars in his eyes and stepped over another velvet rope separating the general club population from the VIPs.

DJ Peter rocked it out with some Doug E. Fresh, and Taye grabbed my hand. "I know you've gotta do your thing, but this was my cut!" Before I knew it, I was on the dance floor. The chemistry between us was undeniable. Taye knew his music. When Peter mixed in yet another hip-hop gem, Whodini's "Friends," we *had* to stay on the floor.

Suddenly, in walked Jacques Beauvais like he owned the place. He headed straight for VIP. Everyone knew him and let him through. I excused myself, leaving Taye alone. Taye was a grown man who'd come of his own free will; I couldn't worry about him. I had to get to Jacques, who was talking to Wyclef.

He had a dangerously gorgeous smile that matched his dangerously gorgeous looks. Looks that are unsettling, yet completely seductive. He's not a big diesel brotha, but I bet even the most hard-core street soldier would think twice before steppin' to him.

"Nice of you to finally show up at one of my parties," I said.

"I thought I'd come see how you livin'. I've heard a lot about you, Destiny Day." His words were drenched with charm. There was this strange cat-and-mouse chase going on. We moved over to the couch and sat down. Taye decided to plant himself right next to me in the booth. I didn't want to be rude, since I'd invited him, but right now I was a helluva lot more interested in talking to Jacques.

"Taye Crawford, this is Jacques Beauvais." An awkward introduction, but I got a kick out of two good-looking men vying for my attention. There was a silent show of testosterone, but Jacques won for now, and he ordered a few bottles of champagne.

"Here's to Destiny!" Jacques said, raising his glass. He leaned over and whispered in my ear. His breath tickled.

"I'm going to call it a night. I've got an early meeting," Taye politely interrupted.

I excused myself from Jacques and walked Taye to the front of the club. "I know there are a lot of people around me, but thanks for coming."

"Yeah, it was nice," Taye said, turning and walking away. I don't know what possessed me, but I stopped him.

"Listen, how about we have dinner sometime?"

"Yeah, yeah, maybe we could check out some music or something."

"That would be nice, since it seems like we both like music and everything," I said, kicking myself for suddenly sounding so goofy.

"Hey, here's my number," I said pulling a tiny business card from my clutch purse and handing it to him.

"This is creative," he chuckled at the one-by-one square card.

"I try to be. That's the one I give to *personal* friends," I winked, beaming. I didn't typically volunteer the private line and cell.

"I feel privileged," he smiled. "I'll call you when I get a minute." Taye exited the club without saying another word, leaving me with a baffled look.

Oh, no he *didn't* take my number and not give up his! Should I pick up the pieces to my cracked face now or later? Had I just been a part of some twisted *Punk'd* episode? I was waiting for *Ashton* and the crew to rush out and announce this was all a setup, but I didn't have time to ponder. I had a hot man waiting inside for me.

Square Biz

Forty-fourth and Broadway, eight-thirty. I'm on time, Taye Crawford is not. Times Square is a world as electrifying as a big-tent circus. Now that the warm temperatures had arrived, the City was even more alive with bodies cramming the night streets. My eyes were transfixed by the flashing Virgin Megastore neon sign overhead. I must be crazy standing out here. I have ten thousand other things I could be doing. I felt a pair of hands on my shoulders and jumped.

"Sorry I'm late. My conference call ran long," Taye said.

"Please don't do that again. I don't do well with the whole surprise thing." I was quite perturbed at this point. This brotha was batting oh-for-one, and the date hadn't officially started.

"You know what, Destiny Day?"

"What, Taye Crawford?"

"Easy!" He threw up his hands in a surrendering gesture. "I just wanted to tell you to stop taking life so seriously."

"You don't even know me."

"I don't have to, *yet*. But I can see everything about you in your eyes."

"Okay, you're a psychic. Great!" I gave an exasperated look.

"Just do me a favor tonight."

"What?"

"Loosen up!"

"I am very loose, Taye."

"We'll see how loose you are!"

Taye took me by the hand and whisked me inside Toys "Я" Us.

"This is our date?" I asked, trying to keep up with his slow jog.

"Who said anything about this being a date? Come on, faster. Can't you just trust me on this, please?"

This man didn't know me fifteen minutes. I must be a fool running around with some stranger. And he has the nerve to say "trust me." Brothaman has me all wrong! I should leave right now. Too late—we'd run all the way down the stairs to the bottom level of the store and were standing in front of a giant ferris wheel. I can't believe this psycho man brought me to the basement of a toy store.

Taye handed the ticket-booth worker fifty dollars and told her to give us the works.

"I hope that's big-ballin' enough for you, Destiny Day."

"Oh, shut up. Stop being so corny!"

"Pick one," Taye said, pulling me in front of the ride compartments. There was a colorful selection of giant-sized kid toys. I picked the Barbie car.

The ferris-wheel operator strapped us in and we took off. It was actually kind of cute, the whole idea of bringing me to a toy store and all, but I wasn't about to give him any points just yet. As we went up, up, and away, and round and round, I felt giggly and silly overlooking the entire store and seeing all the children run and play.

"I'm so embarrassed," I said.

"Why?"

"Isn't it obvious? We're the only adults on this ride and running around this store, outside of the employees and some very exhausted-looking parents."

"What's wrong with just tapping into your inner child every now and then? Reliving your childhood."

"I never had a childhood."

"That's ridiculous! You're trying to tell me you've always been the ever-so-powerful-and-in-control Destiny Day?"

"Yeah, I was," I said sarcastically.

"That's too bad. I think it's kind of sexy when a woman isn't afraid to revert back to her days of wide-eyed innocence. I'm nothing but a big kid at heart, and I'm damn sexy if I must say so myself," he said.

We laughed. Then we went around that thing twenty or thirty more times before the store manager practically put us out of the place.

The adventure wasn't over. Taye dragged me down to 42nd Street to BB King's blues club. I thought to myself, this is way too touristy for my taste. All the giant blinking billboards, throngs of non–New Yorker looky-lou's flashing their cameras and bumping into me. My sentiments were plastered all over my face.

"Don't panic! I'm sure your couture is clashing with this scene, and worldly women like yourself wouldn't usually be caught dead cajoling with all these commoners. Just do your best to blend in."

"I am not like that!" I said defensively, pushing him ahead.

"My boy's playing, so I'll get to really test your music knowledge tonight!"

The place was jam-packed. I sat impatiently at a small two-top in the corner waiting for Taye to get back from the restroom.

"Errhumm," Taye cleared his throat loudly. "I wanted to announce my return, since you said you hate surprises." Taye gingerly placed a Crown Royal Lust down in front of me on the table and sat a beer down on his side.

"Extra peach garnish!" I smiled.

"I hope you like it."

The lights dimmed, and I settled into my drink. I'd already figured I was going to have to get pretty drunk to enjoy Taye's buddy's show. Suddenly, we heard the revving up of an engine pump through the speakers. The crowd began to cheer and clap wildly. Something was vaguely familiar.

Screeeeech!

Then we heard a sound effect of a car slamming on its breaks over the speakers. I looked over at Taye. He winked. I was beaming. Taye had shocked me by bringing me to see one of my favorite groups of all time, the Gap Band, perform live. I leaped out of my seat on the first chord of the song like I had caught the Holy Ghost.

I started clapping and grooving, dancing to the music, and forgot about the room full of strangers. Charlie Wilson stepped on stage followed by his brothers Ronnie and Robert in that famous Gap Band style, shiny suits and all. People were screaming their heads off. The band's Southern-fried funk, rock, and soul was an eighties throwback to my most memorable times as a teenage girl: first kisses, cute boys with the jheri curls, polo shirts with the collars neatly popped and locked, and the tightest pairs of acid-washed jeans you could spray on.

I looked over at Taye again, and he was right there with me. The brotha had rhythm and wasn't afraid to show it. He was singing each line word for word, ". . . *made me just go crazaaaaaaaaaaay . . .*" Taye hit that last note and slid behind me. We broke into the Snake.

189

I followed his lead. Then I faked him out and hit him with the Roger Rabbit.

"Oh, no you didn't," Taye called out, challenging me with the Running Man. We were having our own private dance-off battle. Next the conga player on stage broke it down.

"Watch yourself!" I shouted, hitting Taye with yet another comeback move, the Cabbage Patch.

We both cracked up, still snapping and shaking our butts to the truly funky beat.

For our big finale, we paid homage to the "What's Happening" gang, doing Rog's famous old-school side-to-side ducklike move. I was Peaches and Taye was Herb. Hell, Ashford and Simpson, Rick and Teena all rolled into one.

We tested our vocal-acrobatic skills, going back and forth singing along with Charlie. We looked like an act straight off Solid Gold. For the rest of the show we reminisced and two-stepped to quiet-storm jams like "Yearning For Your Love" and "Season's No Reason To Change." We even did a slow drag to the mid-tempo "Outstanding."

Taye didn't notice, but several times throughout the night, I found myself watching him. I liked what I saw, and it was beyond the obvious physical attraction. I couldn't put my finger on it. After the show, we strolled down 42nd Street. I felt like walking off some of my energy.

"I'm impressed. You *do* know how to get down, Taye. I was afraid you'd be too conservative to get your party on," I said.

"I'm just glad you loosened up long enough to let a brotha surprise you."

"Okay, you had me going when you said it was your boy's band. I didn't know what to expect."

"Well I'm glad the dog-eat-dog world of entertainment hasn't jaded you so much that you couldn't still have some regular fun without out all the paparazzi and bling-bling."

"Wait, you've got me wrong. That world is my job, but it's not me."

"Destiny, I watched you the other night at the Cipriani party and at Show. Then when *Jacques*"—Taye put extra emphasis on the name—"entered the spot, you left me on the dance floor. You didn't have time for a cat like me."

"That was business, *my* business. I'd appreciate it if you stayed out of it."

"Whoa, I got you. I'll just try to remember to come iced out, with my Cristal in tow next time."

"Don't be a hater!"

"No, seriously, I actually get a kick out of guys like that, and I'm turned on by how you can work them over in a room."

"Are you intimidated?"

"I'm the kind of man who's secure enough with himself that I can play the background. I just had to give you crap about it. Don't be angry. Powerful women inspire me. You remind me a lot of my mother."

I'd never been left with a shortage of words before. I felt that same chemistry I'd felt at the club creeping back in.

"It's getting late, and I'd better get you home." Taye raised his arm to hail a cab.

"I'm a big girl, Taye. I don't have to stop by the club until midnight or so. I was actually going to see if you wanted to join me."

"That's sweet. Thanks for the invitation." A taxi slowed to a stop and Taye opened the door for me. "But I've got an early one tomorrow." Taye passed the driver a twenty and extended his hand. "Thank you, Destiny, for a really great night. I'm traveling next week, but I'll call you when I get back."

"Yeah, sure, I had a good time," I said, baffled by the way he was just ending the night. I got into the cab, and as we drove away, I watched Taye cross the street, hop into another taxi, and head off in the opposite direction. Damn, I just *knew* he was going to try to get some. Not even a peck on the cheek. What kind of game is this brotha playin'? We hadn't even made definite plans to see each other again. We didn't even eat dinner! It's after ten and I'm starving, but at thirty-five, whatever I even think about putting in my mouth at this hour is going to go straight to my rear end.

Do Ya Wanna Get
Funky with Me?

 **MESSAGE ONE:**

Curtis: What's going on with you? I've called and left
messages and you're not returning my calls. I'm really
disappointed.

I pressed the THREE key.

MESSAGE DELETED.

Curtis doesn't even have a clue.

Jacques: "Destineee! Wassup, baby. Come meet me for a drink.
Regrets only, baby. Peace."

Jacques inviting me out for drink is no small thing. This man is fine and has money falling out of his drawers. I am so there!

"Destiny Day for Jacques," I said to the hostess when I arrived at the Four Seasons hotel. She led me through the majestic and lavish lounge area to Jacques's table. He stood up like the perfect gentleman. Jacques looked elegant and expensive in his tailor-made suit and shirt. My heart fluttered. He hugged me with his long muscular arms like we had known each other for years. I got comfortable after the arrival of our drinks.

"The elusive Jacques Beauvais!"

"And the gorgeous Destiny Day!"

"I think this is a celebration!" I toasted.

"Where's your man?"

"Where's your woman?"

I could see where this evening was going. Two hours later, I had tossed back another two drinks, Jacques at least five more.

"Let's go."

"Where are we going?" I could feel the effects of the cocktails. I stumbled and giggled.

"Careful, I got you," Jacques said taking me in his arms again. "Have you ever been to any of my restaurants?"

"No, I've been dying to go."

I left my car parked in valet. It was going to be a fortune, but who cared? Tonight we were rolling in Jacques's sweet Bentley Continental GT, humming through the streets of New York City in luxury on wheels. I couldn't help being seduced by the smell, taste, and feel of wealth that surrounded me. This is the kind of seductive setting that makes a girl drop the panties upon contact. I just hope I don't get too excited and christen his passenger seat.

We pulled up in front of Patrois–West Side, a bi-level restaurant and bar that sat on the corner of 20th Street and Tenth Avenue. He probably had millions invested in this place. I felt like a rock star as the bouncers ushered us in. Jacques proudly introduced me to each and every employee like I was going to be sticking around for a while. Within minutes we found ourselves snuggling in on the upper level in a plush booth. A waiter brought us a bottle of chilled Veuve Cliquot. We popped the cork and toasted.

"To new friends," I said.

"To becoming better friends," Jacques said, touching my face and tapping my glass lightly. "I've wanted to spend some time with you for a while, Destiny."

"Jacques, I'm sure you have plenty of women to spend time with." I pulled out a cigarette, and before I could find my lighter, he had a flame waiting. Jacques had pulled yet another move from his distinguished deck of gentlemanly cards. It was like a scene right out of one of those black-and-white classic movies.

We polished off the entire bottle and Jacques motioned for a round of martinis.

"Wait, I . . . *teeeheehee* . . . I'm already a little . . . *snicker, snicker* . . . tipsy! I try not to mix vodka and champagne."

"Baby, I got you," Jacques said, stroking my hair.

He leaned in and kissed me, full mouth. Everything happened really fast from that point on. I downed two cocktails as the groping-and-making-out session continued in front of his entire staff and several patrons milling about.

After sharing a cup of espresso, we tripped out of Patrois and returned to his Bentley, still fondling and groping one another. Jacques broke free from my clutches. Okay, this is a first. Am I not turning him on?

"What's wrong?" I was trashed, but not *that* trashed. Just when I thought I was getting my mojo back, another blow: first Taye the other night, now Jacques.

"Nothing, baby—you're incredible." Jacques reached inside his jacket for his BlackBerry and began scrolling through the messages.

He smiled. "Baby, I'm sorry, but I've got to take care of something for my daughter tonight. Can I make it up to you?"

"Sure," I said unconvincingly. What else was I supposed to say? *No, you can't make it up to me. You're hot and I planned to take you home and screw your brains out!* So he says he's got to do something for his daughter—yeah, right. Come on, man! At least come up with a better lie!

Jacques's Bentley quietly idled next to my Range Rover. He'd given the valet at the Four Seasons a fifty. At least he was a big spender. "Are you sure you're cool to drive?" He asked for the one-hundredth time.

"I'm sure." I fired up a cigarette. I'd gotten sober after he claimed he had an emergency with his daughter. Let me just go back over this whole thing. So, if I had told him I couldn't drive, would he have blown off the daughter? Probably not. He'd have just given the valet a hundred and shoved me into a taxi. "But I will take a rain check," I added.

I kissed Jacques goodbye and he drove away. I was determined that the next time we met, I'd be sure to take the goodies. I started up the engine, slammed the car into DRIVE, and sped off.

Thank You
(Falettinme Be Mice Elf Agin)

A week later Taye called and invited me to that dinner we *didn't* have the first time we went out. I shocked myself when I accepted the invitation to dinner at his house. The portly doorman seated at the guest desk of Taye's West Village apartment building smiled like he knew who I was when I walked up. "Mr. Crawford is on the second floor, unit two," he said, pointing me to the elevator. I guess he *did* know who I was. I caught a reflection of myself biting my lip in the mirror that was hung over a blossoming plant next to the elevator doors. What was I acting so nervous about? Finally, the elevator opened and I stepped inside.

My brain is on overload and this elevator is taking entirely too long to go just two floors. *Okay, deep breath. Exhale. Damn, I need a cigarette. This was a stupid day to stop smoking again. I don't know why I'm trippin' like this. I've probably gone out on a million dates in my life. And this isn't really a date, is it? We haven't even made out or anything.*

This is really just two people getting together to listen to music and hang out over a meal. That's all. I hope this silk skirt and lace camisole isn't too dressy. I wonder how his house looks. Lord, please let the man have some furniture. I can't believe I haven't even kissed Taye. Damn, I should've worn the freakin' jeans!

The doors of the elevator opened, letting me off into a wide hallway. The building didn't look this big from the outside. There were only two doors on the entire floor, and neither one had numbers on it. Great! I pulled out my cell, but couldn't get a signal. When I was just about to hop back on the elevator (I was tempted to run right back to my car and take my butt home!), the door at the far left end of the hallway opened.

"I know you weren't trying to stand me up!" Taye called out.

"You might want to put some numbers on these doors!" I said, turning around to find his big beautiful smile greeting me.

"You look great," he said.

I felt myself start to blush. I guess this outfit was okay after all. "You know my time is precious. I was about to be out!" I smarted.

"Yeah, whatever, tough girl. So, you gonna come in or am I gonna have to come out there and get you?"

Inside was like another world. He lived in a modern, spacious triplex, complete with a rooftop garden terrace and enough space for five studio apartments the size of the one I had when I lived in the East Village. It was one of those New York treasures that you always hear so much about or see in magazines like *Architectural Digest*. Photographic stills covered the walls that had been washed in warm earth tones. It was welcoming, and I was diggin' this man's style.

Taye had bragged about his extensive CD collection and I was here to prove that he wasn't as knowledgeable as he claimed.

"I know you're one of those HM chicks."

"Excuse me?" He'd caught me off guard. I was busy looking around at the amazing photographs.

"You know, high-maintenance," he chuckled.

"Oh, puleeeze! I am so not high-maintenance."

"I've seen you out. Brotha's buying the bar for you and all that crap. So, since I don't typically pop bottles and the Cristal's not flowing around here, would you settle for a simple glass of wine?"

"I guess I could slum today." There I was, doing it again. I have got to get this blushing thing under control.

He popped the cork on a bottle of Merlot and I got comfortable on the couch. Ultrasuede, *nice*! Did I mention this man has great taste?

"So what's up with all the photographs? And what song are you playin' over there?"

"Hey, hey, hey, can a brotha do his thing? Mind yours!" He pressed PLAY on the stereo and Ronnie and Debra Laws's "Very Special" came on.

"Now *that's* my jam!" Taye shouted like he was in one of those old K-Tel Records commercials where the guy gives his buddy that famous line: "*No, my brother, you've got to get your own.*"

"You know, that's the first thing that comes out of a black person's mouth at one of those real good, sweat-your-hair-out, red-light basement parties. Whatchu know about that?" I said.

"Those used to be the bomb!" Taye said.

"Prep-school boy, you don't know anything about basement parties!" I said.

"Oh, there's a lot Taye Crawford knows about and can get down on."

"No, change that. This is one of those back-breakin'-slowjammy-jam songs, like you hear at the after-hours spot. Like the one my mama ran back in the day when I was growing up in the East Boogie."

"East Boogie?"

"East St. Louis, baby!"

"Oh, right, that's where Nelly's from!"

"Not! He's from St. Louis, *Missouri*. I beg your pardon, East Boogie is across the river in Illinois."

"Okay, I feel you. Does your mother still run the place?"

"She died." We both paused.

"I'm sorry."

"No, it's okay. You didn't know." I took a sip from my glass.

"Come on, let me show you around." Taye shifted to a more up-beat subject. I was glad. "These walls are what I call the 'Walls of Fame' because they're photographs by some of the most incredible black photographers in history. Now, this is James VanDerZee's work. This is called 'Harlem.' This is James Latimer Allen's photograph of Langston Hughes." He pointed to several other framed stills. "You'll really like this one by Roy De Carava of Lady Day and Hazel Scott. And here we have the man, the myth, the master, Gordon Parks. This is Mr. Parks's 'Woman Washing Clothes' piece. He's my hero."

By this time we had made it to the second floor, but there was more to go.

"Now I really dig Chuck Stewart. If you really know something about music, you'll dig him, too," he said. "This is Dinah Washington, Max Roach, and John Coltrane."

"Oh, I *know* you didn't challenge me. 'What a Difference a Day Makes,' 'A Love Supreme' . . . do I need to go on?" I said, twisting my mouth. I wanted him to know a sista is cultured.

"Don't go all chickenhead on me, rolling the neck and things! Okay, so you know some musical trivia. I'll give you some points." He gently took my hand and led me up yet another flight of stairs to a large sunroom. There were floor pillows everywhere, beautiful plants, and wonderful-smelling candles. The best part is that there was a feeling of calmness and quiet here.

"Now, these are some of my favorite contemporary photographers. This is Bobby Sengstacke's shot of Savior's Day and another one of Dr. King. And here's my main man, Jeffrey Henson Scales, good brotha and good friend. All these are from his 'House's Barber Shop' series. And finally, these are from a beautiful sista, Jeanne Moutoussamy-Ashe."

"Oh, my God, that's Arthur Ashe's widow. Wow! I didn't know she was a photographer. I feel so stupid."

"Don't sweat it. A lot of people don't know that about her. Yep, she's bad and courageous. I told you I love strong black women." Taye looked me directly in the eye. I quickly turned away, like I was embarrassed or something. He cleared his throat and continued with the gallery tour. "This is her piece called 'Emily's Kitchen,' and these are from her Daufuskie Island, South Carolina series. So that's pretty much it!"

"This room is amazing!"

"I call it my 'peace' room. I come here sometimes to read the Bible, read a book, or just meditate and reflect on life. Everyone should have a space like that in their home."

"I bet the sun is murder in the mornings, huh?"

"Yeah, but it's beautiful when it's setting." Taye led me back downstairs and into the kitchen, where he had prepared an elaborate gourmet feast with shrimp and lobster and pasta. I was in awe.

We both must've been famished because we practically inhaled that food. "I'm stuffed! This was the most incredible meal I've ever had," I said, leaning back in my chair as if I was making room for my expanding belly.

"You don't have to lay it on so thick," Taye said, refilling my wineglass.

"No, I'm serious." I was.

"You probably get meals ten times better than this made for you all the time. Probably by private chefs and things."

"I've never had a man cook for me, Taye. This was very sweet. The least I can do is the dishes," I said, getting up and reaching for his plate.

"Don't you dare," he said pulling his plate back. "I did this because I wanted to. I wanted to do something nice for you," Taye said, starting to clear the table.

I almost didn't know how to accept a man doing something thoughtful for me. I looked down at my bracelet and all its bling-tacular. Taye's gesture meant a lot more than a piece of jewelry. At that moment I realized Malik had never even made me a bologna sandwich.

After Taye cleared the dishes, we went back to the living room to listen to music.

"So let's get into this music thing you've been bragging so much about!" I said.

"How about you pick," Taye said pouring us both more wine.

I started going through his shelves and shelves of CDs like I was an old-school dj diggin' in the crates.

"I've got it!" I announced, holding up a disc as though I had just struck gold.

"Let me see!" Taye reached for it.

"Oh, no! This is a test. Can you remember this one?" I slipped the disc into the CD deck and pressed PLAY. I closed my eyes as the opening strings of the song soared.

"Ooooh, you dug that one up!" Taye said, closing his eyes, too.

"That's right, the one and only, Miss Phyllis Hyman, "Living In Confusion." Gamble and Huff used to lace her tracks, but Phyllis could make a song cry." I took a sip of wine, swaying to the music. "This is one of those heartache songs."

"Oh, really." Taye's eyes went wide. "But then you also know she's thinking about how good the lovemaking was."

"You can feel her pain in every note."

"Maybe the great Destiny Day will write songs or something in her next life." Taye drained his glass.

"You might be on to something!"

"I bet you would write deep tripped-out songs about the meaning of life?"

"That's it! But with me, it's not so complicated. People make more drama out of life than necessary. Life is fabulous if you've got a brotha who can turn it in the bedroom, and a song that can get the party started." I was getting hyped.

Taye broke into laughter as he poured us both more wine.

"The two are damn near one and the same. See, great sex is like a soul-stirring, pulsating, hypnotic bass line. It's utopia. Baby, just thinking about what I can do with some Barry White on the stereo gets the juices pumping," I said.

"Okay, calm down! I feel you. You know, I dig the new-school playas like Usher and Lil Jon, but for me, the last of the great music makers was that shy girl from Yonkers who first asked the world, 'What's the 411?' "

"Oh my God, nobody better say nothin' about my girl Mary J! Oh, and you gots ta put Alicia up in there too! But I've gotta keep taking it back to the hardcore classics—Phyllis; Aretha; Earth, Wind and Fire; Luther; and the list goes on. When I can feel that slow crescendo of the *boombatboombatratatattat*, it's on!"

"I close my eyes," I said, closing my eyes and feeling the moment. "Instinctively arch my back, toss my head back, start grinding my hips, shaking my ass, poppin' my fingers, and throwing up my hands. *Heeeeey, Hoooooooooooo! It's like ecstasy when you lay down next to me!* Music pulls me in and takes me under. It's entrancing, spine-tingling, bone-chilling, orgasmic and leaves me breathless. *Ahhhhhh!*"

"Wow, you *do* love music, don't you?" Taye said, bringing me back down to earth.

"I was born into it. I remember it all used to jump off around one or two in the morning. Two brothers named Baby Boy and Sweet owned a little after-hours club called the Belly Room."

"You're playin', right? Those weren't their birth given names?"

"I never knew anything different. Now that I think about it, it was pretty ridiculous that two big ol' grown musclebound he-men with mouths full of gold should've been calling themselves names like that.

"You would've thought my mother *owned* the Belly Room. Juanita Day was legendary before she *became* legendary. She was only eighteen, and Baby Boy said she was 'one-stop shoppin'. That meant fine, hot-tempered, *and* street smart. Juanita was known to be crafty with a razor and kept her heat strapped to her thigh; a true-to-life, all-the-way-live Cleopatra Jones."

"Kind of like you, huh?" Taye leaned in closer. "I want to know more. I want to know everything about you, Destiny Day."

"I might scare you away if I told you everything," I said, blushing.

"I'll take that chance."

"I don't know if you're ready for East Boogie! Whew! Those were the days, everybody hanging out, dancing, getting their drink on, and of course, plenty of access to whatever your drug of choice might be. Whatever you needed, Juanita could get it for you. And if you had the munchies, Miss Roxy, who ran the back kitchen, could "cue" or fry the hell outta any part of the pig, cow, or chicken your heart desired. I wasn't more than five or six, Juanita had me all up the spot."

"For real!"

"It doesn't get any more real than the Belly Room, Taye. Listen, my mother would be telling patrons, 'Look at my baby, ain't she pretty!' She talked in a sweet and twangy way. But girlfriend was sexy, too. In between mixing drinks and taking a sip or two, or three, or four, for herself she'd snort a line of coke here, take a puff from a joint there.

"Then Juanita would call out from the club's small dance floor, grinding her hips to the music. 'C'mon, dance with me, Carlton!' Man, like Marvin said, she sure loved to ball! Carlton would lift me off his lap and say, 'Wait right here, Sunshine!' And I'd be left there standing by myself in a room full of stinking-drunk, big-haired, big-hat-wearin' Negroes dressed in so much polyester the walls and windows would be sweating.

"Juanita Day had all the money-makin' hustlers coming through. Women eager to have a good time weren't far behind. On the outside, the Belly Room looked like a typical neighborhood hole-in-the-wall joint, but inside it was a decked-out, exclusive spot where the 'hood shot-callers from the East Side and St. Louis gathered after the clubs in St. Louis shut down.

"Two years old, grooving by myself in the wee hours of the morning to "Honey Please Can't Ya See" by The Maestro and his Love Unlimited Orchestra. Now you know Juanita didn't have any business being anybody's mama. That story's crazy, isn't it?" I smiled wistfully.

"I'm blown away. Sounds like you had an exciting childhood. I see why music means a lot to you."

"Exciting ain't the word for what went down in East Boogie." I paused and took a deep, reflective breath. "Most people don't realize how important music is. Whatever emotions you're experiencing, there's a song for it," I said passionately, slipping another CD in, grooving to Michael Jackson's "Off The Wall." "In fact, I wrote a poem, well, kind of like a story awhile ago that I named 'Music Is My Life.' That's corny, though."

"No, let me hear it!" Taye asked.

"For real?" It probably was the wine, but what the heck. I closed my eyes and began to recite the words I'd written in a journal several years ago. "Errrrrum," I cleared my throat. " 'Music gets under my skin, and pumps through my veins. It's that high that I can't get enough of. That headtrip that makes me wanna get up off of *that* and go 'head and sha, sha, sha, sha shake that ass, girl!

" 'You know it must be the music that's turning me on! Like *mama used to say*, girl you'd better *take your time and do it right* even if it takes all night. And you know every now and then *I get around* so don't be all up in my face with that *who is he and what is he to you*. Hold up, wait a minute! This must be *déjà vu*, I know we must've been here before.' " I reopened my eyes. Taye was completely engaged and right there with me the whole time.

"Oh, you got skillz, Destiny!" He stood up and applauded. I took a bow.

"If it wasn't for the music, I'd lose my mind," I said, collapsing on the couch wearing a huge smile. "It inspires, uplifts, drives me . . ."

"And unfurls your deepest desires," Taye said, gently taking my empty glass out of my hand.

"Wow, are you sure I didn't get too carried away?" I asked.

"You were supposed to have a good time tonight." He flashed that winning smile again.

"Well, if I said anything crazy it was because of the wine."

"I won't hold it against you." Taye checked his watch. "I know you have to be at the club tonight. So, thanks for hanging out with me."

"Are you putting me out?" I said, taken aback. *Okay, what is really going on? This was his second time shutting me down for the night.*

"No, I'm just being considerate of your schedule," Taye said, giving me a long hug. It felt good being in his arms. In the past, I've

206

compared *this* guy with *that* guy, but even Taye's hug was different. It was warm, it was secure, it was gentle. *I don't know what it is about Taye Crawford, but I think he's pretty cool.*

He walked me out to my car, after he made sure I was okay to drive.

"Honey, it takes more than sharing one bottle of wine to have me trippin'."

We laughed as I started up the car and slowly pulled off. I could still see Taye in my rearview mirror when I stopped at the corner of Greenwich and Eighth. I'd never really hung out with a guy without the intimacy. Well, Rico doesn't count. I smiled to myself, still blushing like a schoolgirl.

Super Freak

I decided to take Jacques up on another offer to meet at his Brooklyn Heights restaurant. I hoped it would at least be another shot to find out what all the hype was about. I strutted into Patrois–Brooklyn Heights in a sexy Roberto Cavalli silky-sheer frock and four-inch Cavalli snake-skin sandals. I wanted to give Jacques a look to remember.

To say Patrois is out of this world is an understatement. The main dining room's large bay windows, lining the back wall of the restaurant, overlook the East River. The Brooklyn Bridge is on one side, the Manhattan on the other, and the FDR Drive is in the distance. It's the perfect postcard shot.

It was closing time, so the dinner crowd had pretty much filtered out. The hostess showed me to a secluded patio area that was tented with large bamboo ceiling fans spinning lazily. Jacques was holding court with two other women who looked like Victoria's Secret models. Great. Just what I needed. They were giggly, obnoxious, and clearly drunk, as evidenced by the two empty bottles that were turned upside down in the ice buckets.

"Destiny, wassup, babe!" Jacques stood up and pulled out the chair next to him, then kissed me on the lips. I softened up. They must all have just been friends for him to kiss me like this. Okay, I could deal with their annoying presence for the time being.

"I'm Gina," the one with skin the color of desert sand, hazel eyes, and bright blond dreads said. She extended a long, slender hand. "I've heard so much about you." I immediately went on the defensive. *What the hell has she heard? I don't know anything about this chick.* I gave her a phony smile and quickly put my order in for a Lust while we were waiting for more bottles of champagne to arrive.

"And I'm Kiki. I hear you're in the club business?" The other one said with a heavy African accent. She had the same long neck and high cheekbones that Iman has, but fuller lips. She looked like an African queen. I had never seen anyone with skin that rich and dark before.

"Sort of, I give a lot of parties in the city and do some special events other places, too," I answered guardedly, gingerly sipping from my frosted cocktail glass. I wasn't trying to tell all my business to this chick.

"Kiki owns a few clubs in London and one in Paris," Jacques interjected, sensing my apprehension, and winked. "Destiny, you've heard of Chez Enchantée?"

My eyes lit up. Who hasn't heard of Chez Enchantée? It's the biggest nightclub in Paris. Maybe allowing Jacques to hold court tonight was permissible considering the possibility of hooking up some international business. The waiter placed another chilled Lust in front of me. I examined Kiki more closely.

209

"You have amazing skin," I said, taking a sip.

"Thank you. It's called incredible sex!"

The table erupted with laughter. Kiki had a good sense of humor. The night should prove to be very interesting.

"Kiki's my sole investor in my future restaurants, Patrois–South Beach and Patrois–Beverly Hills."

"Yes, next we'll be doing Patrois–Paris!" she said excitedly, raising her glass to toast.

Two more bottles of Veuve and four Crown Royal Lusts later, I was officially trashed and had caught up with Kiki, Gina, and Jacques. It was two a.m. and Jacques had turned the restaurant into our very own private club (the upside of being its proprietor). The staff had gone home, and Jacques had taken post behind the bar and started mixing up a new batch of cocktails for the gang.

I had taken over as the dj and popped some Jay-Z in the CD player. I was dropping my ass like it was on fire. Kiki drained her entire martini in one gulp and shimmied over to my makeshift dance floor. Jacques glided in between us and began to grab and fondle my breasts. Gina decided she didn't want to be left out of the picture and worked her way over to where we all appeared to be bumping and grinding in sync. I closed my eyes and let the moment take over.

Jacques slipped the delicate straps of my dress off my shoulders, revealing the satin-and-lace bra I was wearing. It must've signaled the freakfest to begin. Within seconds Kiki had slipped out of her Swarovski-crystal-trimmed minidress, and she was standing buck naked, Brazilian waxed and bald like a baby from the neck down, in a pair of Gucci bronze studded sandals. Kiki grabbed Gina and they started touching and fondling each other. I stopped dancing to watch.

Jacques began to undress, removing his jacket and shirt. He kissed me on the mouth. I was feeling warm and tingly all over. He stepped back and unbuttoned his linen pants. I could taste the anticipation. I'd wanted Jacques the first night we met, when he walked into Show. I wasn't into girls, but at this point, I didn't care if I had to screw Kiki and Gina *both* to get to him.

Jacques dropped his trousers and I thought I was going to have cardiac arrest on the spot. My breathing ceased. My face was frozen in terror. The man had no drawers on when he removed his pants. He was packing, but I don't know what *it* was. His penis was as thick as a tree trunk, and almost as long as a third leg. No, actually, it *was* a third leg! Hello, where did he think he was going with that *thing*? Nowhere near me, I guarantee!

Kiki and Gina were now pawing all over me. I still couldn't move, but I'd regained the power of sight, zeroing in on his penis again. What the hell? I squinted. Good Lawd, the man was uncircumcised! Jacques's penis was like something in a circus sideshow. This wasn't normal. I knew they'd have to put me in the hospital if I tried that one.

I was suddenly ill. I grabbed my evening clutch, put on my underwear and was out of Patrois faster than O-Town's career had come and gone.

Que Sera, Sera
(Whatever Will Be, Will Be)

SLY AND THE FAMILY
STONE VERSION

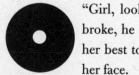 "Girl, look at the bright side: If Jacques ever goes broke, he *can* join the circus!" Izzy snickered, doing her best to sit still while Rico tested new makeup on her face.

I ordered sushi and helped myself to another tuna roll.

"Chile, I still can't get over him having a little hoodie on his wee-wee!" Rico curled his upper lip and rolled his eyes. "Now *that's* some stankonia stuff!"

"Voilà! How does she look?" Rico said, spinning Izzy around to unveil his latest creation. He was testing out new makeup designs on her for his book. "This is what I call 'Zee Lioness'!" He growled, snapping a quick shot of her face with his digital camera.

"Bravo, bravo." I stood up and started clapping loudly.

"Destiny, on the real, thanks for the pep talk. I'm working hard to get my dream out there into the universe!" Rico said.

"You sound focused. I'm happy. Speaking of focused, how's celibacy?" I asked, popping a tuna roll into my mouth.

"Wonderful. I really think I'm getting to know myself better. I met someone, and you will be happy to know, he's practicing celibacy, too. It's hard sometimes when we're together, but we put our energies into other things like good conversation. I told you hens, I want it to be right and forever the next time. So, Legendary, wassup with you and Taye?"

"We're just friends."

"Des, you don't have male friends! Don't tell me Jacques scared you that much, Ma?" Izzy said, biting into a piece of eel, careful not to ruin her makeup job.

"Maybe Taye is scared to step to you romantically, because he doesn't want to get hurt or risk losing his friendship with you," Rico added.

"What do you mean?"

"Chile, you eat men for breakfast."

"I'm not as tough as I used to be. Malik worked a number on me."

"I hoped you've softened up, because I know I got drama and ain't one to talk, but seems like Taye's a good find. A keeper. One day you'll wake up—I just hope it's not too late. On that note, I'm out. I've got to do inventory tonight." Rico packed up his kit and jetted. Izzy and I finished off the last of the sushi.

"Des, I haven't spent that much time around Taye, but he's a good guy. Sometimes you have to just let your heart guide you, Ma. I think you should really think about getting serious with Taye," Izzy said.

"You sound like a Hallmark card, girl. Look, the last thing I want

213

is anything serious with anybody. I'm barely over all that drama with Malik."

"Des, why are you so down on love and relationships?"

"I got nothin' against other people having relationships, but seems like most people don't even understand love. I hate getting into this all the time with you and Josephine. Right now, I'm back to being focused on business, and that's always good for me. I never want to make the mistake of putting all my hopes and dreams into loving somebody again. They only go away!" I didn't want to go there, but Iz had struck a nerve. "People disappoint you. You put all these expectations and emotions out there, and then it hurts. It cuts deep when something goes wrong!" I took a deep breath and confessed. "I did the dumbest thing I could've ever imagined. I gave Malik fifty thousand dollars. I just didn't tell you and Rico. It was supposed to be an investment, but he screwed me and took off with my money. Now, I'm over it. I got that huge Garcel party at the end of the summer. Hey, I can make paper. It's the principle. If he needed money that bad he could've just been straight with me."

"You know I can come out of retirement if you want to go find that motherfucker!"

"See, that's why I didn't tell you. I don't want to find him. I don't want to know why. I don't care. I just want to get on with my life, but I'll tell you one thing: I'm about to be on a new page when it comes to people. If I don't know you, I don't trust you! Nobody made Destiny Day a household name with the club kids but *me*."

"Des, you can't just come hardcore like that. I know you, and I know you ain't like that."

"My mother was."

"But you're not her, and tha's the one thing you always said you'd never be. Des, I know you don't like to talk about things, but what happen' with your parents made you believe tha' love is gonna walk out on you or maybe tha' you're not capable of love. I used to

214

feel that way, Ma. Look at how bad my family is. Do you know what that feels like, when you wait your whole life for somethin'? Then you get it right there in the palm of your hand and it jus' blows away like dust. And now Carmen might be dead in less than a year."

"You told me you didn't care."

"I lied. How can I not care? Carmen is still my mother. I was going through some old photographs the other day and I saw how pretty she was back in the day. She jus' wasted her life, Ma. I hate her for that. But I know God has somethin' real for me. I know you're gonna be mad, but I still think it's D-Roc. But whether it's him or not, I know I'm a good person and I deserve true love." Puddles of tears formed in Izzy's eyes.

My heart connected with hers. I could feel myself fighting back my own tears. Now you see why I don't like talking about this stuff. "No, Iz, I'm capable of love. I love Ainee and Uncle Charlie, Josephine, you and Rico. Y'all are my family. And you will find real love one day, but I can tell you it won't be with D-Roc." My voice was shaky. I didn't want to cry. I quickly wiped my eyes and nose and cleared my throat.

"But Des, whatever I do with my life, support me. I've never once judged you or held anything against you. I love you no matter what!" An invisible wall of tension suddenly shot up between us. Izzy's cell rang. "That's D-Roc," she said looking at her caller ID. "He's been trying to work things out. I just didn't tell you." Izzy looked back at her phone, then at me. Her phone kept ringing.

"You'd better get that."

"Nah, he can wait, Ma. I jus' want you to know that this guy Taye sounds like something special, for real, Ma, but you won't even give him a try. What if the Malik drama was supposed to happen to get you ready for the real man you supposed to have? And for me, jus' try to understand me better. You think I don' want to be happy, you're crazy!"

215

I closed the door behind Izzy and stood in my foyer. My feet wouldn't move, like they were cemented to the floor. I remembered what Josephine said about her ex-husband Mr. Sanchez. She said he was a "keeper," but she was just too foolish and hardheaded to see it. Is Taye a keeper?

I almost drove myself crazy trying to stand by Malik running on that wheel like Josephine's ex-husband Willie Williams and the lab rat, just running and running, never getting anywhere. And that piece of moldy cheese dangling forever, because that rat's too stupid to realize it's attached to a string. I had sense enough to know that Malik was that rat, and he was never going to finish that Freedom album! I could just kiss my money goodbye.

Josephine's analogy made sense, and I appreciated Izzy's good intentions, but only *I* could know what *I* needed in my life! *Destiny is in control of her feelings, and that's all I've got to say about it!*

Disk Six
When The World Turns Blue

{1} 'TAINT NOBODY'S BIZNESS IF I DO

{2} NEED A LITTLE SUGAR IN MY BOWL

{3} I'D RATHER GO BLIND

{4} ALL OR NOTHING AT ALL

{5} BORN UNDER A BAD SIGN

{6} THIS BITTER EARTH

'Taint Nobody's Bizness if I Do

Just three weeks and counting until the Carcel event, and it will be the biggest Labor Day party the Hamptons have ever hosted. In the meantime, temperatures in Manhattan hit the high nineties this week, but with the humidity, it felt like triple digits. Jenna and I were keeping cool at my place, putting the final touches on the party. I could sense something was on her mind.

"Destiny, can I . . . um, never mind." Jenna was anxious and fidgety.

"What's up with you, girlie? This is your second time starting a sentence and then stopping. What's the problem?"

"I just think we should talk about the Peter situation."

"There is no Peter situation." I was aggravated at this point.

"Yes, there is, Destiny. He's unhappy creatively. He's really talented, and the only reason why he hasn't gone out and signed with another company is because of his loyalty to us."

"Hold up, there ain't no 'us'! This is my world, and you're just running around in it!"

"Destiny I didn't mean it like that, I just . . ."

"You just *what*! Got too damn comfortable. The company is called Destiny Day Productions, *not* Jenna fuckin' Cohen Productions. And what is all this with you and Peter? Does he tell you every time we screw, too?"

"All this isn't necessary. I'm looking out for your best interests."

"You're looking out for Jenna, and I'm not mad at you!" I began to chuckle maniacally. "You've learned from the best. Me! I'm always gonna make sure Destiny gets hers. But the mistake you made is that you can't outcon the Queen of Con.

"I can be ruthless and cutthroat. I told you on Day One you and I would get along famously, as long as you didn't overstep your bounds when it came to how I ran my business and my personal life. And you've done pretty well so far. I even brought you into my tight circle. But the truth is, you've liked Peter for a while. I've seen it in your eyes. I thought you wised up after that night we had our talk at the club."

"Destiny, I think Peter's really nice, but I know he's off-limits. I just believe in his talent."

"Talent my ass! Girlfriend, you're out of your league. I made DJ Peter a star! I made you a star! I took this whole club game to the next level! So, as far as I'm concerned, your work is done here!" I spat out those words before I could even think about what I was doing.

"What? I've busted my tail for you, Destiny, and I take a lot of crap from you. But I love my job, and you and I go deeper than this. This whole thing has really been blown out of proportion!"

220

I folded my arms and cocked my head to the side. "This ought to teach you never to put that much faith in anybody or anything. You don't know me."

"You can't be serious!" Jenna was beet-red and sweating. Her breathing quickened. She was blinking her eyes rapidly.

"I'll send your final check in the mail. Your services won't be needed for the Garcel party, either." I looked away.

"That party's my baby! It's not about the money."

"Then you won't mind not being compensated for anything having to do with Garcel's party?"

"This is so unfair!"

"Get over it! Haven't you heard? Life is unfair!" I whipped my head around, facing her and standing. Jenna stood up too, challenging my words. We were face to face. Heated fury was the only thing that separated us. "Look at the bright side: Now you can pursue Peter to your heart's content. Just remember, I come for girls like you in the outside world. So be ready!"

Jenna's eyes welled up and her bottom lip quivered like a wounded lamb's. I was uncomfortable seeing her like this. She couldn't hold back the tears any longer. In all my years working with her, even after my most volatile explosions, I'd never seen Jenna cry. She was visibly shaken, traumatized. I felt queasy, but I stood firm.

I wanted to reach out and comfort her. Tell her I was sorry, maybe take it all back, but forget that! Then I'd be the one looking stupid and weak. I fired up a cigarette instead. Jenna snatched her purse off the table so fast all the contents went flying across the floor. It was too painful to watch her shaking and crying like this.

I took a puff and exhaled as Jenna scurried to put everything back inside. She was so nervous she left several coins, a lipstick, and her compact behind. Jenna ran out of my apartment and never looked back.

I collapsed into my large chaise lounge and took another long drag. I had just lost not only my best assistant, but a dear friend. I'd hurt her deeply. The first day I met Jenna, I'd felt a connection. She became the little sister I never had. My tight inner circle was complete: Ainee, Uncle C, Izzy, Rico, Josephine, and Jenna.

Damn, I guess it's too late for sorry.

Need a Little Sugar
in My Bowl

"Okay, three more steps up, now we're making a little turn to the right, and we're here. Now open your eyes." Taye guided me into a closet-sized room at his house that had photographs hanging up like clothes on a clothesline.

"You didn't show me this the last time I was here," I said, looking around. I'd actually visited Taye at his house a couple of times since he cooked dinner for me. We'd gone to the SoHo flea market one Saturday afternoon, and another night we watched a bootleg I picked up from my man Unique.

"Well, I decided I was ready to share my secret with you. It's a darkroom."

"Duh! I see that!"

"I've always had this dream of being a photographer, and I've never really told anyone, but I felt like I wanted to tell you."

"Wow, thank you. But nowadays isn't it all about the digital thing?"

"I do that, too, but I also like developing things the old-fashioned way. Kind of how you like the new music, but it's the classics that get your juices running."

"You so nasty! I said the classics get my juices pumpin'!"

We laughed.

Taye set up the "peace" room with cheese and crackers and wine.

"Why aren't you married, Destiny?"

"Whoa, I don't think me and marriage would be a good mix, but you, *you're* the settlin'-down family-type brotha," I said, placing a slice of brie on a cracker.

"I love the idea of one day getting married and having a kid or two. I'd be happy just being blessed with one. I'm getting old, you know."

"Old! You're crazy. You're only thirty-six."

"Yeah, but I ain't feelin' being that old man tryin' to keep up with my son out there on the baseball field. I'm ready to start planting some seeds, poppin' some off!" he said.

"Oh, yeah?" I felt uneasy. Taye had never been this assertive. You know, the way a man is when he's interested in a woman in more than just a sexual way.

"Yeah. So, tell me again why you're so against marriage, Destiny?"

"Urgh! I hate this subject."

"I'm not letting you get out of this."

"People get stupid when they get that into each other. It destroys the beauty of freedom and great sex. Marriage is so confining!"

"That's absurd! The beauty of two people loving each other is exploring life together sexually and mentally. You're so jaded."

"I'm not jaded. I'm a realist!" I proclaimed, taking a big swallow of wine. "Can we forget all that other stuff? I'm more interested in hearing about this dream of yours."

"You think you're slick, Destiny Day. You only want to talk about what *you* want to talk about. But I'll let the princess have her way today."

"Thank you! Now, spill it!" I said as we tapped our glasses together in a toast.

"You're gonna think it's corny, but I love the way a photograph tells a story. A good photograph can show you the history of a person in their eyes, and you know the eyes are the windows to your soul. That's why Gordon Parks is so brilliant!"

"So why aren't you doing what you love?" I asked.

Taye took a deep breath and a big gulp from his glass. "My mother died of cancer when I was ten."

"Man, I was ten when I lost my parents." Things were starting to get spooky with Taye. There were too many things we shared.

"Then you know how hard it is at that age. I mean at any age. Anyway, my father was always a hard-nose. He graduated at the top of his class from Morehouse College, and then years later got his MBA from Howard. He's a successful businessman now. He wanted me to follow in his footsteps, but be even more successful, be better. That's why he pushed me and worked hard to pay for me to go to Stanford. He wanted me to make my mark, get my JD, MBA. I didn't care about all those letters after my name. I just wanted his love."

I could see Taye becoming more and more on edge the more he talked about his father. "I wanted him to hang out with me, go to the barbershop, a ball game, just regular stuff. Do you know he's never once told me he loved me? I mean, I guess I've always known it, but sometimes a parent needs to tell their child that kind of stuff. A child needs to hear that."

"You can't keep living your life for your father. You need to just do your thing, Taye."

"Destiny, I've contemplated many times just giving it all up and moving to Paris to do my art, or just packing up and traveling the world to shoot pictures of people from every culture. I just feel like my soul is withering away. I'm making big money, sure, but there's more to life than that. Don't you think?"

How was I supposed to answer something like that? Money's always been the first thing on my mind when I wake up and the last thing on it when I turn the lights out. Hell, no, there *isn't* anything more to life! Money is power. But I didn't want to sound shallow, so I lied. "I feel you. Life is about more than money."

"You do *not* sound convincing," he laughed. Taye saw right through my paper-thin answer.

"Okay, so you busted me. I just didn't want to come off materialistic, but all I've known is hustlin' and being on that grind to make money."

"Do you think money makes a person?"

"No," I said defensively. "The person makes the person! But money makes big things happen in life for that person."

"Destiny, all the money in the world can't bring my mother or your parents back."

Taye had struck a nerve. A chilling, spine-numbing nerve. I felt my eyes puddle up.

"I'm sorry, Destiny. I didn't mean to bring up something bad." Taye caressed me gently and I felt myself melting into his arms, wanting to pour my heart out to this man.

"It's just kind of hard when you say it like that. I always looked at money as something that was more important than people." I began to cry.

"Just let it out," Taye said softly stroking my hair.

"But it's what killed my mother and father. Money was always too enticing to Juanita. She got greedy. I remember it all like it's happening right now. Juanita was using and selling drugs, and she got my daddy hooked, too. As smart as she was, you'd think she would've known not to get high on her own supply. That's supposed to be the first rule you learn in Dealin' 101, right?"

I pulled away and wiped my face with a wad of tissue Taye handed me. I began to recount that fateful morning for Taye, every second of it. "See, Juanita was stealing from Baby Boy and Sweet; they owned the Belly Room. She was gonna pay them back, though. She just needed more time." I closed my eyes tight.

"Open up, bitch!" Sweet yelled from outside our apartment door.

"Carlton, we gotta get the fuck outta here!" Juanita was rushing around throwing everything she could into trash bags: fur coats, shoes, money, drugs. Carlton was trying to help me get my stuff together. He was so nervous he dropped everything on the floor. I'm pretty sure he was high, because he kept scratching his arms and he was sweating pretty bad. "Hey, Sunshine," he said, jumpy, forcing a smile.

"Open up, bitch!" Sweet yelled again.

Then they kicked the door in. Carlton told me to hide in the closet. Baby Boy, Sweet, and their crew of about five started blasting away. Bullets ripped through the air. Sweet made sure Juanita went first. He pulled the trigger himself. Her bullet-riddled body was sprawled over the living-room couch. The rest of the goons opened fire on Carlton after that.

● ● ●

I stood in front of Taye's large patio doors and felt the sun's rays on my face. "And that was how it all went down. They were gone just like that. I know Juanita loved me the best way she could love anybody. I remember she always told me that I should never give my heart away to anyone. It was like she was mad she'd gotten hooked up like she did with Carlton. She was born to be free. My aunt and uncle took me as far away from East Boogie as they could. A nice, clean, quiet town called Markum, Illinois, just outside Chi-town."

Taye walked over to me and put his fingers on my temples and began to massage them.

"Are you okay?"

"Josephine always says, 'That which doesn't kill you, only makes you stronger,' and I believe that!"

"Then you must also believe that 'God never gives us more than we can handle,' right?"

"Right."

"Would you mind if I took some pictures of you?"

"Now?" I said patting my face. "I look a hot mess."

"I love the way you look!"

Taye picked up his camera and started snapping away.

"What do you dream about, Destiny?"

"That's a crazy question."

"You've gotta have a dream."

"You wanna know for real?" I said, striking a pose. "I've always wanted to own my own club. Not a big one, maybe just a cool lounge with great drinks, great atmosphere, and of course great music. Hell, maybe I'd even be the damn dj."

"Okay, let's make a deal from here on out that we're not going to let anyone stand in the way of our dreams!"

"Deal!" We shook hands.

"But I need your help."

"What?" I said, eyeing him suspiciously.

"Let me photograph you for real."

"As long as you don't sell them on the Internet and cut me out of the profits, double deal!" We hugged on that one.

I really liked hugging this man. It hit me that I had just told Taye my entire life story *and* cried. I'd never even given all the details to my friends. What was happening to me? I'm not even sure I know myself anymore. I guess there's only one choice for now . . .

Just keep going with the flow.

I'd Rather Go Blind

Tonight, multi-platinum-selling Southern rapper Lil Nitty, famous for that ignorant saying, "*Gittin'thatnit-tygritty,*" was getting on my last nerve. But it was adding the pig-snort sound effect that made him and his posse truly obnoxious. If one more gold-tooth, white-tee, saggy-pants-wearing fool called me *shorty* and made that God-awful sound, I was gonna start kickin' some ass.

I agree with Josephine; hip-hop has created some important, culturally advancing opportunities for black folks of our time, but it's also helped mass-produce ignorance. I am ready to choke one of these little illiterate scrubs, if they order one more bottle of Hennessey or Hpnotiq. Thank God, their record label, Universal, is footing the bill for this little 'hood extravaganza.

"*Gittin'thatnittygritty,* duurty!" One of Lil Nitty's cohorts snorted at me, before grabbing my ass. Oh, hells no! Just for that I'm billing Universal another ten Gs. I didn't have Jenna here to watch my back and deal with this mess, either. I'd really just fired her to flex. I expected her to come back begging for forgiveness the next day, but she didn't. It had been a week.

I was finally fed up with everything. "Party's over! Hit the bricks." I started grabbing unopened bottles and motioned for Big Tom to remove Lil Nitty.

"Fuck you, beeyach!" Lil Nitty flashed a mouthful of diamonds and gold.

Too bad he had no idea just how crazy Destiny Day could be. Before Lil Nitty could blink . . .

Kabam!

He was wearing an ice bucket, courtesy of the Princess of East Boogie. Me! Big Tom and his security squad were doing double duty to round up the *gettin'thatnittygritty* posse. A calamity was unfolding right before my eyes.

The party had officially been shut down and the club cleared out. When the last Hpnotiq bottle was thrown away, Peter slowly walked over to me and sat down. My face was buried in my hands.

"I don't want any company tonight, Peter," I said, raising my head. He began gently stroking my hair.

"I'm not trying to go home with you, Destiny. I just wanted to tell you that I've gotta make some other moves."

I should've known it was only a matter of time before the other shoe dropped.

"What!" I jumped to my feet. "Don't tell me Jenna put you up to this!" I was yelling at the top of my lungs.

"I didn't want things to go down like this, Destiny." He let out a deep sigh. "Look, this has nothing to do with Jenna, but everything to do with her. I think it's foul what went down. Lately, she's the one who's shown her support. She believes in what I do. Not you! She told me to stick with you. But she's gone now, and I gotta be out. When you want to step to me for real, you can call me." Peter started away. I yanked him by the arm.

"I made you! You were spinnin' in a no-name dump, and I put you on the map as a dj and gave you some of the best ass you ever had. I laced you! If you walk out, it's over. You can't come back!"

Peter pulled away and stared at me long and hard. He had that same sick-lamb look that Jenna'd had in her eyes. He turned away and kept walking until he was out of sight. I was too weary to run after him. I just wanted to go drown myself in a tub of vodka.

All or Nothing at All

My buzzer rang, and I was shocked because I wasn't expecting company. I figured it was Izzy or Rico and pressed the DOOR button on the intercom system like I always did. The door opened and Taye was standing there with a fiery look in his eyes. He barreled in, and I didn't even have a chance to make an excuse for how bad I looked.

"What's going on?" I asked self-consciously, taking the do-rag off my head and smoothing out the wrinkled T-shirt I was wearing. I normally didn't let my male friends see me looking like this. "Excuse my appearance. I thought you were Izzy or Rico."

"I'm sorry to just storm in your place. I'm just angry and frustrated and I didn't know where else to go."

"What happened?"

"I just had a major run-in with my father about closing my business and becoming a full-time photographer."

"And he said . . ."

"He asked me if I was on drugs!" Taye's voice cracked. "And then told me that I needed to give myself a reality check and quit thinking like an idiot. This is my dream, Destiny! This is not about him anymore! Screw Stanford and Wall Street. I don't want to stand in the shadow of the great Aubrey Crawford anymore!"

"Taye, you need to calm down first. Maybe your father has a point and you do need to think through things a bit more."

"Destiny, you saw my work. I need to take this step in life. I see you and you aren't afraid to live. You do your thing and don't worry about what other people think. Ever since my mother died, my father's been on my back to do all these things that are really just for the sake of other people's perceptions. Go to Stanford, get every degree a black man can get, and show the establishment that you are an above-average Negro!" Taye buried his face in his hands.

I felt a tug on my heart. The years and years of pent-up aggression this man had inside was oozing from every pore. Taye had been in search of himself for a long time. Unfortunately, the moment the real Taye Crawford stepped out of the shadows, his father was waiting to crush his dreams. I felt helpless. Was this all my fault? Here I had gone and encouraged this man to go and tell his father off, quit his seven-figure gig, to become *a what?* A *photographer*! I had to fix things.

"Taye, you can't keep being unhappy. I mean, look at me. I gave up what Ainee thought was everything when I dropped out of NYU to be a promoter. She thought I had just thrown my life away. If I'd stayed, I would've been living my life for her, because she never got the chance to go to college." I placed my hand over his. "Maybe you need to show your father that you're not out just taking snapshots at children's birthday parties," I said, smiling. I had successfully gotten Taye to laugh.

"I'm glad you were home."

"You'd better be glad I didn't know it was you, or I wouldn't have let you in. Look at me. I look terrible."

"Yeah, you do look pretty bad. Did you even take a shower today?" he teased. "I'm joking. Even when you look bad, you're beautiful. Let me show you something." Taye reached into a leather satchel he had on his shoulder and pulled out a portfolio. "Check this out."

I took the book from him and slowly opened the cover. My jaw dropped. There were several photographs of me taken during an afternoon we'd spent hanging out in SoHo and at the flea market.

"These photos are great!"

"You act so surprised, like you didn't think I'd be this good. What's up with that? If I'm talking about giving up hundreds of thousands, even millions of dollars, I'd better know what I'm doing!"

Taye and I shared a laugh, but as the laughter was dying something came over both of us. He leaned in and kissed me. His lips, soft and supple, gently parted mine. This time I couldn't fight the connection. Our kisses became more intense, passion-filled, and there was electricity between our bodies. Taye pulled his shirt off, revealing his well-toned, conditioned torso. I nuzzled in his muscular, hairy chest. His crisp, clean, spicy scent filled my nostrils.

I could feel a throbbing between my legs. He pulled off my T-shirt, too, then unhooked my bra, and hungrily began sucking on my nipples. I reached into his pants and felt his thick manhood. *Yes!* I was relieved that the boy had been blessed, almost too blessed. Suddenly, insecure thoughts began to swirl in my head. If we made love, would things change? Would he still want to be my friend? Was this turning serious? We needed to slow down.

He started to unzip his pants. "Stop!" My chest was heaving. He was panting. I couldn't believe what I had just done. My body was saying yes, but my mind was confused. "Taye, this is just going to mess everything up," I said, putting my bra and T-shirt back on.

"What are you talking about, Destiny? Isn't this what we've both been wanting?" Taye leaned back. His chest glistened from the light layer of sweat he'd worked up.

"Yes, but I'm unsure about things." What the hell was I talking about? In the past I could have sex at the drop of a dime, anyplace and anytime, sometimes with total strangers. I'd definitely given it up to worse! But Taye was someone who seemed to care for me on a deeper level.

Taye released a frustrated puff of air. "It's cool if you're not attracted to me."

"No! I am," I said stopping him as he re-dressed. "Taye, I just want to figure some things out first. I don't want to blow this," I said.

"No pressure," Taye said, stuffing his portfolio back in his satchel. He kissed me on my forehead. I noticed the bulge in his pants and tried to quickly look away.

"Hey, um, wow," I mumbled, trying to downplay a creeping blush. "Look, I wanted to know if you're going to come to the Garcel party in the Hamptons. You could get some great shots there." Dammit! I keep shoving my foot farther and farther into my mouth. First, I deprive the man of a great lay, now it seems like I'm giving him a pity invitation to my party.

"Yeah, yeah, that should be cool." Taye tried to bounce back from the awkwardness of the moment, but he was doing a terrible job, too. "Destiny, I've gotta go." Taye grabbed his portfolio and bag and made a fast exit. I collapsed on the couch, sinking into the cushions.

Scenes from the Velvet Rope

Labor Day Weekend and the long-awaited Garcel party had arrived. I need a vacation desperately, but this weekend was the closest I was going to get to one for a while. The best part was that MTV had extended their twelve-million-dollar summer home to me for the entire weekend as a thank-you for pulling this shindig together.

Izzy and Rico were of course the first to pack their bags. I was happy Taye hadn't changed his mind. Chryssa and Nikki (two-thirds of the now-defunct "Girls" since the Heather debacle) were part of the gang, too. It was supposed to be a happy time, but the mood was somber. Both Jenna and DJ Peter were gone.

Luckily, my Rolodex is a mile long and I was able to get Biz Markie to spin in place of Peter, and Doug E. Fresh to make a guest appearance. Not too shabby, and Biz and Doug E.'s names made MTV even more excited. I hadn't missed a beat.

Yeah, right, that's the Destiny Day illusion!

Part of me felt empty, because Jenna and Peter had stuck it out with me in some of the leanest times, and now the company was riding high. But the *other* part wasn't about to let that part get the best of me. Before I had Jenna or DJ Peter, I was practically single-handedly pulling off major events like this Garcel party. Two monkeys don't stop a Destiny Day show, and I am not about to go back and beg for forgiveness and hang my head in shame. Hey, it is what it is. There are millions of girls out there who are waiting in line to walk in my footsteps, and DJ Peter ain't the only white boy who can spin a record!

A who's who of young and old Hollywood came out in full force to Garcel's "Single 2 Mingle" album-release party and MTV taping at the Star Room. Usher, Paris Hilton, Salma Hayek, Don Cheadle, Denzel, Cameron Diaz, Justin Timberlake, Jamie Foxx, and a slew of other million-dollar movie babies, hip-hop and rock stars were greeted with hugs and kisses from yours truly as they entered the club.

One last limo pulled up, and out stepped Garcel, who looked stunning in her Gucci dress and strappy stiletto sandals accented with Swarovski crystals. She was followed by Mama Kelly, overdone in a harsh mixture of Dior and Baby Phat. Her hair was the color of burnt straw and done up in cascading curls.

"Des-ti-nee! Hey, boo-boo!" Mama shrilled. "Listen, is the VIP setup 'cause my feet hurt already and I need a drink." Chryssa ushered them in. You could hear Biz Markie blasting on the ones and twos.

By eight o'clock, the crowd out front was out of control and the Star Room was at capacity. It always happens at these star-packed parties in the Hamptons. You've got more people on the guest list than the club can allow. I spotted Taye, Izzy, and Rico and frantically waved them over.

"I see you made it!" I said, giving Taye a big hug. I felt strange because I wanted to kiss him on the lips, but he pulled away.

"Yep, we got in about an hour ago."

"Hey, Mami! The party looks hot!" Izzy gave a round of smooches and skipped right in.

"Just breathe. It's pumpin'!" Rico gave an encouraging wink, taking Izzy by the hand.

"I hope you don't mind I put my stuff in the extra bedroom downstairs," Taye said.

"You could've put your bags in my room, Taye," I said, blushing.

"It's cool, I didn't want to assume," he said, giving me a sly reminder of how I'd shut him down the other day.

"Look, it's hectic and I've gotta get back to Garcel, but enjoy the party and I'll find you inside." Just as we were about to turn and enter the party I heard that all-too-friendly voice.

"Taye! Destiny!" Lindsay Bradley rushed over to us.

"Girl, you almost didn't make it in. The fire marshal says I'm at capacity—hurry!" I pushed her along.

"Wow, nice to see that you two kept in touch." She was hinting and I wasn't budging with the details. Neither was Taye. "Well, I'll just head over to my crew, but why don't you both meet us at Keith Riley's house after the party? He's having post-party cocktails."

Keith Riley is one of those names I can only talk about when I'm in the mood. And right now I'm not. But I will say this: Yes, we did have a fling. It was torrid, dramatic, and very very passionate. He's a major egomaniac and either we had to stop sleeping together or I was going to jail. He had too many women and thought he had more game than the Queen Gamer.

Since curiosity always gets the best of me, I wouldn't pass up making an appearance. Nothing like seeing an ex after lots of time has gone by, just to let him see that you're still fly. The last thing I want to do is go to his house alone. I guess Taye *will* actually come in handy.

Born Under a Bad Sign

The party was in full swing.

The MTV film crew was following Garcel around in Wardrobe Change Number Ten, a fuchsia, two-piece satin-and-lace hot-pants ensemble. She had the legs and abs of life. Nikki was responsible for making sure the changes went smoothly. She gave me a weary look. She was no Jenna, but she'd have to do. I shot her a nod of encouragement. Only fifteen more changes to go!

Over the next hour, Garcel dazzled the crowd in satin, silk, organza, feathers, and linen, each dress, skirt, or pair of short-shorts more elaborate than the one before.

By Wardrobe Change Number Twenty-Five, I thought I was going to have to have Nikki carried out on a stretcher. I handed her a glass of champagne and gave her the rest of the night off. Chryssa had managed to run velvet-rope interference at the front door, and we were all exhausted and feeling the Jenna void. A huge success, but with more stress than I'm prepared to handle again. I'd done my job giving *Hamptons* magazine and *InStyle* exclusive shots. Biz Markie and Doug E. Fresh took us all the way up to midnight. I was over the entire scene and anxious to get to Keith's with Taye.

● ● ●

At Keith's, a petite light-brown-skinned beauty who looked to be a mixture of black and Filipino answered the door. I heard that's his new "thing." Translation: Asian-inspired chicks. She led us through a renovated country cottage that had been turned into a chic bachelor's retreat with Moroccan flair, influenced by his travels to India and Africa.

That's one thing I could always count on with Keith—a fabulous trip to some exotic getaway. Sometimes it was as simple as a flight to the Paradise Islands in the Bahamas and barricading ourselves in a suite at the Ocean Club for the weekend. Other times, it could be Christmas in Costa Rica and a luxurious and airy treehouse-style room, seaside at the Four Seasons at Peninsula Papagayo. Five-star meals and a spa to die for.

He definitely knows how to splurge. The problem is that an arrogant attitude and a tiny penis don't mix. I know my typical attitude toward a man challenged in the manly-man area is to give him the boot without hesitation, but I admit the whole *Fabulous Life Of . . .* syndrome got to me.

Everyone was gathered in the large dining room, where Keith sat at the head of the table. About fifteen people were all sitting around having various conversations. Here it comes . . .

"Destiny, you made it! And you brought a *friend*." Keith couldn't wait to rush over and make a scene. "Damn, girl, you look good," he said, hugging me and kissing me on the neck. "Still smell like a fruit tree and shit!" Keith was being his usual facetious self. "Wassup, B?"

"Hey, man, Taye Crawford." Taye extended his hand.

"It's the Hamptons, relax!" Keith slapped Taye on the back. Taye was agitated.

"Keith, shut up and offer us a seat," I said, taking Taye's hand and leading him over to the table where the rest of the guests were seated. I knew Taye wasn't digging the scene. "We won't stay long, promise. Just one drink and we're out," I whispered.

Taye and I mingled for a few, and he found himself trapped in a conversation with another former Wall Streeter but seemed to be enjoying himself more. I found myself sipping on my third glass of wine.

"Destiny, I know your ass wants another drink," Keith smarted as he reached over to fill my wineglass, lightly brushing against my breast with his arm. One of those accidentally-on-purpose moves.

"Oops, my bad."

"Still down for the cheap thrills, huh, Keith?" I said, waving him off.

"How about you, B?" Keith lifted the bottle and nodded at Taye.

"I'll pass," Taye said, annoyed.

Keith made it a point to scoot his chair closer to mine. I scooted away, taking a healthy chug from my glass. The only way I was going to be able to tolerate this fool was to get as drunk as possible.

"Where you going, D?" Keith said, throwing an arm around my bare shoulders, pulling me toward him. I could see Taye's anger and disgust with the situation all over his face.

"Get over it. I did a *long* time ago." I sloppily slammed my hand on the table. Four glasses of a good Merlot always works. Hell, four glasses of anything will get you tipsy.

"I think we should go." Taye was perturbed.

"Me, too!" I said, spinning on my heel, following Taye out the door.

I must've passed out in the car on the drive back to the MTV house. The next thing I remember, Taye was shaking me.

"Come on out, Destiny," he said, standing with the car door open. His body was outlined by the bright porch light.

"Are we home yet?"

"Yep, and you need a bed," Taye said helping me out the car.

I put my arm over his shoulder and we quietly walked into the house. Taye helped me sit down on the couch and then immediately rushed off to the room where his bags were.

"Where the hell are you going?"

"Home," he called out from the bedroom. When he returned, a leather Coach duffle was hanging from his shoulder and he was holding a smaller leather bag. He placed them on the floor. "And I'd appreciate it if you didn't drag me around with your ignorant music-industry cronies."

"Excuse me?" I tried to get up from the couch, but I had to struggle to keep my balance.

"I'm not one of your playthings, Destiny, and I'm not a punk! You take me to some party at one of your little ex-boyfriends' houses and you treat me like I'm nobody. He was disrespectful to you and to me. The only reason why I didn't kick his short ass was because I'm more of a gentleman than that, but one more comment and it was gonna be on!"

"I don't look at you like a plaything!"

"Well, what is it? Do you not like to be treated respectfully and decently? What do you think this is, some kind of game you're playin' with me?"

"Taye, stop! Everybody in my life either dies or disappears, so I don't count on nobody or nothin'!"

"That's a messed-up way to look at things, Destiny!"

"Well, my life is messed up!"

"No, it's not your life. It's your thinking that's messed up! You're so filled with fear and hurt that you won't let anybody in. You won't let yourself be loved. I've been patient. I've swallowed my words about a lot of shit you do. Don't you see I'm trying to build a real friendship with you? I thought there was something special between us, especially after the other night in my darkroom. I guess I was wrong."

"Maybe you were! I mean, damn, here you are this straitlaced guy, and that's not my get-down. I just flow."

"What the fuck is 'flowing'?" I had never seen this side of Taye. He hardly ever cursed. As a matter of fact, I couldn't remember ever hearing him use any profanity at all. He looked at me long and hard, then picked up his bags. "Drunk isn't very becoming, either."

"Taye . . . wait a minute . . ." I had to lean against a bookshelf to stand up.

"If you just wanted a puppy to drag around, then you should've been straight up from the jump. How 'bout that's not *my* get-down. Is that enough of a flow for you? Perhaps you need to think about what you want in life. I'm out!"

I was bracing myself between the wall and the bookshelf now. The front door slammed. I wanted to run after Taye, but what would I even say?

This Bitter Earth

There are only three words that can describe me right now: PI-TI-FUL. I sat sulking at a small table in the back of The Uptown Tea Café, waiting for Josephine to finish with a customer. She walked over and carefully placed a cup of hot chai and a tiny clay teapot on the table.

"Are you going to be okay, Destiny?" She asked, patting me on the shoulder, sitting down across from me.

"I'll be fine." *So* not true. I was dying a slow death.

"I figured when the Spirit felt it was time, you'd show up. It all fell apart, didn't it?"

"Taye, Jenna, Peter . . . I don't know what to say to anybody. I just lied. I'm *not* fine. Things are terrible," I said, inhaling the soothing aroma of cloves and cardamom. "I don't know how to feel, because I've lost all feeling. I've never cried this much in my life. I'm just hollow."

"Well, my dear, I think you've finally come full circle with Destiny. Your soul is shattered and your heart is broken," Josephine said softly, pouring a cup of tea for herself.

"I never told you some things because the time never seemed to be quite right. But another reason why I always felt a connection with you, Destiny, is because I see pieces of me in you. I remember about twenty years ago I found myself standing at a crossroads. I had been on a very dark journey most of my life and it was the death of my fourth husband, Mario, and a baby that made me realize that I could either begin a healing process, spiritually and physically, from self-inflicted degradation and emotional pain or die.

"I don't mean death of the flesh, but death of the soul. Did I want to continue to flounder through life aimlessly? I was drifting between failed marriages. I had been the abuser in all of them. I had become this bird confined to the ground, using my legs to get around, unaware of the Glory above. I had never given myself a chance to discover that I had beautiful wings to fly.

"Mario's death and losing my child happened at the culmination of my addiction to alcohol, drugs, and a very negative lifestyle. When he died, I didn't have any direction. Mario loved me, but I didn't know how to accept his loving me, even though he'd accepted my alcoholism. I'd only had one really good friend, and I abused her, too, so she was gone. I never bothered to let anybody else in.

"I was alone. I was stuck. I didn't remember the skills I used to have. I was just sitting in the first café I ever owned and the bills were piling up. That's when I gave it all up, sold the place, and moved back home to Louisiana for five years. That five-year sojourn reintroduced God to my life. But God being in your life isn't the same for everybody. For some it's going to church, for others it's just finding a connection. Could be on a park bench, or even at the Fairway."

We shared a laugh.

"See, Destiny, I had to develop my own relationship with Him, and I did ultimately find peace and solace in meditation. But honey, before that, I had false courage. Alcohol will do that to you. It helped me lock away all my feelings of abandonment by my own mother and father. When I got back to Baton Rouge, the first stop I made was at my grandmother's grave. She had raised me, and maybe that was all I needed, just to be back to where it all began. I then went and made peace at both my mother and father's graves.

"I eventually kicked the drinking altogether, got into exercising, and could finally see that ray of hope peeking though the dark curtain that was being lifted. I was shedding my selfish and egotistical ways. Through the power of prayer I let go of my anger, hurt, and disappointment. I had been delivered.

"But Destiny, becoming whole and holy is a process, and one that only you can take on. I am telling you that it's time you began to let go of that embedded fear of love and self-acceptance. That boy might just be the angel God placed on your doorstep."

Her words echoed in my head . . .

"That boy might just be the angel God placed on your doorstep."

● ● ●

When I got back to my apartment, Izzy was in the kitchen sorting through bags of groceries, mostly fresh fruits and vegetables.

"Girl, where are you going with all this food?"

"To my *abuela*'s. I'm gonna spend some time over there and give you a break."

"You sure? You don't have to. *Mi casa es su casa*."

"No, I need to do this. She's gettin' older and I think she really needs me righ' now. Plus, I was readin' up on AIDS, an' even though there's no cure for it yet, I can tell Carmen about some herbal teas

247

and good vitamins and vegetables like garlic, soybeans, shiitake mushrooms, and a lotta otha' stuff I can't pronounce. Here it is, Ma," she said, handing me a thick book on natural healing. "Oh, and speaking of the whole *mi casa es su casa* thing, I got fired from La Familia because I couldn't speak Spanish."

"Girl, I told you!"

"Yeah, I know, and I fired my agent, too!"

We let out a round of laughter, but as it began to die, Izzy's facial expression turned more serious.

"On the real, Mami, we gotta talk about something else, too."

"What's up, girl? Are you okay?"

"I'm pregnant, and before you ask, yes, it's D-Roc's."

"What are you going to do?"

"I'm definitely gonna keep it. I'm too old to do anything else."

"Wow, we're gonna have a baby!" We hugged. "How far along are you?"

"About six weeks."

"How do you feel?"

"Damn, you gotta lotta questions, Ma! I'm excited. And I've been thinking about my life a lot lately. I know I've got to make some changes. I don't even know how to begin, but I'm *not* tellin' D-Roc. I just need to try to build a healthy life for my baby and me."

"He has a right to know, Iz."

"Ma, it ain't like me and D-Roc are gonna to be together. So you gotta just respect how I feel."

"I don't agree, but I got your back, girlie."

"I also been thinkin' about Carmen. I don't think I can be a good mother until I at least work some things out with her. But it's got to be on my terms, and my *abuela* understan's tha's what I want. So I'm outta here. I'll call you later and see you in a few days."

Izzy trekked out the door with four large bags from Whole Foods. It seemed like she just grew up overnight. I was excited about the baby, but I gotta be honest, my girl needed a baby like she needed a hole in her head, but she didn't have a choice now. Hell, *we* don't always have a choice.

It was really going to take a village to pull this one off. But this baby didn't ask to come here, and we'd better make damn sure that between the both of us, he or she has a *real* chance to know what *real* love is in this world.

Disk Seven

Body and Soul

{1} IT SEEMS TO HANG ON

{2} YOU ARE MY FRIEND

{3} REAL LOVE

{4} GO AWAY LITTLE BOY

{5} SIGNED, SEALED, DELIVERED I'M YOURS

{6} LOVE AND HAPPINESS

It Seems to Hang On

I stood outside Taye's door, nervous and awkward, just as I was that first day I set foot in his building. I took several deep breaths and contemplated making a mad dash for the elevator. My palms were sweaty, my stomach did a light dance, and my heart pounded so loudly my brain was shouting for it to shut up. I closed my eyes tightly and started to practice my lines in my head. Before I could rehearse them well, Taye had opened the door. He was wearing a faded Stanford T-shirt and jeans and was barefoot. He looked unshaven, but still as fine as ever.

Taye invited me in, but not before giving me one of his much-missed hugs. I buried my face in his chest and inhaled. I wanted his scent to soak into my skin so I could carry it with me every day. My steps were cautious as we made our way over to the sofa. He offered me something to drink. I passed. A bad case of nerves had me parched, but I didn't want to waste another minute.

"I came to tell you that I'm sorry and I didn't mean to hurt you." My heart was pounding. Taye just sat there. He sat, and sat, and sat for what seemed to be an eternity.

"Don't you have anything to say?" I said sharply. I began to tremble. Dammit! My stupid ego was showing out. The last thing I needed to do was come over here and blow it again.

"Destiny," Taye reached for my hand and placed it in his. I think I stopped breathing around this time. "I really care deeply for you," he said. "I don't think I've ever felt this way about anyone in my entire thirty-six years. Your spirit, fire, and energy woke me up, and I'm so thankful for that. I'm at a place in my life where I want a lifelong companion, a best friend, a lover . . ."

I was starting to regain consciousness.

"You are intense, insightful, and undoubtedly the most incredible woman I've ever met." Taye flashed me a spine-tingling smile and then gave me the most sensuous, orgasmic kiss ever. He slowly pulled back. I could still feel the impression of his lips on mine. He cleared his throat and turned away.

"What's wrong?" I said.

"I just came to the realization that in the end, we're just not compatible."

I placed my hand over my mouth as if putting it there was going to keep my face intact. I stopped breathing again. I felt like I was cracking into a million pieces inside.

"But you're the one. The keeper that Josephine told me about!" I wasn't making any sense to him.

"I want so much for you. I want you to be happy, Destiny. It's just too late."

"But I can be happy with you. It's never too late."

"It's not you. It's me. I've decided to step out on faith and do my thing, like you've always suggested. I've merged my firm with a larger company, and I'll still consult every now and then, but it's going to be all about me and my camera from now on."

I felt those God-awful tears filling up inside my head, ready to overflow, but I had to kick Emotional Destiny to the curb and get it together.

"I— I— think this is great . . . really great news," I said, clearing the lump lodged in my throat. Trying my best to play the role of the good sport.

"Yeah, it is. My father has no choice but to deal with it now. The contracts are signed. I'm also getting an award and a grant from the Museum of the African Diaspora for my photography work next Friday night in San Francisco. Maybe a change of scenery after that. Hey, I'm even considering Paris for a while."

I was wearing the heck out of the biggest, fakest happy-go-lucky face on the planet, nodding my head in agreement, even giggling a few times. After Taye finished laying out his big plans to move forward in life without Destiny, he offered to walk me out. I passed. He didn't need to waste any more time with me.

I held it in really well, all the way out of his building, down the elevator, back to my car. But something happened when I got in and closed the door. A moan buried deep in the crevices of my bones came bellowing out. Between the howling and hollering and weeping and wailing, and howling and hollering again, I was suddenly the main attraction on the block.

I was an alarming sight even for New Yorkers who are immune to the insanity running rampant up and down the streets of Manhattan. A gawking passerby didn't know whether to call the cops or the nuthouse. I could see the headline on Page Six in the *Post* tomorrow: THE PARTY'S OVER! DUMPED "IT GIRL" HAS NERVOUS BREAKDOWN.

I just wanted to snap my fingers and make everything shiny and sweet again . . .

You Are My Friend

Rico asked me to come to the store. He sounded excited and said he had a surprise for me. I'm glad one of us was feeling happy about life. When I got there, Izzy was already inside. The store was closed. They greeted me with hugs and kisses. They had been doing a lot of that lately. I think they just felt sorry for me. In the middle of the laughs, there was a knock on the window. All eyes shifted to me.

"Go open it," he said, giving me an encouraging nod.

I turned around and saw Jenna and Peter on the other side of the glass door. A smile crept over my face. I opened the door and without saying a word threw my arms around both of them. The only thing better than seeing them would be seeing Taye. I took them each by the hand and didn't waste any time with the apologies.

"I'm not very good at doing this kind of thing, but I want you both to know that I was a jerk. It's been miserable without you and I don't ever want to lose either of you again." It took all my strength to get those words out. My eyes welled up with tears.

"We forgive you!" Jenna said, looking to Peter for assurance.

"I know I've been selfish, and I'm asking for another chance, Peter."

"Yo, I came here because Jenna said it was the right thing to do. I'll come back, but you've got to promise to get behind my music." Peter wasn't giving in that easily, but whatever I needed to do to show both of them things would be better this time, that's what I intended to do.

"You've got my word, starting right now!"

"Bet, and, um, another thing: I don't want to mix the whole business-and-pleasure thing anymore. I'm feelin' Jenna and I wanna do right." Peter glanced over at Jenna for assurance this time.

Jenna and Peter had my blessing and we were like one big happy family all over again. But Rico wasn't done.

"It's showtime!" He directed everyone to a cleared area of the store, where an easel covered in black cloth stood.

"I know it's taken me a lifetime to finally do this, but I did it, and I couldn't have done it without my fabulous model, Izzy, and the loving support of you, Destiny . . ." Rico choked up. Since I had turned into Weepy Woman lately, tears had started to form in my eyes, too.

"Destiny, you're like the glue that keeps us all together, and without your strength I wouldn't have completed this. You inspire me!" Tears were streaming down Rico's face, and he unveiled his long-awaited book. The next thing you know, Izzy had joined in the tear-fest.

"Can we get this celebration started, please?" Rico said. He cracked open a bottle of champagne and poured everyone a round except Izzy, who was drinking sparkling cider. We flipped through page after page of Rico's book. His work was so good you'd have thought he was beatin' faces for the top magazines already. He had Izzy looking like she was straight off the pages of *Italian Vogue*.

There was another knock on the glass. "Rico, you've got a customer!" Izzy called out. We all still had our faces stuck in Rico's book.

"Chile, whoever it is better come back, we are clo—" Rico stopped dead in his tracks. "Oh, there is a God!"

Rico rushed to the door and unlocked it. His hands were trembling. The door flew open and standing there was Tyra Banks in the flesh. We were all speechless.

"Thank you for lettin' me in. I'm desperate and I need makeup! And MAC is closed." She was a frantic hot mess. "My makeup artist missed her flight, and I left my makeup bag on the plane, and I'm running late for a major press event at President Clinton's office down the street!" She had gotten all that out in one breath.

"Rico, this is your time to shine," I said, whispering in his ear.

"Chile, you betta breathe and come get in this chair, girl!" Rico ran into the back to get his kit. He almost couldn't believe what he'd just gotten himself into, but he held his own, and did a helluva job selling himself, too. "This is my new book, and I'm comin' for whoever you got workin' for you. I live for you, Tyra!" Rico was on a roll.

Twenty minutes later, Rico had transformed Tyra into a red-carpet goddess. Boyfriend had saved the day. Tyra was wowed, and she hired him on the spot to be one of the makeup artists on her new reality series, *Runaway Runway*, a follow-up to her hit show, *America's Next Top Model*. It follows the top-model winners as they strut their stuff on the runways all over the world, and ultimately hit the runway during New York's Fashion Week at Seventh on Sixth in Bryant Park.

"Can you be ready to leave for Paris in two weeks?" Tyra asked.

"What! Baby, I can be ready to leave tomorrow!"

Tyra was barely outside when the room erupted into screams.

After several minutes of jumping around and shouting with joy, we calmed down—only for a moment, and then we started up all over again. I made another announcement.

"Guys, I'm gonna take a break for a while." Everyone sighed in disappointment. "I didn't say I was shutting down. You know I gots ta get paid!" I gave a sistagirl two-snaps and a circle.

"Hello!" Rico shouted.

"I think Jenna is fully capable of handling things for a while. I know she'll be busy setting up meetings for Peter and all," I gave him a wink. Jenna and Peter were elated. "But I think she's ready. And I'll still be around. Don't get it twisted! The sign still says Destiny Day Productions!" Izzy topped us all off with another round of bubbly and poured herself another glass of sparkling cider. We'd be celebrating all night.

Real Love

Despite Taye's heartbreaking news just two days earlier, I didn't have time to be depressed. Destiny Day had a business to run and a pregnant best friend who desperately needed her. I guess in a city like New York there's always too much drama swirling around to keep you from crying your eyeballs out longer than ten minutes.

After a wake-up phone call from Josephine telling me I'd better "Kick the Devil in his ass and get a move on," I agreed to tuck my tears away for the day. Izzy and I got dressed, picked up a stack of books on parenting and motherhood from our neighborhood black bookstore, and made it to The Uptown Tea Café just in time for lunch.

Josephine was just the inspiration I needed to start building my village. I'd say we were off to a great start with some of Josephine's food for the mind, and some healthy sandwiches and salads for the body. That Spirit she's always talking about must've been operating in overdrive.

"You have some work to do on yourself, Isabelle," Josephine said, calling the tribal session to order. "But I'm proud that you're taking the steps now while that baby's growing inside of you instead of bringing another child into this corrupt world, unbound by love, only to be sucked into the same type of pain we all know too well. It's time to break the cycle!" Josephine preached to a wide-eyed Izzy who was soaking in each word like a thirsty sponge. We tapped our teacups in agreement.

"You know, sometimes we can be our own worst enemies, but now God can open the door," Josephine continued. "He can give us the ammunition, but it's up to us to fight the good fight! What I'm saying to you both is that it's time for everyone to get quiet in the stillness of our spirits and focus on walking away from negativity for good.

"Focus on walking away from loveless relationships for good. Focus on expanding and generating new and innovative thoughts!" Josephine's words had both Izzy *and* me paying attention and nodding like five-year-olds.

"You may not see it right now, but the Spirit spoke to me and I'm seeing a change in the air. You are both beautiful and strong women, but you've been hitting a wall and feeling lost. You've got to dust off your faith, and if you don't have any you'd better get some real quick! God wants us to be surefooted and forthright with what we want and what we need. Haven't you ever heard of 'ask and ye shall receive'?

"Well, my dearies, it's time to speak it, or better yet, put what you want in writing to God! 'Cause babies, I don't know about the Easter Bunny or Santa Claus, but my God is real! I know you're tired of disappointment, tired of the struggle for love in your personal lives. Tired but don't know where to turn. When it gets this bad, you've got to turn to your faith, and get with God and the person looking back at you in the mirror!"

It was time for me and Izzy to get our minds, our hearts, our spirits, and our faith right. I think our village tribunal with Josephine had turned into more of a "Come to Jesus" meeting. There wasn't a dry eye at the table, and Izzy and I were both ready and willing for God to release the chokehold of life that we'd gotten ourselves tangled up in.

However, I don't think either one of us was ready to go sign up at the corner church, put on our white robes, and go get baptized in the Hudson River. Going to church for me right now might be right here at The Uptown Tea Café, it might be the Fairway, or it might just be at First A.M.E. down the block. Change is a process, but the first step is opening up your spirit, and I am more than willing to do that. I've got a lot of issues that I've got to deal with *and* work on, and I know Izzy does, too.

When Izzy and I got back to my apartment, we started on our own housekeeping. She got online and looked up all the free programs for mothers-to-be, and tons of prenatal- and post-natal–care information. Then we did like Josephine suggested and got out two sheets of blank paper and wrote down all the things we wanted in life and love and addressed them to God.

"I been thinkin' about everythin', Des. I wasn't going to tell D-Roc at first, but I thought about it, and he needs to know he's going to have a child."

"I'm happy you're making the right decision, Iz."

"*But*, I'm not tryin' to, like, he wit' him like that. Me an' him got bad blood. I don' need to be fightin' no more over a man, either. I jus' wanna do the right thing wit' my baby. I don' want her growin' up not knowin' who her daddy is, or that she got one. I don' want her growin' up angry at me 'cause I never told her the truth!" Izzy was making more and more sense every day.

"I think it will all work itself out in time, girl!"

We sealed our letters to God in two envelopes, and I placed mine in an old Bible Ainee had given me. Izzy had managed to keep up with one her *abuela* gave her. It was in Spanish, but it would suffice for now. We made a pact that we'd reopen them in a year. One never knows what could happen . . .

After Izzy left, I knew I had to take care of one more thing today. I picked up the phone and called the two most important people in my life, Ainee and Uncle Charlie. I hadn't been calling home or returning Ainee's calls, and when we did talk, I'd been rushing off the phone. I was finally seeing how life's twists and turns can toss you the unexpected, and I didn't want to lose anybody else and be left with a lapful of regrets. She answered on the first ring . . .

"Ainee, I know it's been a while, but I just felt like I needed to call home and tell you and Uncle Charlie how much I love you . . ."

Go Away Little Boy

I woke up this morning in a panic. Taye was getting his award tonight in San Francisco and off to start a new life halfway across the world after that. I couldn't let him get away. I had to make one last effort. Damn! I was in desperate need of another pep talk from Josephine. When I got to the café, it was closed. A small sign on the door said, BE BACK IN AN HOUR, OUT FOR THERAPY. I knew she could only be at one place. Fairway. A gypsy cab had just rolled to a stop in front of the café. I jumped in and we sped away.

It had to be the busiest day in shopping history. I barreled my way through the throngs of people picking out fresh fruits and vegetables, calling out Josephine's name like a maniac. I finally found her.

"Good Lord, Destiny, what is wrong with you?" Josephine said, whipping around from the self-serve coffee stand, where she was re-filling her cup.

"I can't let Taye get away! He's getting an award in San Francisco tonight and then he's leaving for Paris!" I was out of breath and panting. Josephine just started to laugh.

"This is not a joke. I need your help. I think I'm in love with this man!" I almost swallowed my tongue saying those words.

"Don't tell me the woman with the heart of steel has joined the rest of the human race?" Josephine continued to laugh.

"I understand now what you meant when you said Mr. Sanchez was a keeper, and I made up my mind I don't want to be that lab rat or that piece of moldy cheese." Now I was confusing Josephine.

"Destiny, slow down." She pulled me close. "If a person wants goodness in their life, they have to really open their spirit up to good-ness. Are you ready to do that for real? Because Taye doesn't deserve to get messed around like your old boytoys."

"I think I'm ready. I'm just worried, because he already turned me away. What if I show all my vulnerability, and I get rejected again?"

"You'll never know, now, will you? Why don't you give yourself a chance to be open to love? Let go and let God. Give up the control for a change and see what happens. Can you allow yourself a chance to be loved?"

"I can certainly try."

"Then what are you standing in the Fairway wasting away for? Don't you have a flight to catch? You'd better go get that man!"

Rico called the airline and booked me a nonstop flight out of JFK to San Francisco. I had exactly one hour to pull it together. I was rush-ing around the apartment throwing shoes and underwear and everything but the kitchen sink into an overnight bag. Rico and Izzy would be here any minute to take me to the airport.

The bell rang, and I automatically pressed the buzzer. There was a soft knock at the door.

"It's open," I yelled, stressing over what jacket to carry onto the plane.

I walked out of my bedroom and Malik was standing in the middle of the living room.

"Did I come at a bad time?" he said, taking off his baseball cap and turning it to the back.

"I've gotta catch a flight," I said gripping the handles of my Louis Vuitton duffle tighter, as if doing that was going to help me stand my ground with Malik.

"I heard you're seeing somebody else."

"Is that what you came here to ask me?" I smarted.

"I brought you something." Malik pulled a tiny square box out of his jacket pocket. I swallowed hard. My heart started beating fast. I put my bag down. "Remember I promised to make up for missing your party that night at the studio?"

I took the box from his hands and opened it. A magnificent diamond pendant covered in pavé diamonds, hanging from a platinum chain, sparkled at me.

"Oh, my God!" I screeched excitedly.

"I thought you might like it, and it would look good on you." He cleared his throat. "This is for you, too." He handed me an envelope. Inside was a check for fifty thousand dollars. "I'm sorry I had to just break out like that on you, but things got really bad. I came out of it though—finally finished the Freedom record, and got a label deal through Sony."

"Thanks for paying me back. I should make your ass give me interest."

"You're so crazy." Malik flashed a smile then cleared his throat. "Destiny, I know you're seeing some cat, but he ain't me and we got history. I could see myself falling in love, getting married, the whole nine, one day. But right now the timing just isn't right. I just need to have you with me helpin' me to build."

My buzzer rang. I knew it was my ride to the airport. I had a choice. I could either relent and fall right back into the old Destiny, running on that wheel or being the moldy cheese dangling from the string, or I could live up to my name. I had momentarily gotten thrown off by the bling. I closed the box and handed it back to Malik.

"You know what, Malik? it's not even about all that stuff you just rattled off. It's about treating me like a friend. Having some consideration and decency for my time and my feelings. The really disappointing part is that I've been so caught up in myself for so long, I didn't even see how ludicrous the whole situation was between us until after you left. I needed that wake-up call."

"I thought you wanted to just flow?"

"Somehow flowing sounds very *unappealing* and *unsavory* to me right now. I'm not into flowing anymore and I'm just not that into you."

"I know shit's been crazy. I'm just trying to get this album out."

Malik leaned in and kissed me, and I got scared. Did I still feel something for him? I felt myself being pulled in, and I liked it. I missed his smile, his teeth, that . . . *sniiiiiifff* . . . that Irish-Spring-clean smell. His masculine thang.

"Shit's just been crazy, but I miss you, Mama. Who's this cat that's been up in my nookie?" Malik whispered.

What? Had I just heard him correctly? I pulled away from him. This man didn't know anything about me. He didn't know my favorite song, or color, or food. He didn't know what my dreams were. He didn't know because he never bothered to ask.

"I've gotta go, Malik, and so do you. The situation isn't healthy for either of us."

I picked up my bag and left Malik standing in my living room. I had a flight to catch and a man in San Francisco to get to.

Signed, Sealed, Delivered
I'm Yours

I'd endured a nerve-wracking six-hour flight, sitting in the back of the plane on the last seat available, next to a screaming sick baby, but it was worth the agony. I'd miraculously made it to San Francisco in one piece.

I was determined to show Taye that I loved him, and I was willing to open up my spirit and let all the goodness come that I deserved. I checked into a cheap hotel, showered, and dressed, all in time to make it to Taye's award ceremony. This letting-go-and-letting-God take-over idea was something I had been needing in my life. When all this was over, me and God were overdue for a good long conversation.

The taxi was moving in slow motion. "How far is the museum from here, sir?" I didn't want to flip out on the driver. That would only piss him off and make him drive even slower.

"A few more blocks, ma'am."

"That's what you said a few blocks ago." My attitude was about to show its ugly head if this taxi driver didn't get me to my destination fast.

Finally we made it! I bolted up the steps and through the doors of the Museum of the African Diaspora as fast as I could in four-inch heels. I walked slowly into the main gallery, where a large crowd of distinguished-looking men and women in tuxes and evening gowns had gathered. Gordon Parks was standing next to Taye. The MC introduced Taye, and as the audience clapped I began to walk forward. A series of photographs were hanging from the ceiling.

"Someone once told me that music was her life, and that without it she'd lose her mind . . ." Hearing Taye's voice gave me a case of the jitters. I can't believe he remembered what I told him. All of a sudden I wondered if coming here was a rash decision. I hope this man doesn't just go all the way off on me. What if he's here with a date? Then I'll really be mad and ready to pull an Izzy. I took a deep breath and stepped through the crowd. Taye spotted me and his eyes lit up.

"Her exact words were, 'It gets under my skin, pumps through my veins. It's that high that I can't get enough of.' Music can indeed inspire, uplift, and unfurl a person's deepest desires. So, ladies and gentlemen, thank you for this award, and without further ado, I present to you my work-in-progress composition, 'Last Night a DJ Saved My Life.' "

The audience cheered. Taye strode off the stage, and right into my arms.

"I love you, Taye Crawford," I said, staring deep into his eyes.

"I love you, too, Destiny Day!"

Taye planted his soft lips on mine and kissed me deeply with all the emotion he had inside. Spontaneity was never so sweet . . . My Chéri Amour!

Dear Izzy,

Love has taken full bloom in Paris. I left New York a week ago with two pair of underwear, a toothbrush, a pair of jeans, sneakers, a pair of Jimmy Choos, and a dress. Now I'm halfway around the world, but who needs clothes when you're in love?

We are living large, girlfriend, at the fabulous Hôtel Plaza Athénée. I danced and drank champagne all night. I can see the Eiffel Tower from my balcony and it all feels so glamorous.

Today we took a cruise on the Seine, and yesterday we shopped at both Galleries Lafayette. Tomorrow I'll visit the Champs-Élysées and walk through the Louvre. Each morning I have tea with croissants and brioches at a cute sidewalk café, while Taye takes more pictures. He's been inspired to do his next exhibit. I am loving this man! Together we plan on conquering all corners of Paris: Île St.-Louis, Tuileries Quartier, the Marais, Beaubourg, and Les Halles.

Enough about me, I bet your belly's getting big. Scrap that, you've got those genes women commit murder for—I bet you don't even look five months pregnant. I miss you, Rico, Josephine, Jenna, and Peter madly. I hear Rico's in Italy. I'm sure he's turnin' it! See you soon.

Love, Des

After a romantic dinner at Le Regence, inside the Plaza Athénée, Taye guided me out to the ivy-decked terrace for a moonlight stroll. An older Parisian couple, also admiring the night, walked past us.

"Look at them. Wow, that's how I wanna be with my wife. Grow old, still in love . . ."

"Still sexy!"

"Yeah, man! That's what it's all about. Gotta keep that love thang goin'."

"You never told me how your parents met, Taye."

"My mother went to Spelman and my father went to Morehouse. They met at a Greek party, fell in love, and the rest is yours truly."

"That sounds like something out of a classic love story."

"Tell me more about your parents, Destiny."

"The story isn't as sweet as yours. I mean, our lives are so different."

"Listen, Destiny, I'm never going to judge you, and I just ask that you do the same," Taye said, lifting my chin gently with his hand. "I love you unconditionally, everything about you, the good, the bad, the ugly, even your breath in the morning." We shared a laugh. "So who is the real Juanita Day? And what about Carlton Day? They say little girls go after men who are like their fathers."

"I'd agree with that last one. Carlton was a good-hearted man, and fine, too, just like you! He couldn't help it that he fell in love with the wrong woman." I took a deep breath and slowly let it out. "My mother Juanita was a trip. She was one of those high-yella sistas who would be ready to throw down if you *ever* made the mistake of thinking she was anything other than a *real*, soul-sista, number one. She had a body like Pam Grier's and Jayne Kennedy's packed into one.

"She'd be moving so fast, shaking her butt and tossing her hair like she was in the Ike and Tina revue. One minute she'd be serving a drink, the next, seducing a loyal patron with her electrifying moves. And when she felt like it, she might even jump on the turntables and play some records if the dj was playing something 'jive'!"

"Damn, your daddy was lucky."

"That's exactly how she got my daddy. She trapped him with that good lovin'. Got 'em every time." Taye and I laughed some more. "I think my controlling thing is definitely *all* Juanita. That woman used to have men fawning over her, *especially* the high rollers, but for some reason she noticed Carlton.

"I think it was his boyish smile that was so perfectly pearly you could stare at it for hours. Carlton Day was just a simple Midwestern boy from a good A.M.E family. He was fresh out of college and new to East St. Louis, and as green and wet-behind-the-ears as he wanted to be.

"Juanita told me she put on Al Green's, 'I Can't Get Next To You' and practically forced her good stuff on him. She had that college boy so whipped he couldn't see it coming. He was hooked and determined to get her."

I slipped deeper into the story that Juanita once boasted about during one of her drinking-and-doping binges. "She said it would be brick-cold winter and Carlton would wait in ten inches of snow until four or five in the morning, when she got off work. He'd say, 'Juanita, come on, girl, let me take you away from all this!' Then she'd say, 'Negro, please, this is my life. You need to go on home to yo mama and find you some nice simple girl.'

"Carlton would watch her dancing all up on other men. His partners thought he was crazy. *'Man, she like a wild tiger. You can't tame her!'* But Carlton didn't want to tame Juanita. He just wanted to love her."

Taye held me closer. "One day she just said yes. I'm pretty sure it was because she was on the outs with this sugar daddy named Teddy she was always on-again-off-again with. But Carlton never tried to change her. I imagine there was a whole lot of that good old sweaty, back-clawing lovemaking going on, too.

"When Juanita got pregnant, she wasn't happy, but Carlton was ecstatic. He didn't care if it was, as my Granny said, 'right by God.' He just wanted to be with her. At least she slowed down on the drinking during her pregnancy. I think she realized she was too vain to have a messed-up baby.

"After twenty-two hours of labor, I made my debut on the first day of the New Year. Juanita was pissed off because she'd missed the big New Year's Eve jam at the Belly Room. Carlton said Juanita couldn't take her eyes off me. I think she was just shocked that I'd actually come out of her.

"They eventually went to the Justice of the Peace, made it official, and Juanita tried her best, but after just a week of having me on the tittie, she was O-V-A-H it! It was back to business at the Belly Room in her high heels, a micro-mini, and that brick-house, back-breakin' body, like she'd never even thought about having a baby. She was tossin' back shots of Jack to 'Let's Stay Together' all over again. She couldn't wait to show me off and show me the ropes, either."

When I was finished telling what turned out to be a pretty good story, Taye leaned in to kiss me.

"What was that for?" I asked.

"Just because I love you. And you know what else? I think Carlton fell in love with the *right* woman. Now, c'mon, Destiny girl, let me take you away from all this!"

● ● ●

Taye stretched my naked body out gently on the hotel's large antique bed. The French doors to our balcony were open, and a light breeze brushed over my skin. Then he spread my legs open wide, kissing me from my toes, up my calves, around my knee caps, over my thighs, in between the walls of my sweetness, up to my belly, around my belly button, up to my breasts, and brushed each nipple lightly with his tongue. My baby had some tricks, and tonight I didn't care if all of Paris could see us.

Our eyes locked. I was with the man who had saved my spirit and helped me set my dreams free. Taye thrust himself deeper and deeper, slowly, steadily, inside me. He pressed his lips gently against mine. I wrapped my legs around his back, as he gyrated gently. Then he started all over again, stroking, licking, and kissing every inch of my body and then some . . . here and here and here and here and there and there and *here* . . . Taye had discovered my spot and all the nooks and crannies in between to get there, tasting and touching, tickling and teasing.

I know we were in Paris, but a brotha was working it so good he had a sista wanting to take it all the way back to Alabama, real country-folk style, and cook him up one of those good soul-food meals with collards, fried chicken, black-eyed peas, cornbread, sweet potatoes, fish and grits, *and* peach cobbler. I was ready to throw down buck naked and barefoot for this man after all that good loving. And like I was a freshly changed, fed, and burped baby, Taye put a sista to bed.

● ● ●

Juanita visited me in my dreams that night. She couldn't believe I'd come all the way to Paris for a man.

"You really in love, Destiny aren't you?" Juanita said, pouring us a round of drinks.

"I really am, Juanita. We talk about our dreams, our fears, and we laugh together."

"I always wanted that."

"You could have that with Carlton, but you keep fighting happiness like I used to."

"Humph, ain't that some shit, *you* tellin' *me* about love." We burst into laughter.

I hadn't seen her laugh that hard in a long time.

"Wait a minute, that's my song playin'." Juanita closed her eyes and began to sway and snap her fingers. "Can you hear it? It's a song just for you, Destiny, 'The Makings of You.' I love me some Gladys Knight and the Pips. She's singing it just for you, too. C'mon, dance with me, Destiny. I can't find Carlton's old jive ass." She took both of my hands in hers. "Quit actin' so shy." I followed her lead and started swaying side to side. "Aw, that's it, now you feelin' it."

"The song is beautiful, but why does it sound so sad?"

"It's not sad, it's just soulful. Anyway, you'd better go. Sweet's gonna be here soon, and I've got some business to handle with him."

"Wait, can you give me a sign, or a message, or something? Taye is a very special man, and I don't want to mess it up this time."

"Yeah, I've got a message for you: Live your life for you, and don't end up like me. Now go on."

"Can I come back?"

"Anytime you want, Destiny. Good night, baby."

Love and Happiness

Paris opened a chapter in life for me, and by the following March (six months and fourteen hours of labor later to be exact), Izzy had delivered a healthy baby girl and named her Journey. The moment Izzy laid eyes on her, she said that baby's journey in life would be filled with love and happiness. As her godmother, I plan on making sure life for Journey is full of everything—as Josephine calls it—"sweet and shiny."

I also decided that I needed to start practicing what I preached. What's the sense in stackin' all that paper and not doing something productive with it? I found a nice little spot right here in Harlem and plopped down a fat check on the down payment. There's even an apartment available in the building for Izzy and Journey.

Welcome to my new club—Belly!

You know I had to give a shout-out to Juanita and Carlton Day. And of course I had to give my girl Izzy a hostess gig, because Lord knows Journey's gotta eat. Jenna's my new manager, and Nikki and Chryssa are working the floor. DJ Peter, well, Jenna and I agreed to co-manage him. He got a phat deal over at Def Jam Records, and his first single should be droppin' soon. Every now and then he agrees to drop in and guest-dj. Like tonight, DJ Peter was just getting started, giving the crowd a variety of Marvin, the O'Jays, and the Isleys.

"I want to thank everyone for coming out to my new club, and tonight I want to introduce Taye Crawford, one of New York's premiere photographers, and his award-winning exhibit, now completed. I'll let the music tell the story!" Josephine and Abraham Paul were in the front row, cheering me on. I blew Taye a kiss.

Just as the unveiling was about to take place, Taye stopped all the action and grabbed the mic.

"I'm sorry for busting up the show and all, but I have a little surprise for Destiny, the woman who showed me that true love can stand the test of time just like a great song."

Suddenly, Rico walked in with Ainee on one side and Uncle Charlie on the other. I ran as fast as Gucci would allow me to, threw my arms around Ainee, and inhaled her scent of fresh gardenia. Tears poured out of my eyes. This was their first trip ever to New York City. They had proud looks on their faces. I know Ainee had put on her "good" dress for this one. Uncle Charlie still looked spry, with his short silver 'fro and dark skin. He was clean in his tweed three-piece, suspenders, and wing-tips.

Ainee looked petite and dainty. Although she had wrinkles around her mouth and eyes, and almost a full head of silver strands, you could tell she had been one of those redbone beauties back in the day. I closed my eyes and remembered how she used to starch and iron my dress for church in the kitchen while Uncle Charlie shined my patent-leather shoes.

We all got dressed in our Sunday best—Ainee in that big church hat and gloves, Uncle Charlie in his suit, and me in my eyelet-and-organza dress. When I'd get sleepy during the sermon, she'd let me lie in her lap, and I could smell that gardenia all in her dress. I did have a family, and roots, and I was loved.

DJ Peter dropped the needle on Indeep's classic disco track, "Last Night a DJ Saved My Life" (that's right, he took it way back on wax, to punctuate Taye's unveiling of his collection of photographs that were presented in San Francisco). There were the various shots of me dancing and working the room at different clubs around town.

However, on a deeper level, Taye had captured my evolution from the old Destiny, callous and unhappy, to the new Destiny, who was liberated and overflowing with goodness. A dj had indeed saved my life from a broken heart with a song! A song with a melody so memorable and lyrics so meaningful that it speaks to every fiber of my soul—all the heartache, the joy, the laughter, *and* the love.

Taye's photographs were a hit. I grabbed a glass of bubbly and gave DJ Peter the go-ahead to take it up a notch with "The Boss," by the boss herself, Miss Ross. I grabbed Taye's hand and he grabbed Ainee's. Uncle Charlie was right behind, followed by Josephine, Abraham Paul, Izzy with little Journey in her arms, Jenna, Nikki, and Chryssa. I was "turnin' it," as Rico would say, getting the crowd going with every black family reunion's favorite, the Electric Slide.

We laughed and danced the night away, keeping Ainee and Uncle Charlie up well past their bedtime. Just when you think love can't happen to you, it has a way of proving you wrong. And you'd better answer the call when it comes, because as Josephine would say, "You only go around once on this earth!" I did find a moment alone to stand back and watch the crowd from the dj's booth. I closed my eyes, and I could see Juanita and Carlton out there in the middle of the floor doing a slow drag. Carlton whispered in her ear, and a smile crept across Juanita's face so big she started to laugh. She was finally happy.

After the Dance

I knew, the moment we bonded over Whodini, that Taye Crawford was the one for me. The pain and fear from my past that I struggled with most of my life tried to make me believe otherwise—think I wasn't good enough to deserve such a man. That same pain and fear shrouded my spirit for so many years I didn't have a clue that life wasn't supposed to hurt so bad. My soul was void of love.

I still have to tell myself every day to let the fear out and the good in. What I discovered is that all the scrapes and scratches weren't in vain. It was *all* worth it, especially Malik. I guess I owe him a huge thank-you.

Oh, and that letter I put in the Bible? I opened it a little early. Okay, six months early. But my prayers were answered—I had to! See, I asked God for a man who was handsome, loving, kind, well-off financially (you know I couldn't forget that one), and a few other things that will remain just between me and God. Funny thing is, Taye just *happened* to fit the description. I actually asked *for* Taye.

But the biggest thanks of all goes to God, the Almighty, All-Powerful, All-Knowing, All-Fixing. If it weren't for Him, I wouldn't have discovered the truth: I *can* love. Destiny Day can love unconditionally. And now there's someone standing by my side, sharing that same depth of emotion with me. Taye and I are friends, partners, lovers, and the best is yet to come.

. . . I want you, and you want me, so why don't we get together after the dance . . . (Marvin Gaye, "After the Dance").

Set the Party Off
Destiny Day Style!

 *Destiny's Top Ten Old
School DJ "Must" Plays:*

{1} Tom Browne, "Jamaica Funk"

{2} Parliament, "Knee Deep"

{3} Michael Jackson, "Don't Stop Til You Get Enough"

{4} Mary J. Blige, "Real Love"

{5} Junior, "Mama Used Ta Say"

{6} Prince, "DMSR"

{7} Chic, "Good Times"

{8} Chaka Khan, "Ain't Nobody"

{9} Tenna Marie, "Square Biz"

{10} Kano, "I'm Ready"

● ● ●

● *Destiny's All Time Greatest "Sweat-Your-Hair-Out" Jam:*

Guy, "Groove Me"

● *Destiny's All Time Greatest "Red-Light-Basement-Party" Cut:*

Al Green, "Love and Happiness"

● *Destiny's All Time Greatest "Last-Call-For-Alcohol" Joint:*

Teddy Pendergrass, "Come On and Go With Me"

● ● ●

● *Destiny's Choice Elixir— The Crown Royal Lust:*

.50 oz Crown Royal
1 oz Peach Schnapps
Splash of cranberry juice

Shake well to combine. Serve over ice and garnish with a peach wedge or purple orchid.

About This Reading Group Companion

Destiny Day is, as Chaka would say, "Every Woman"—smart, sexy, savvy, and the shrewdest, most ambitious sista walking around Manhattan in a pair of Christian Louboutins. She is calling her own shots in the seductive A-list nightlife world. Destiny is also strong and resilient, having escaped hardscrabble beginnings in the small Midwestern town she calls "East Boogie," East St. Louis, Illinois. The questions that follow are designed to spark a discussion that is poignant and compelling. I hope that your reading group finds inspiration in her story as you discover who the real Destiny Day is, after the dj spins the last jam and the party's over.

1. Destiny lives by the rule "Get in, get yours, and get out." Discuss how she applies this philosophy in both her professional and personal life.

2. Prior to meeting Taye, Destiny has a string of men and manages to separate herself emotionally from all of them except Malik. What makes her so vulnerable when it comes to him? Why do so many women fall victim to this type of passive-aggressive behavior when it comes to relationships?

3. What is the significance of Josephine's comparison of Malik to the main character in the children's book *Where's Waldo?*

4. In the chapter "Love Rollercoaster," the laundromat scene is an important eye-opening experience for Destiny. Discuss the revelation she has after spending the afternoon with Malik at the laundromat.

5. Destiny's mother, Juanita, appears in her dreams and reflections throughout the book. What is the significance of her presence?

6. Destiny begins to question the meaning of love. Discuss where in the book this occurs and her ultimate journey to discover love.

7. Destiny is determined not to be *like* her mother, Juanita, but in many ways she is. How is she like Juanita?

8. Josephine's therapy is going to the Fairway Market, while Malik's is going to the laundromat. What special places or activities provide "therapy" for you, and how?

9. Destiny has special connections with Rico, Izzy, and Josephine in

terms of their life struggles. What is that connection? Discuss Destiny's trust issues when it comes to friendships with people outside her small circle.

10. Spirituality plays a big part in Josephine's character. Recount and discuss the chapters that reveal various revealing moments in the story for Destiny that eventually lead her to find her own spirituality.

11. When Destiny meets Taye Crawford, she quickly finds herself moving in a direction she never anticipated. Discuss the emotional challenges she is confronted with. How does he help her face her painful past and let go of fear?

12. Taye is able to break through barriers as no man has ever been able to do before with Destiny. What makes Taye so different than all the other men in Destiny's life?

13. Josephine encourages Destiny to be open to something "shiny and sweet." What does this mean to you? How do Rico and Izzy find that "shiny and sweet" gift in their lives?

14. Music plays a major role in Destiny's life. She believes music can "unfurl a person's deepest desires." Explore and discuss how music is used in the story. What is its significance in Destiny's life, and how does the dj's presence metaphorically save her life?